"YOU ARE A REAL MAN!"

Princess Litei watched Jean with shameless pleasure
as he built a fire in the cave. "I was prepared to die but
I am too young for that," she whispered.

The Oriental beauty had been teasing the Crusader
ever since they met at her father's court. But his
was a sacred mission—taking the princess to Rome to
become a Christian.

Now they were buried under an avalanche in a mountain
pass high in the Himalayas. Help was far away.
And the little time left to them—what better use for it
than to show her he was every bit the man she
thought?

The Wicked Blade

Robert Carse

POPULAR LIBRARY • NEW YORK

CHAPTER ONE

The wine had been served in small porcelain cups. Jean Baignault reached for the flagon on the table beside him when his was empty and refilled it. He drank steadily while the Syrian woman sang. This was pleasant here, he thought, and at least he wasn't bored.

Shutters over the long windows kept the room cool. It smelled faintly of patchouli and attar of roses and the perfume the woman wore. She sat opposite Baignault on a low ottoman and held a lyre that she played well. Her songs were new, most of them troubadour ballads just out from Europe, and she gave them tender accent. He could take her to bed before the afternoon was over, he realized; the invitation was in the songs. Still, several that she sang in her lisping French troubled him.

Their words were not only about love; they told of the Provençal court, the France he had never seen although he called himself a Frenchman. He rose nervously from the ottoman and crossing the room, stood at a window. The woman put down the lyre and followed him. She stood close at his side.

"You can look at the colt later," she said, "when my husband is home."

5

"I'm not interested in the colt," he said. "That was just a pretext to get here with you."

An ornamental pier glass hung from the wall between the windows. He caught their dual reflection in it as she said, "Oh," slowly, then slid an arm around his waist. She was quite swarthy in her prettiness, her dark looks accentuated by the bright scarlet of her jacket and the pearls twined through her hair. He stood over her almost giantlike, bulky and blond despite his brown eyes and deeply tanned skin. His body armor showed beneath the collar of his surcoat, and on his left shoulder the Knight Hospitaler cross of his order was distinct in the sunlight coming obliquely through the shutters.

Nothing, he thought, was strange in the scene, though. Not here in the Holy Land. He smiled wryly at the mirrored images: the wife of a merchant who was more interested in his business than he was in her, and a Crusader without a crusade. The woman had her head lifted. Her lips were ready. But Jean Baignault merely kissed her glancingly; his attention was drawn beyond the window.

The courtyard below flanked the Roman road. Beyond it stood a grove of ilex trees, and Baignault had just noticed a movement there. Mustaf, his father's turcopole sergeant of bodyguards, was half-hidden among the trees, next to his horse in a patch of shade. Baignault cursed without sound. He stepped away from the woman and crossed to where he had left his sword against the ottoman.

His rage was so great he hardly heard her. She said, "What is the matter? You know that my husband is in Latikya. He shan't be home until tomorrow."

"I am sorry," Baignault said. He bowed to her before he buckled on the sword. "But I must go."

She was about to cry, he saw. Her slightly plump body was trembling. He felt oddly sorry for her, but the rage drove him past her into the hall. A wise-eyed servant lingered near the front door; when Baignault clapped his hands he jumped and opened it, muttering, "I kept your horse saddled, Sir Knight."

Baignault gave him a gold piece from his belt pouch. "Thank you," he said. "Open the gate."

His horse was a pure-bred Arabian, big for the breed and very fast. He sent him at a walk through the gate and at a slow trot on the road. Then he took the reins short and swung rapidly off into the grove. His sword was out; he let

6

the blade touch Mustaf under the chin. "My father must have sent you," he said. "You're a poor spy, though. I could see you from the window. You didn't pick a very good spot."

"That's right," Mustaf said. "Your father sent me. But I wanted you to see me, and now take the sword out of my face."

Jean Baignault got down from the saddle, his sword back in the scabbard. He moved to Mustaf and seized him by the shoulder. "I've had enough," he said.

"Look," Mustaf said, "your argument is with the Sieur Amboise, not me."

Mustaf was a small, beak-nosed man with a mustache that trailed thinly down over his chin. He rested motionless beside his shivering, panting horse, one hand gripping the mane, the other on the reins. His thick woolen caftan was flecked with fresh lather, Baignault saw; the horse must have been ridden hard.

"How did my father find out I was here?" Jean Baignault said. "You must know."

"No, I don't," Mustaf said. "But I can guess. The Sieur Amboise gets word from all kinds of people along this road. Even Syrian merchants."

Jean Baignault laughed, the rage still hot in him but turning to laughter against himself. "So I'm supposed to come home," he said. "Back to the farm. Then—"

"Let go," Mustaf said quietly. "You hurt my shoulder, Sir Jean." The little man's eyes were squinted. His right hand had left the mane of his horse and was lowering gradually toward the curved tulwar that hung in the scabbard at his side. "The Sieur Amboise sent me for you, but not to keep you from some Syrian's wife. And if I don't obey orders, I don't get paid."

"*Dieu me damme*," Baignault said. He was looking into Mustaf's eyes. "No good. You and I cannot fight." He had known Mustaf all his life. Mustaf and his father were the first two men who had put him in a saddle. This was for him and his father to settle, not the sergeant. He moved away from Mustaf with small strides.

"Very well," Jean Baignault said flat-voiced. "Let us ride."

On the road he kept a pace or so ahead of Mustaf. The old sergeant sat slumping wide-kneed in the saddle in traditional turcopole style, head down, eyes nearly shut

7

against the late, low sunlight. Mustaf sensed and respected his desire for silence, Baignault knew, and that was good. He needed time in which to think.

His call upon the Syrian's wife hadn't taken him far from home. He and Mustaf would be back at Beth-Haggan a few hours after dark. The broad white way the Romans had built was already deserted, the caravans, fearful of robbers or Saracen attack, gone for the night into tavern corrals the other side of Baalbek.

Baignault cursed aloud in his morose mood. This was just about the heart of the Holy Land—what people like himself, born and raised here, called *Outremer*. It had a nice sound for those who hadn't seen it. And it was still supposed to be the great bastion of Christianity against the infidel. But in these last years of the thirteenth century Jerusalem was lost, held and held very strongly by the Saracens. Yes, there were the great Crusader fortresses to the north and to the south. Yes, the ports along the Mediterranean coast were open and did a great deal of business with Cyprus and Venice and Genoa, even France. The contact with Europe grew steadily less, however, and for a number of reasons *Outremer* was in extreme danger.

Jean was twenty-three years old, the grandson of Crusaders. He had been brought up in what was fervently spoken of as the True Faith, and in his early teens had started as an esquire at the famous Knight Hospitaler fortress of El Kerak. Then, under his father and other veteran commanders, he had fought along the Lebanese border and helped clean out bands of hashish-crazy Assassin fanatics, catch and kill remorselessly the Saracens who dared to come down from the Anti-Lebanon hills and raid this rich, narrow plain. He had been just nineteen when he was knighted for bravery in action.

But along with the sword and lance work and the archery and horsemanship he had been taught at El Kerak he had learned that there were no more leaders like Robert of Normandy or Richard Coeur de Lion. The tremendous waves of popular emotion that had brought such men from Europe were gone, seemingly for good. Europe lived within itself, occupied by its own wars, exhausted by plagues, and Rome was too weak to give much help to get back Jerusalem, recapture the Holy Grail. The two great knightly orders, the Hospitalers and the Templars, who for centuries had carried most of the fighting in *Outremer,* now de-

8

lighted in scheming against each other. His father had shown his dislike of them when he had refused to join either; despite all the pressure put on him, Sieur Amboise remained an independent knight.

Jean Baignault smiled at his estimate of his father. What bothered him, he knew, was that Sieur Amboise was content to stay at home at Beth-Haggan and be a farmer instead of leading a life of intrigue and the planning of campaigns that were never fought. He was wrong, he told himself, if he blamed his father for that. The Sieur Amboise only shared the general theory of all the senior knights: *Outremer* shouldn't strike out at the Saracens until they had been heavily reinforced from Europe. Meantime, men of his age, ambitious, highly trained, chased Syrian women to fill an empty hour. Baignault spit down into the roadside dust. His mouth had a bitter taste.

Darkness came and the moon rose and the limestone road was pale under it, while in the fields beyond crickets cried and rabbits scuttered at the sound of the horses' hooves. "We should eat," Mustaf said, breaking the silence of hours. "My spine is up against my belt buckle."

"Your own fault," Baignault said. "What is an old-timer like you doing without a haversack? We'll have to wait until we get to Beth-Haggan. And that will be after midnight. There's another ten miles to go."

"The Sieur Amboise sent me off in haste," the turcopole said. He had reined down his horse to a walk. "But I have flint and steel, and over there are plenty of rabbits. It wouldn't take me long to make a snare, then a fire."

"No, not tonight," Baignault said softly. He had stopped his horse and sat immobile, straight in the saddle. Off to the left, out of sight, lay the Mediterranean. To the right climbed the steep Lebanon hills. A mist that would be gone with dawn veiled the hills. But some ridges lay stark, and staring up at one he believed that he saw mounted men. They were a mile or a little more from the road. And ahead the road wound up into those hills, through a narrow pass.

Baignault stroked his horse's neck and shut his eyes an instant to rest them. Then he looked at the ridge again. The men were there, all right. It was one of the proudest Crusader claims, he remembered, that the enemy was kept out of the territory east of the hills. But a shrewdly led Saracen war party could enter from there at night, cutting in between the guard posts.

9

Mustaf had begun to watch the ridge too, and he said, "That's a Saracen *rezzia*. I count over a dozen. No patrol as big would be out from the guardposts. They'd like to meet us up where the road goes through the pass." Without seeming to change his posture, he took the powerful bow from his back in one easy motion, tried the bow string, drew an arrow and fitted it.

"I am not sure they're after us," Baignault said. "They are strung out as though to watch the pass, with men on either side of it. But they have seen us, and if we ride through they will meet us. Are you willing to go against them?"

Mustaf lifted the bow. "I didn't set this up," he said, "to shoot rabbits."

Riding at a canter and almost knee to knee, they went up toward the pass. They rode through mist. The moonlight penetrated here and there, to throw distorted shadows. But Baignault knew the place. He had hunted all this country before starting his esquire service at El Kerak. There was an olive orchard somewhere here on the high side of the road. He recalled the terrain beyond it and the angles of the rough stone walls that Syrian farmers had built to save the trees from being ripped loose in the spring rains. Leave the road now, he decided, and stay well away until clear of the ridge.

He tapped Mustaf on the arm, then swung his horse on a short rein and jumped a low stone wall. The light here was dim, a grayish blue, and he could scarcely see the trees. But the ground was soft; his horse and Mustaf's made little sound. He bent to miss the branches, trying to adjust his eyes and listening for the enemy.

The Saracens were in the orchard too, and considerably closer than he had thought. He heard the creaking rustle of saddle leather. A horse snuffled and his beast nearly whinnied in answer before he leaned and got a hand across its muzzle. Then he dismounted and moved back to Mustaf. "Go on," he whispered to the sergeant. "Take my horse. Keep straight. When you reach a wall, swing left and I'll meet you there."

"I can open up a hole through them with the bow and then the tulwar. We could both ride out wide."

"That was an order," Jean Baignault said. He took his bow and quiver from his saddle. "I want it obeyed, sergeant.

10

These people will be looking for us both as mounted. Your job is to make them think we are."

He moved from Mustaf quite soundlessly in his soft boots. But then he stepped on a loose stone and it turned and threw him against a tree. He went down on his hands and knees, the bow in his left hand, an arrow in his right, and began to crawl. He could smell the other horses; they had been harder ridden than his and Mustaf's, and they were lathered, sweaty. He wondered for just a moment why Saracens would push their mounts so far into enemy territory. If this *rezzia* ran into a guard detachment it would be in a very bad way before it got anywhere near the border.

But then he saw the men who sought him and he moved too fast for conscious thought. There were four of them at the edge of the olive orchard where the mist was thin in the small breeze, and he believed there was a fifth, probably a sentinel, beyond them alongside the road. The men made no attempt to hide. They wore the pointed steel Saracen cap, the white headcloth fluttering below, and they carried lances and rounded, steel-studded shields and scimitars. Their horses were stocky, with long tails and manes.

One man, who appeared to be the oldest and wore a beard, stared at Baignault and then grasped his scimitar blade in a characteristic movement, bent it double, released it whanging. That was a signal to the rest of the warriors. They whirled around toward Baignault.

Baignault chose to shoot the man with the pliant scimitar. He put the arrow into his throat at the point of the beard. Then he fitted another arrow and shot the next man, who spun his horse and yelled before he fell. The other two now knew Baignault's exact position. They rode in where he knelt by a tree trunk. He dropped the bow and drew his sword and was chased between the trees until Mustaf reached him.

Mustaf came out of the orchard at the gallop, erect, guiding with his knees. He had his bow taut and he killed one of the Saracens instantly with an arrow that tore grinding through socket bone. The fourth man reared and wheeled his horse and tried to get away. Baignault lunged and struck a sword blow that merely wounded the horse. It was Mustaf who killed the man with the tulwar.

"Hold my horse," Baignault told Mustaf. "I want my

11

bow and quiver." His lips were stiff with tension and when he walked to the tree where he had dropped the long bow and lacquered, crested quiver, his strides were uneven, he stumbled and was suddenly aware that he was terribly tired.

But he ràn to rejoin Mustaf and mount. They must get out of here. The sentinel down at the road was calling. Men further on in the darkness responded to him. "Up-slope," Baignault told Mustaf. "They have left the ridge open and we can get along it, then down into the valley."

Looking back into the mist, he heard overhead the whine and slur of arrows in flight. But there was no pursuit. The rest of the warriors in the *rezzia* remained at the pass. It seemed that they had fixed posts there, had been ordered not to leave them. "We are lucky. They would fight us, but they are after something else."

"Let them worry about that, then," Mustaf said. He was beating his horse with blows of the tulwar to keep the animal in motion. The horse moaned and swayed and staggered, and blood was in the muzzle froth. "You'll have to take me on your crupper, Sir Jean. I'm a worthless turcopole when I walk. My legs wouldn't get me to Beth-Haggan."

They were down from the ridge and again on the powdery limestone of the Roman road, Mustaf astride behind Jean Baignault when Baignault saw the man in the field. He was prone and lay very still. The spread of barley almost hid his body. But Baignault was able to trace his footmarks off into the field, and in the ditch near them lay a horse just as dead as the animal Mustaf had been forced to kill a few minutes ago.

Baignault dismounted with a single smooth movement. He put the reins in Mustaf's hands. "Stay here. I can catch him—or kill him."

He went into the field with his bow lifted, an arrow fitted, and he allowed the man to hear him. A standing target would be better, and if the man ran it would only be for a pace or so. His feet flattened the green barley and the stalks made a whispering as if in complaint, and he thought curiously that he was enough of a farmer's son to regret this. The field was about ready for harvest, and the crop good.

Then he stared keen-eyed and tense at the man. He was part erect a short bowshot away, and he had veered around

12

to run. The moon-touched valley mist exaggerated his silhouette and Baignault saw that he wore a caftan such as Mustaf wore, and a peaked felt cap in the turcopole style. He was armed too; there was a tulwar at his side and he pulled at it stiffly, with groping effort. The broken haft of an arrow protruded several inches from his left upper arm.

"I am not out to kill you," Baignault said in Arabic. "Stop, man. Let go your weapon."

"No," the man said harshly. Then, spraddle-legged, grunting in pain, he threw the tulwar. It was a terrific cast, superbly aimed and executed. Baignault had to tumble flat as the blade whipped drumming in an arc that chopped the barley beside his head. He swore more in surprise than anger. This man was a real fighter. But the cast had spent what had been the last of his strength. The other took an uncertain stride, reeled, and sagged to his knees. He was almost gone in coma as Baignault reached him.

"*Salaam aleikum,*" Baignault said quietly to him. "I will not kill you. But I must search you."

The man started to bite his hand when he took the long poniard out of the belt scabbard. "You were warned," Baignault said. He batted him on the jaw and made the coma complete. Then, picking up the tulwar on the way, he went out of the field, the body slack in his arms.

"He looks like one of your tribesmen," he told Mustaf after he was on the road.

Mustaf bent down where Baignault knelt. "He could be," he said. "Turcopoles work for a thousand masters, though. This one smells like a cameleer, and the boots are of Mongol make. He's come a big distance in them. They're about done."

"But the arrow," Jean Baignault said, "is of Saracen design. Look at the work on the haft. Then go over there and take a look at what killed his horse. I will tell you right now it was the same thing."

Mustaf moved to the sprawled carcass in the ditch, came back and stood silently beside Baignault. Then he knelt and his hands passed expertly over the man's body, examined the lining of the cap, the caftan, emptied the belt pouch. "The Saracens must ha' been after him," he said. "Still, I don't know why."

"Not that it matters immediately," Jean Baignault said. He had begun to tug tentatively at the arrow haft. Congested blood welled up around it from the wound. It lay

13

cruelly in the flesh just below the shoulder. "If we fail to get this out, we will never know. Hold him. I am going to pull."

"Go ahead," Mustaf said. He set himself, his hands broad upon the unconscious body.

The man screamed with the wrench of removal. He sprang up writhing and almost knocked Mustaf away from him. Mustaf muttered in turcopole, then Arabic. "Stay still, man. We're your friends. We don't make you trouble."

He stared at them, the sweat of agony on his flat face, his body shivering, but his eyes very sane. Baignault realized that he studied the Knight Hospitaler cross, the surcoat and armor, and each article of Mustaf's clothing. Then he spoke. "I'm looking for a place called Beth-Haggan. And a Sieur Amboise Baignault."

"You are not very wrong," Jean Baignault said slowly. He had ripped a strip from his surcoat lining to serve as a bandage for the wound. "Beyond here a couple of miles is Beth-Haggan. Believe me, I don't lie to you. Because I'm the Sieur Amboise's son."

The man smiled, as if at some marvelous and secret joke. "I've come a long way," he said. "I'm tired. The shoulder sorely hurts me."

"Get him on the horse," Jean Baignault said to Mustaf. "Then you take one stirrup and I will take the other. We want to get to Beth-Haggan before dawn."

The farm which had been held in fief by the Baignault family for over two centuries was off the Roman road in the Valley of Eleutherus. Walking the weary horse, Jean Baignault and Mustaf entered the walled lane as dawn began to turn silver into crimson across the fields and vineyards. The Sieur Amboise's greyhounds barked and roused sleepy roosters. Then the turcopole guard who had the duty at the front door of the house came running at the double. He saluted and said good morning, but he was looking at the man sacklike over the saddle.

"All right," Jean Baignault said, short-tempered in his fatigue. "Now you have had your look, go call my father."

"The Sieur Amboise is still asleep, sir," the guard said.

"Wake him," Jean Baignault said harshly. "He sent for me. This is my turn."

CHAPTER TWO

The Sieur Amboise came quickly along the hall to the front door of the low, long, two-story house. His face was expressionless, but his eyes serious as Jean Baignault greeted him, then indicated the wounded man. "We found him on the road," Jean said.

"A bad wound." Sieur Amboise had lifted the rough bandage. "He will be brought in the house. But Lady Baignault is not to be disturbed. I'll send for a surgeon from El Kerak. You are dismissed, Mustaf, but stay in your quarters. I will want to see you later. Sir Jean, you must talk with me."

"I am ready, sir," Jean Baignault said, standing at his full height and aware that the guards who had gathered in the dooryard curiously watched him and his father. Sieur Amboise was dressed in a plain surcoat without distinguishing marks. He wore cambric hose and short, light boots of red Damascus leather. Still, his manner was much more that of a soldier than a farmer and scholar.

The Sieur Amboise had fought with the Crusader host years ago, and been gravely wounded at the savage battle of Ain Jalut. Jean's mother, who was a descendant of Bohemonde of Antioch, had read to her husband from ancient scrolls and he had continued his other studies while he made his slow recovery, and he had since been recognized among the higher ranks of both the Hospitaler and Templar orders as an authority on the border regions. He spoke, read and wrote Arabic, had mastery of a number of Syrian dialects. But as he turned into the house, Jean was impressed once more by the effect of his father's old wound. The Sieur Amboise wasn't entirely crippled, yet he would never ride out again as he had in the past. His left leg dragged heavily with each step he took.

Jean Baignault recalled his anger of yesterday against his father and had a feeling close to remorse. He might well have been wrong to condemn the Sieur Amboise for his own inaction. To be lamed so must change any man's thinking. But there was no time now for consideration of that.

15

His father had entered the big, tiled living room where night tapers still burned and seated himself in his favorite leather chair. "Sit down, Jean," he said. "You must be just about as tired as Mustaf."

Jean Baignault lowered himself onto an ottoman beside his father's chair and the saddle stiffness made him grunt. He heard out in the hall the shuffled passage of the guards carrying the wounded turcopole. One of the maids, a woman competent at the dressing and care of wounds, was with them.

"Now how about this fellow you and Mustaf brought here?"

Jean Baignault looked squarely into his father's eyes. He put his hands on his sword hilt to support the weight of his aching body. The turcopole he had found was somehow important. He had begun to believe that when he was in the barley field, and by his father's intent though quiet manner he was made certain of it.

"Mustaf found me where you expected me to be," he told the Sieur Amboise unsmiling. "We came home along the Roman road, but where the road goes up through the pass between the olive orchards I saw Saracens. They were dispersed along the ridge in skirmish formation and covered it on both sides. You know the place."

"I do," Sieur Amboise said. "How many of them were there?"

"A dozen. Maybe more. But not many more. I came at them through the orchards. We killed four before we could get past onto the ridge and cut back to the road. The rest could have caught us possibly, if they'd chased us after the fighting started. They stayed, though, and I think they were on fixed posts and under strict orders not to leave them. The turcopole was in a barley field about two miles from the pass."

Jean Baignault paused, allowing his father the chance to speak. But the Sieur Amboise sat silent, his hands crossed loosely on his chest, his eyes unblinking on his son's face.

"I have the idea," Jean Baignault said, "that the *rezzia* was looking for the man in the field. But they missed him somewhere up on the ridge. They'd wounded him already, probably down on the eastern side, and yet he slipped past them. It was misty and dark, and he could have got through pretty much the same way we did. He was still full of fight when I got to him. He almost took my head off with a tulwar cast. His trouble was that the Saracens had wounded his horse too, and the horse died, and he wasn't strong enough to go ahead on foot."

"I share your idea," the Sieur Amboise said. "The man would be some sort of messenger. You see, yesterday I got private advice from the border that one was on his way to me. My information was given by people in the north, beyond Aleppo. They're trustworthy. But the Saracens might have got the same information, or just met the fellow trying to ride in across the hills. Maybe you understand now why I sent Mustaf for you."

"Yes," Jean Baignault said slowly, "I do."

"Then you'd better eat and sleep," his father said. "I shall call the servant for you." A brass gong was on the table alongside Sieur Amboise's chair and he touched it musically with a leather-headed stick. "The turcopole won't be in shape to talk to anybody until tonight. While you rest, the surgeon from El Kerak can tend to him."

Jean Baignault nodded and stood up, a number of questions pressing in his brain. But the desire for sleep was more insistent; he yawned despite himself, and when the maid came along the hall he could hardly tell her the food he wanted. The Sieur Amboise sat quietly and smiled at him. "It's good to have you home, Jean," he said. "And I'm sorry I had to interrupt you yesterday."

"Think nothing of it, sir," Jean Baignault said. He was going slowly out into the hall after the maid toward the dining room.

"What attracted me was not much. I was bored, that is all."

"But no longer," Sieur Amboise said in a low voice.

"No, sir," Jean Baignault said. He looked back and smiled, then went stumbling down the hall.

He undressed and bathed after he had eaten and gone to his own room. He massaged his body to get rid of the saddle cramps and lay on the bed and, soothed by the household sounds, slipped into sleep. But the excitement of the action and his father's words had been too great. He dreamed fitfully, then out of the dreams emerged certain memories.

He remembered this house when he was in his teens and his grandfather was still alive. It was in the middle of the night and during the intense heat of summer when the wind from the hills dropped, that his grandfather usually cried out. The old man was blind and strong almost beyond belief, so Jean would get up and go in to him. His excuse to his parents if they awoke was that without his presence his grandfather might hurt himself.

The old man would sit up on his bed, eyes open, and behind him on the simple bedstead were his suit of armor and the Crusader sword with the cruciform hilt and the three-foot-long blade. He spoke to Jean, holding his hands, and he went off into the past which was as immediate to him as the heat of the room. The talk reached far back, and Jean realized that part of it was family history told from generation to generation, the rest from troubadours' tales and the sober accounts of the Knights Hospitalers and Templars.

It told of Dorylaeum at the time of the First Crusade when the host of half a million emerged onto the salt plain and before them were the Turks in a shouting sprawl. Sun glossed the flanks of the Turkish horses; the arrows tore the air in unseen furrows. The Baignault who fought in that battle was named Marc and he was barely twenty-two, in the service of Robert of Normandy, the son of the Conqueror. Before noon, he had killed more Turks than he had years.

Then there was Antioch. The siege towers were erected, and the gangways reached to the parapets. Below, the carcasses of men smoked greasily where they had toppled under the boiling oil. Yet this was victory and Marc Baignault and the others cried in their eagerness, "Jerusalem, Jerusalem!"

The city, even among the unbelievers, was known as The Golden. It held the Grail and it was holy. That night the men who had taken the Cross slaughtered through the streets, raped, burned, ravaged and were mad.

Jean would stand back from his grandfather both shocked and proud. He knew that the old man told the truth, but also that his mind wandered. Now he spoke of Jean's great-grandfather and how he had died at the second siege of Damascus. The heat had been too great. There was not enough water. The horses had been weak for the attack, and for the Crusaders who rode them in their weighty armor. They had been slaughtered by the Paynims who were fresh and fought light-clad.

The rough and deep voice thudded on; Jean stood and listened to a description of Normandy, which his grandfa-

18

ther had visited in his youth. That was the birthplace of the Baignault family. In the spring, it was beautiful; apple blossoms were like a rose-white lace over the fields, and in the hedgerows the thrushes sang all night long. The winters were foggy. Great fires were needed, but in the buttery were cheeses big enough to keep a fighting man going for a week.

Jean's grandfather would at last fall back asleep. The gray, scarred head rested slack. The mouth gaped loose from the broken butts of discolored teeth, and the immense hands relaxed. Jean stroked the hands just before he left the room, and touched the hilt of the sword. Very soon, with the death of this man, it was going to be his. And, from what he had been told, he would have need for it. The Holy Land must be fought for over and over again. . . .

Jean Baignault stirred, partly awake. He had gone a long way into memory, he realized, and maybe that had done him good. The light through the window shutters was faint with dusk, and the heat was less. He rose and splashed water from the ewer on his face, began to dress. Maids moved through the hall outside, and he could smell dinner being cooked. He told himself that he would eat twice as much as when he had come home, but drink very little wine.

There was the talk with the wounded turcopole ahead. He wanted his wits sharp for that. He had waited enough, dreamed enough. It was time that he had his share of action, and the turcopole's presence here might very possibly give him the chance that until now he'd missed.

He was at the door, had opened it to step into the hall, when he saw his mother. She wore a soft brown velvet dress with a train, pearls around her coif and a pearl necklace. The light of the hall sconces showed her slim and graceful as she moved toward him, but bending to kiss her hand he noticed that she was taut with strain. Her eyes were haggard; lines cut at the corners of her mouth, and it was his belief that even in the short time he had been away the gray streaks had spread through her hair.

"You are all right?" she said.

"Yes, I am," he said.

"But who is the wounded man you brought here?"

"Mother, you should not worry," he said. Then he took her arm and led her steadily toward the dining room. He spoke little during the meal, letting his father and mother talk about the crops, the grape yield and the annual early fall request for supplies from El Kerak, which lay close up behind Beth-Haggan on a crest that dominated the entire valley. At the end of the meal, without a word, Lady Baignault rose and the two men stood and bowed to her.

The Sieur Amboise took time to drink the last of his wine. He seemed quite calm. But there was a note of tension in his voice as he said, "Come to my study, please, Jean."

"Gladly, sir," Jean Baignault said.

Mustaf was on duty at the front door. He gave a salute, the tulwar pommel at his chin. "The man is ready, sire," he said.

"Help him in," Sieur Amboise said. He sat in his worn chair, his hands spread out after he had worked the lame leg into a comfortable position. Mustaf stood in the doorway, and with him was the turcopole. The man wore a loose coat of Mustaf's over his shoulder bandages, and he was pale and haggard, but he could walk all right, and his small eyes were keen, careful within the pouched lids. "Enter, sire?" Mustaf said.

"Yes, sergeant," Sieur Amboise answered. He was gazing at the man's boots and caftan. The sides of the boots were chafed ragged; the caftan was slick, stiff with dried animal lather. "You would be a turcopole and a cameleer," Sieur Amboise told him in the turcopole dialect. "Tell me why you are here."

The eyes slanted around in the flat brown face at Jean Baignault. "I'm a cameleer, yes," he said. "But this man—"

"We met in the barley field," Jean said. "You threw your tulwar at me. A very nice cast. Recall it?"

"Not much," the turcopole said. "I was in great pain."

The Sieur Amboise made a quick gesture. "Sit down," he said. "Let us not wait any longer. You know who I am. This is my son, Sir Jean Baignault. I have asked him to be here for special reasons. And the sergeant can listen to anything you might have to tell us."

Jean Baignault felt a flush of pride. He had never before known just how much his father respected him. He had fought only in small border actions, and although they had been severe and he had conducted himself well, he had until now believed that he was just one of several thousand ambitious young knights who lacked the chance to prove

20

capable of advancement and leadership. The Sieur Amboise had a definite reason, then, some plan of real consequence in mind when he'd sent for him.

"Then," the turcopole said, "I bear you the greetings of the Il-Khan Arghun, Khan of all the Mongols, Master of Thrones and Crowns. He sends them from his *ordu* at Karakoram. I come from him to you."

"Why to me?" Sieur Amboise said quietly.

"Because at the battle of Ain Jalut you stood fast beside the Khan Hulagu against the Saracens. You took a blow that would have cost Hulagu his life. It hasn't been forgotten by the people of the Golden Horde."

"Go on," Sieur Amboise said. "The battle of Ain Jalut was a long while ago."

"There has been at the court of the khans a Frankish trader known variously as Buscarel or Bendosi."

"He is a Venetian?"

"No, sire, but Genoese. A trader who has traffic with Cathay in the same way as the Polo family."

Jean Baignault sat very still, watching his father, then the turcopole. His father had just tried to trip up the man. But if this was really a messenger from the Il-Khan and the Golden Horde, it could mean a very great deal. Every point had to be checked.

"On his left cheek he has a mark from the pox," Sieur Amboise said.

"On his right, sire," the turcopole said. "What I tell is truth. There's no need to trick me to show lies."

Mustaf took out his tulwar and very lightly prodded the turcopole in the good shoulder. "Nothing like that," he said. "Leave out the loose bazaar talk."

"But you must know, sire," the turcopole said, "that Buscarel brought a scroll from the Il-Khan to the Pope, His Holiness, at Rome."

"That I do," Sieur Amboise said. He was leaning forward, his arms broad on the chair, and from where he sat Jean Baignault could see the little flicker of nerves through his father's jaw. Now you begin to know fully, he thought. This is a deep business. Deeper than any in which you've had part or even knowledge. The Il-Khan is very powerful. Right now, he is more so than the Pope. If an alliance could be made between them . . .

Jean Baignault stared narrow-eyed in complete concentration at the turcopole. He weighed each word the man said. The slow, rough voice went on regularly in the stillness of the room.

"His Holiness was asked," the turcopole said, "to enter into alliance with the Golden Horde. It was in the message borne to him by Buscarel. You must have heard."

"I did," Sieur Amboise said. There was a slight note of impatience in his voice. The narrow and angular-boned face held a grayish shade that came from exhaustion, Jean realized. His father was forcing himself to be calm. It must take all of his will to continue to talk. "But His Holiness refused to do anything in answer to the message from the Il-Khan. Except—" his voice was harsh—"that the Pope sent back word that the Il-Khan should be baptized in our faith."

The turcopole bobbed his head up and down. He opened his thick hands in an almost supplicant gesture. "Yes, sire; yes. I'm a good Christian. So I can say to you that I think it was a very bad mistake, that. But I have been months on the trails. The other side of Marghrab a Saracen *rezzia* nearly got me and killed all my companions. Then up in these hills I was chased again, and wounded. If I anger you, understand that I am weary, and sad."

"Save your tears for outside," Mustaf muttered.

But Sieur Amboise said, "Go easy with him, Mustaf."

The turcopole smiled in gratitude. He said, "The Il-Khan hasn't given up. It is for me to tell you that he wants an alliance between the Mongol people and the Franks. That would mean very much to the Golden Horde. So he is willing to send his son to Rome. He would have Chagan go and talk in person with the Pope."

"I cannot quite believe it," Sieur Amboise said, so low that only Jean Baignault heard him. "But it could be." Then his voice took strength and he asked the turcopole, "You would tell me that Chagan will go to Rome to see Pope Nicholas?"

"As God helps me; yes, sire."

"Then from that there might be military alliance. Those of us who hold the Holy Land joined with the Golden Horde." Sieur Amboise's eyes were very bright. He seemed suddenly young. "We'd kick the Saracens into the sea of Galilee, pickle them in brine." But the youthful look went from him, and his eyes were dark and cautious again, and his voice hard-edged. "Do you have written word of this?"

22

"No, sire," the turcopole said. "I learned the message by heart, like the litany. Maybe the Il-Khan knew best not to put it in writing. I'm a simple man. There are many spies of all sorts along the border."

"I know of them," Sieur Amboise said. "Still, I should be given proof. Without it, I am unwilling to trust you."

The turcopole glanced around at Mustaf. "Give me help," he said. "The proof is in my boot." He pointed and Mustaf knelt and pulled off the scuffed, ragged yak-hide boot. Mustaf ripped at the lining in the upcurling toe and fumbled loose a stone that was almost as big as a hen's egg and shone with sheer green fire.

"For you, sire," the turcopole said. "A gift of the Il-Khan. With it, his friendship and good faith." He took the stone and stepped forward. Then, clinging to a chair arm for support, he bowed and gave it to Sieur Amboise.

Sieur Amboise turned the emerald on the palm of his hand. He walked with it to the candles on the table, examined it in their light. Then he came to Jean Baignault and dropped it in Jean's hand. "That is from Cathay," he said in French. He touched one side of the superbly cut and faced gem. "The symbol carved there is very old. It represents the Tree of Life."

Jean Baignault felt a profound sense of awe, and a fierce exultation and pride. He had seen many gems since he had begun his Hospitaler service; a considerable part of the wealth of the Orient passed through the Holy Land, and some of it had gone no farther than the Crusader citadels. But this was absolutely magnificent. It had been tendered, too, as a gift of faith to his father. The purpose of the gift and the Il-Khan's message could bring tremendous help to the Crusader cause.

"The man must have told you the truth," Jean said hoarsely.

"I have no more reason to doubt him," his father said. But he turned to the turcopole. "You have finished your message?"

"Not all of it, sire. The Il-Khan has this to ask of you. Don't take anger. He asks it only because of what has gone before. His son Chagan must make the journey to Rome and then home again safely. Harm to Chagan would be a sign of bad faith, and instead of peace between the two peoples, there would be war."

Sieur Amboise laughed with his head back. "If we can

afford to trust the Golden Horde, they can afford to trust us. But it is a fair condition. Across the Gobi from Karakoram to Rome and then back is a great distance. And both people have their enemies."

"Yes, sire."

Sieur Amboise held the emerald. He rolled it on his palm, then stared quickly at the turcopole. "The Il-Khan must have paid you well."

"He has been very generous. Yes, sire."

"But allies should be generous." Sieur Amboise went to a coffer behind his chair. He came back with a bag of gold bezants and opened it and let the turcopole see them. "To help you get home. I don't know your name, and I don't want to know it. Enough that I know your face, and that my son and sergeant do. Tell your story anywhere between Mecca, Samarkand and Byzantium and I will hear of it. You will be found and killed. Now get out of here. Go with my thanks to the Il-Khan."

"You have no message for him?"

"Not until I have talked with my people." The smile that creased the corners of Sieur Amboise's mouth was harsh. "When we are ready, the Il-Khan will hear from us. He is in command of a million fighting men. We are just a few thousand. But you are smart enough to know this or you wouldn't be here. Take him away, Mustaf."

The turcopole bowed despite the wound. His topknot almost brushed the floor tiles. Then Mustaf grasped him and they backed out the door. In the hall, Mustaf said, "Hide the gold, man. I'm going with you to your caravan, and I'd like to be alive tomorrow."

"But I can get to it alone," the turcopole said. "All I need is a horse."

There was a short, flat sound. Mustaf had just smacked the messenger lightly on the jaw, Jean Baignault thought. "I'm going with you," Mustaf said. "I have my orders. Do you walk to the horse, or do I carry you there?"

Jean Baignault gave his father a grinning glance. He said, "Mustaf has no liking for his duty as orderly."

But the Sieur Amboise sat in a posture of utter fatigue. The grayish shade had drained away from his cheekbones and they lay white under the drawn skin. His eyes were shut, and his hands hung lax. "I must tell you," Jean said, "that you ask too much of yourself. You drive yourself too hard. I am worried by it. So is Mother."

"Why?" Sieur Amboise said very softly. He stared up in the candlelight. "We are all the same here in *Outremer*. The danger threatens all of our lives."

"You're very tired," Jean Baignault said, "or you wouldn't talk so. How about that?" He indicated the emerald. "That should mean victory and then lasting peace."

Sieur Amboise shut his eyes again. "It might," he said, "if the Il-Khan's son can be taken to Rome and back without treachery. If we are not betrayed here in the meantime. And if—" He stopped, then pushed himself upright from the chair. "Enough. I am absolutely fatigued, and must go to bed. But, with your permission, I will use you as my deputy."

"What would you have me do, sir?"

"Go to El Kerak. Seek out the Grand Master, who is there now, and report to him. Give him the entire story, from the attack upon you and Mustaf in the pass, the finding of the messenger, and each detail of the conversation just finished. Take the emerald with you. It will convince even such a skeptic as the Grand Master."

"Yes, sir." Jean Baignault picked up the emerald, put it in his belt pouch and then saluted his father.

"But you will need an escort," Sieur Amboise said.

Jean Baignault nearly laughed. "To El Kerak? I shall be up there in less than half an hour."

"I do not propose to give you an order," Sieur Amboise said. "But the emerald is very precious. If it were lost, all of *Outremer* might be taken from us. You see, Jean, I trust only a few people any more."

Jean Baignault looked at his father for a moment in silence. "Then I will muster a strong guard," he said. His father was old, he realized. But, more than that, Sieur Amboise was tired to the point where hope could no longer sustain him. It wasn't frightening to recognize that; he was too much of a man, had enough reliance upon his own skill and strength. Still, he had always thought of the Sieur Amboise as indestructible, indomitable, the kind of man who was at the core of all that was strong in the Crusader spirit.

He moved to his father's side and stooped down and kissed him on the cheek. "Good night, sir," he said. "Sleep well. I love you very much."

25

CHAPTER THREE

A breeze from the sea had taken the mist and both moon
and stars shone on the Beth-Haggan fields as Jean Baignault rode through them. The corporal in command of his
escort of men-at-arms called out the password at the guard
posts; they were sent quickly on up toward El Kerak, solitary on the stony height. He stared at it, urging his mount,
yet reflective.

El Kerak meant many things. The old Arab name for it
was Hisn-el-Akrad, the Castle of the Kurds. It was also
known among the Saracens as Flame of the Franks, and by
the Crusaders themselves as the Castle of the Knights. Like
Marghrab, the Watcher, the other huge, grim citadel to the
north, and El Kerak of Moab to the South, it was a challenge to any enemy. Five thousand men answered to the
garrison muster. A thousand horses were stabled in the
lower corridors of the main work. It held supplies, water,
forage, food and wine for a five-year siege. No more than a
day's ride away and within sight, were other castles with
which communication could be maintained by fires at night
and from which patrols rode the countryside in regular ro-
tation.

The Il-Khan was not wrong, Jean Baignault thought,
when he came to us to be his allies. We are not what we
were in the days of Melek Richard and Baldwin. Still,
we are powerful. We can fight and win.

Torchlight splashed the white limestone walls ahead. The
corporal had halted; the party was at the sally port of the
barbican tower. "Sir Jean Baignault," the corporal shouted,
then turned back with his men as Jean dismissed them. The
drawbridge swayed down, soldiers ran to hold torches aloft
and Jean rode in.

"Take my horse," he told a sentry. He dismounted and
went rapidly up the steps into the main work.

Sir Guillaume Prunel met him where a yellow flare of
cresset light filled the arch at the head of the staircase. He
was a tall, lean and sour Breton, one-eyed, a veteran of forty
years of *Outremer* fighting. Jean Baignault had known him

26

since he had first entered El Kerak as a small boy perched on his father's shoulder. Now he gave him a short salute; Sir Guillaume was in his final glory as the constable of the citadel. "With your permission, sir," he said, "I seek the Grand Master."

"At whose request?"

"That of the Sieur Amboise, and my own."

The constable gave him the cold, straight stare of the one eye. "Sir Matthew de Clermont went to bed back some hours ago."

"It is important, sir. Let me assure you."

Sir Guillaume almost smiled. "Because you and your father's sergeant fought your way through some Saracen *rezzia?* Because you brought home a wounded cameleer? Make certain, Sir Jean."

"I have, Constable. Thank you." Jean Baignault spoke quite slowly, unwilling to show his surprise at the accuracy of Sir Guillaume's information. There are forty years between us, he thought, and a little jealousy. The young Crusader against the old. Not a new story. This man could remember him when he was less than sword-high. But he was respected; Sir Guillaume was wheeling to call to a sentry.

"Take Sir Jean to the Grand Master's quarters."

Jean Baignault saluted again before he began to climb the flights of steep, curving stairs behind the soldier. He moved eagerly, in elation. If Sir Guillaume had passed him with such ease, then very probably the Grand Master would see him at once and the matter could be pushed forward fast. But when the soldier knocked discreetly on the big oak door of Sir Matthew de Clermont's quarters there was only a sleepy grumble. A serving brother-of-arms finally showed his head. "Get away," he said. "The Grand Master is not to be disturbed until morning."

"Then wake him," Baignault said. "Tell him that Sir Jean Baignault is here. I have a message. The Sieur Amboise knows of this and has asked me to carry it."

The serving brother pulled his head inside and Baignault could hear Sir Matthew's deep, hoarse voice, and it was no longer sleepy. He came to the door barefoot, a big man, powerful and dignified even in his rumpled night shift.

"You will excuse me, sir."

"Of course." Sir Matthew had recognized him. "Come inside. You have something that is written?"

"No, sir. It is a report that I must make to you."

"Let me get slippers and a robe," Sir Matthew said. He stalked across the room with enormous strides, came back and sat down and signed to Baignault to take a chair beside him. "Go ahead. I would understand that this is a report from your father. And that he has charged you with it."

"Only in part, sir," Jean Baignault said. He looked around to make sure that the serving brother had gone off into the alcove away from the room where they were. Then he opened his pouch and took out the emerald. He raised it so that it glittered in the candlelight. "From the Il-Khan Arghun. Sent to the Sieur Amboise as a token of good faith. The Golden Horde would make alliance with us against the Saracens, sir. You see, last night—"

"Give me that," Sir Matthew de Clermont said. His blunt fingers gripped tightly and his eyes were bright and narrow as he stared at the jewel. "Now tell me. But without hurry. I would understand the entire thing."

"Yes, sir," Jean Baignault said. He took a long breath, and impressed by this man's grave, almost straining attention, began to speak in a deliberate and calm voice.

"So why isn't the Sieur Amboise here?" Sir Matthew said when he was finished. "I have need of him in such a matter. He knows more of what goes on beyond the borders than any other officer we have."

"He was very tired tonight, sir," Baignault said. "His old wound gives him pain. After the turcopole was through, Sieur Amboise could hardly talk to me. But in the morning he should be all right."

"Then I will send for him early," Sir Matthew said. "And I will send for Henry and for the Templar too. It will make history in itself. Never has a Grand Master of the Templars been here before. But you have quarters for the night?"

"I can find them, sir," Baignault said. "I have been on detached service under my father's command. But I can stay with friends who served with me when I was esquire."

"Very well," Sir Matthew said absently. He had taken the emerald close to a candelabra and was once more intently examining it. Jean Baignault started for the door and then stopped. Fatigue had gained on him so that he wasn't certain of what he should do or say. The "Henry" who had been mentioned by Sir Matthew was King Henry of Jerusalem now in residence with his court on Cyprus.

28

The "Templar" was Sir William de Beaujeu, the commander of that order, and with King Henry and Sir Matthew one of the three most powerful men in *Outremer*.

Sir Matthew obviously gave the greatest consideration to the Il-Khan's offer of alliance, had faith in the message, was willing to move in the matter or at least explore it further with the other Crusader leaders. Still, the Sieur Amboise hadn't ordered that the emerald should be released. It was up to him, Jean Baignault, to see that his father kept his gift.

Jean Baignault moved to stand in front of Sir Matthew. He bowed to him. "If you would excuse me, please, sir," he said.

"Dieu me protige," the Grand Master said. He laughed, but without mockery and with pleasure. "The Sieur Amboise's gift is in good hands. I will turn it back to him in the morning. You are dismissed now. But, before you go, I will tell you that you have done well. Good night."

"Good night, sir," Baignault said. He let his breathing go with a rush then, and walked quickly to the door.

The hall was in shadow, seemed empty, but he knew that sentries were stationed in recesses along it. He clapped his hands softly and a pikeman wearing a dish-shaped morion and a chain-mail shirt responded. "Is Sir Coidovic de Cressy in quarters?" he asked him.

"Yes, sir," the sentry, an Englishman, said in flat French. "You'll find him there."

Jean Baignault knocked hard on the door at the end of the hall. He had lived here in his esquire days and the man who now occupied the room had served through them with him. De Cressy grinned in delight and said, "Jean, the prodigal," and at his shoulder was a smaller and younger man, Pablan Ecorches.

"Let him in, prodigal or not," Ecorches said. "He's just come from the Grand Master. Wine and song aren't enough. He has a new assignment—to smuggle girls in to us."

"I could use some of your wine," Baignault said.

"Then come in and sit down," De Cressy said. "Get out of your gear. We have a fresh flagon of the well-known Cypriot product. And Pablan has a song he will sing for you."

Jean Baignault looked at the familiar room with pleasure as he put aside his helmet and sword and the wine was poured. It was spare, simple in the Hospitaler tradition, but there were small strips of Bokhara carpet beside the pallet beds; gerfalcons fluttered high-headed on their perches, and near the door on a gazelle hide stretched a very small and very tame brown Syrian bear.

This was his second home, he thought. These men were glad to see him and there was always a bed for him. De Cressy was a Norman and Ecorches a Catalan, and they had come out among the sons of over two hundred other noble families of Western Europe to become aspirant knights in the Order of Hospitalers. Their lives were given to the service, and yet they were gay, happy, quite content to accept the fact that because of his record in combat he had received his knighthood several years before them.

Ecorches sat cross-kneed with his lute in his hands and Baignault was oddly reminded that it was like the one the Syrian woman had played for him. But Ecorches had a much better voice, and sang beautifully:

> Oh, there sat upon a linden tree a bird,
> A bird, and sung its strain;
> So sweet it sung that as I heard
> My heart went back again.
> It went to one remembered spot,
> It saw the roses grow,
> And thought again the thought of love,
> There cherished long ago.

Jean Baignault told Ecorches at the end of the song, "Your life's wasted. With that voice, you should have been a troubadour. And with your looks, you'd go far at the Court of Love in Provence." It was difficult for him, though, to bring forth the bantering words for the Catalan. Behind them, stark across his mind, lay the thought of the Golden Horde.

It was another sign of the lack of Crusader leadership, he told himself, that Ecorches spent a lot of his time in song. There was little military duty for him or De Cressy. They rode out on routine patrols; they drilled the men-at-arms and the esquires, passed hours in the tilting yard galloping and hacking at straw dummies, then went back to their singing, their drinking. The fine skills they possessed were almost entirely wasted.

Baignault ran a hand up over his face. His head ached, and the wine did him no good. "I'm tired, friends," he said. "Do you mind if I go to bed?"

30

"No," De Cressy said. "Take the spare pallet. We have a patrol and will be out of here early in the morning. Sleep as late as you like."

"But tell us first," Ecorches said, "what brought you back to this place, Jean."

"I cannot," Baignault said. He stared levelly at his friend. "I'm under orders not to."

"Let the fellow be," De Cressy said. Then he got up and began to snuff the candles on the table. But Baignault was aware that De Cressy was also curious about him. He wasn't as warm a friend to these two men as he had been before; a certain, small constraint was upon them. They regarded him differently, and he was remote from them and from the other men of their age and rank here in the citadel. The realization saddened him, made him abruptly conscious of how great his responsibility was. He lay down on the pallet with his cloak over him and tried hard to sleep. But the turcopole's words rang in his head, and his father's words, and then Sir Matthew's, and he thought, at last drifting toward sleep, that the road that led to the Golden Horde was very long and if he traveled it, he would be quite lonely there.

He stayed alone, though, most of the next day and evening, nervously waiting to be summoned by Sir Matthew or the Sieur Amboise. He passed his time in the library room of the citadel, studying the scrolls and manuscripts and maps that he could read. Père Malachi, the bald-headed old chaplain who had been born and educated in the ancient Danish city of Dublin and was a real scholar, helped him, but his language knowledge was too limited. He gave up after trying to decipher a Roman map whose finely drawn characters made his eyes smart.

He was out on the upper battlement, near the southern tower with its creaking windmill, when he saw the party that climbed the main trail from the valley. It was too big to be a patrol, and instead of men-at-arms the escort was formed by knights in polished and bossed armor. King Henry, he thought. Henry has come in from Cyprus, and that hulking knight who's beside him is Sir William de Beaujeu, the Grand Master of the Knights Templars.

The party moved unchallenged to the sally port of the barbican. That was the least courtesy the Hospitalers could extend the Templar commander, Baignault thought as he leaned down over the parapet and stared. Then he saw the

Sieur Amboise, who rode with Mustaf and a pair of men-at-arms from Beth-Haggan. Sieur Amboise sat erect in the saddle; he gave a quick greeting to Sir Matthew de Clermont at the sally port and Jean Baignault could hear his father's voice. It was firm, and strong and calm.

Muted trumpets were being sounded within the barbican tower. This cannot be done without panoply, Baignault thought. Remember what Sir Matthew said; it is the first time a Templar of such rank has been inside El Kerak. Then he realized that very soon he would be called. He left the battlement and was about to cross the hall to De Cressy's room when the party advanced from the staircase.

Pages and trumpeters were in front. Jackmen with torches stood in close rank along the walls. Jean Baignault moved back into a recess out of the light. He wanted his hair combed, his surcoat brushed and his body armor polished before he was presented to these officers.

They marched the hall with King Henry in the lead. He was a slight and dapper man, and marvelously graceful. A small, soft beard covered his rounded chin. He wore an orange velvet jacket of Byzantine design over his body armor and he smelled of perfume. Sir William de Beaujeu was enormous; he clanked with each step he made. Beside him, Sieur Amboise, who was Jean Baignault's height and six feet tall, seemed a small man.

The Templar was like some figure out of the tapestries that were shipped to *Outremer* from France, Baignault told himself. But he had caught the Sieur Amboise's sharp sidewise glance at him, and he had also been seen by Sir Matthew. The Grand Master of the Hospitalers was hard-mouthed, his hand was on his sword haft and his eyes were like strips of steel in his darkly tanned face. "Be prepared to present yourself in my quarters within a half-hour, Sir Jean," he said low-voiced. "You will answer any questions asked you. But you will take orders only from me."

Jean Baignault saluted in silence. Sir Matthew had gone on with the party. It entered his quarters and the pages and trumpeters filed off and the door was shut. Jackmen stood there with their pikes at the ready, Sir Guillaume Prunel in command, rigid, his sword in hand.

Get out of here while you have the time, Baignault thought. Then he ducked across and into De Cressy's room. De Cressy was by the window. He said nothing when Baignault went to the round steel mirror on the wall and began to comb his hair. But then he asked hoarsely, "Will Pablan and I be in on it, Jean?"

"I hope so," Jean Baignault said. "Still, I am not sure."

"That is all you can tell me?"

"Yes," Baignault said. "But be patient. Maybe, when I come out from talking with them, I can let you know more."

He was ready when the page summoned him. But nerves jumped a bit in the backs of his hands, his throat was dry. This could be the biggest thing in his life, he knew. The page shut the door behind him and he halted and saluted and looked forward into the vaulted, brilliantly lit room.

King Henry sat half-slouched on an ottoman. Sir William de Beaujeu sat in a chair at one side of him and Sir Matthew de Clermont at the other. Erect in front of them, but flanked around toward the door, Sieur Amboise stood with his lame leg supported by his sword. He said, "My son, Sir Jean Baignault." There was open pride in his voice. "King Henry, shall I tell him?"

"Yes, do." King Henry had a bowl of olives next to him on the ottoman. He dropped a pit delicately into the bowl, then leaned and stared steadily at Jean Baignault.

"The matter of the Il-Khan's offer has been discussed among us, Sir Jean," the Sieur Amboise said. "It has been decided to send a mission to the Golden Horde. That will treat with the Il-Khan and then attempt to take his son, Chagan, from Karakoram to Rome and safely home again."

"Understood, sir," Jean Baignault said. His nervousness was gone. He was part of this now; he lived it, and it moved too fast for any emotion to be felt.

"You will go as a member of the mission," the Sieur Amboise said. "With you and in command of it will be Sir Gerard Montvilliers Louvic of the Knights Templars. The third man will be my sergeant, Mustaf, for the reason that Mustaf knows a great deal of the territory through which you will travel and some of the languages spoken there."

"Understood, sir," Jean Baignault said again. He was obliquely watching the Grand Master of the Knights Templars. Sir William de Beaujeu stirred in his chair and the frame creaked. Then he made a gesture with his hands flung wide. "I would prefer another knight. One of more experience. This is a vast venture that we propose."

Sieur Amboise stood motionless. Jean Baignault sensed suddenly the tension that held him and also held the rest. There must have been a lot of bitter dissension here, he realized, before anything like an agreement was reached. Now the Templar was ripping that apart and the whole matter might be lost.

For years, Baignault remembered, the Templars had been opposed to the Hospitalers. The Templars, who were once mostly monks, had grown rotten-rich. They held huge wealth in both *Outremer* and Europe, and they put a tax upon pilgrims, mocking the Hospitalers when they said those folks should go over the roads free. So in return the Hospitalers taxed the Templars when they entered Hospitaler territory. The Templars got back at them by selling at a high price the salt from the mine they owned at Château Pelerin. It was a stupid, galling situation, and Sieur Amboise who belonged to neither side was caught between them.

But the Sieur Amboise had decided to speak. His pale face was sharply lined. He looked at the Templar commander almost as though he were his enemy. "I insist," he said, "that Sir Jean Baignault be a member of the mission."

"We have already reached agreement," Sir Matthew de Clermont said roughly. "Sir Jean is our choice. He has distinguished himself in combat; he is the best of our young knights. Remember, too, if you would, Templar, that there is a personal element. The messenger came straight from the Il-Khan to Sieur Amboise. And the gift of the emerald was made to him. His son will go as his deputy, and as such will have real effect among the Golden Horde. He will carry the emerald too. But if you are not satisfied by what we tell you, name another knight, one of your order whom we can trust more."

"Messieurs les chevaliers," King Henry said in a smooth voice before Sir William de Beaujeu had time to speak. "There must not be among us any question of trust or distrust. I am in favor of Sir Jean Baignault for the reasons given. You might recall, Sir William, that an officer of your order is to lead the mission. I can say no more."

"You need not," the big Templar said. He reached across King Henry and took a handful of olives. "I accept the choice. You have convinced me. Even among our people, we have heard how clever Sieur Amboise is in dealing with the tribes over the border. So, let the son go. He looks like a real fighting man. Good luck to him. Good luck to the mission. It may pull us out of a very deep hole."

Sir Matthew looked at the Templar as if about to smile.

34

"I am pleased that the matter is settled. Come to my serving room. It is late, but there is still time for supper. King Henry has eaten couscous here in the past. He will tell you how well my cook prepares the dish."

"Fine; very fine," King Henry said.

But Jean Baignault was listening to Sir Matthew. "You will stay, Sir Jean, and talk with your father. There are details of the mission to be discussed. When you are finished, report to me. I will have a final word for you."

"Yes, sire." Jean Baignault saluted. Then he stood stiffly until he was alone in the room with his father. Sieur Amboise went to a chair and sprawled in it and propped out his lame leg. He massaged the knee with rhythmic strokes, and his head still lowered said harshly, "If I did not have this, I believe that I would be on the way to Karakoram and Rome myself. But I make a small joke, Jean. Right from the start, I have known that you would go. It will be difficult, still I have faith in you."

"Thank you, sir," Jean said. "But I thought for a moment here that my chance could not be too much."

"That is a stubborn lot." Sieur Amboise nodded toward the serving room where tankards clinked and there was laughter. "I had to argue with both sides before I was through. As you know, there is more bad blood than good between Templars and Hospitalers."

"But when do we leave, sir?"

"Before dawn. We want you down the mountain and away from here as soon as possible."

"Have you met this Templar officer who's to be in command?"

"Louvic? Yes. He was with us for some time before we sent for you. He has hennaed hair and painted fingernails and the same soft ways as King Henry. But he has a real battle record too, and is supposed to be one of the best Templar knights. Your worry will not be with him, and I was able to get you Mustaf."

"Then there is not very much else to worry about," Jean Baignault said.

His father looked up at him with a short, bleak smile. "There'll be treachery on every side," he said. "And intrigue within intrigue. Nobody has come forward yet to explain how you can reach Rome unharmed with Chagan. But this Templar, Gerard Louvic, has been mixed up in intrigue for years. If he is a true knight, which I think he is,

35

he should know how to recognize treachery and deal with it."

"You make him out a good deal smarter than myself," Jean Baignault said.

"The greatest fault you have," the Sieur Amboise said unsmiling, "is that you are young. But you will get over that. Now I must go and discuss the journey with Louvic. You should report to Sir Matthew. Give me your sword."

"Could I ask why, sir?"

"Of course. Louvic and you and Mustaf are to ride out as if the party is made up of a Pisan merchant, his clerk and his bodyguard. You will have bales of trade goods and pack mules to carry them. Louvic can talk like a Pisan, knows the place and the dialect well. Along the way, he will instruct you. But you and he will both carry your swords and body armor inside a bale. I want to have the armorer fix the emerald that came from the Il-Khan in the hilt of your sword. That you can show as proof of who you are when you get to Karakoram. And I am quite sure that no matter what happens you will keep your sword."

"You can be very sure." Jean Baignault unbuckled the belt and handed his father the weapon. "But will I see you in the morning when we leave?"

"No," the Sieur Amboise said slowly. "You will go over a trail distant from Beth-Haggan. I shall say good-by to your mother for you. Now I say it for myself. The armorer will bring the sword to your quarters. Ride with all my love."

"Thank you, sir." Jean Baignault assisted his father up from the chair. He stooped and the Sieur Amboise kissed him on the cheek, then went straight toward the door. Jean thought that he might turn or look back. But the Sieur Amboise kept on into the hall and out of sight, the long sword under his arm, his lame leg giving a scuffing sound as he dragged it over the tiles.

Before he saw his father again, Jean thought, he would have gone halfway across the world and back. But he was able to smile at himself. If the journey was so big, he'd better get started. He went to the entrance to the serving room and signed to a page to call Sir Matthew de Clermont.

The Grand Master smelled of spiced wine, but was extremely sober. They moved to a window recess and he said, "Your father has explained the matter to you clearly, Sir Jean?"

"He has. I will be prepared to leave at dawn, sire."

They stood in almost total darkness and it was difficult for him to see the Grand Master's face. But Sir Matthew put a grinding grip on his shoulder. "So there remains little left for me to tell you. If we come to an alliance with the Golden Horde, and if we are not betrayed meantime, *Outremer* will belong to us a very long time. We will regain Jerusalem and the Grail."

Jean Baignault did not speak. Emotion had finally caught him and he was shaken by it. He imagined the Holy City he had never seen; he knelt before the Grail, and triumphant singing pealed, and Jean Baignault was a Crusader who would be remembered in history. . . .

"Go to the chapel," Sir Matthew said. "Pray for yourself and the success of your mission. But do not stay too long. And, along the way, keep a sharp eye on every man. Yes, and woman. Good night, Sir Jean. I wish you luck."

"Thank you, sire," Jean Baignault said, and knelt in the manner of his order and kissed the Grand Master's scarred hand.

But he prayed for only a few minutes in the drafty, empty chapel. He had experienced his moment of ecstasy and of hope. Now he was impatient to make the dream reality. He was nervous, quite tense when he entered De Cressy's room. Both De Cressy and Ecorches were there, and he could tell by their eyes that they wished him to let them know where he was going, and why, and why they could not go.

"I am sorry," he said. "There is nothing that I can tell you. Later, you will hear. It might be a long time, though. I'm not sure."

"Get to sleep," De Cressy said, his fair face flushed. "We don't seek after your secrets. But when you are away from us, remember that we still are your friends."

"I will," he muttered, and lay down on the pallet and tried to sleep. But then the armorer was at the door with his sword, the emerald exquisitely set in the hilt. A serving brother behind the armorer had brought the clothing that an Italian clerk would wear, a knee-length woolen smock, a round cloth cap, woolen hose and sandals with ankle thongs.

Jean Baignault looked around in the light of the single candle burning on the table. His friends pretended to sleep; he tiptoed past them and lay down and listened to their

37

heavy snores. Those reassured him. De Cressy had meant it, he realized, when he had said that they were still his friends.

Baignault shut his eyes, the sword beside him, the Italian clothing at the foot of the pallet. The road to Karakoram was long. From there to Rome was longer yet. Then all the way back again . . . Sleep. Sleep. He must sleep. Snoring, he slept.

CHAPTER FOUR

A serving brother called him at four o'clock, deftly and without noise, and handed him a cup of sugarless but strong mint tea, then whispered, "You're to go to the barbican, Sir Jean."

"Very well," Baignault muttered. He drank the tea and dressed in the Italian clothing. The serving brother had brought a plain cape and he put it on, wrapping the sword in the hem, and went to the door. He had an overwhelming desire to get out of here. Last night had separated him from the past. He did not even glance at De Cressy or Ecorches, and was glad that they hadn't awakened to say good-by to him.

Only men-at-arms on night guard were in the halls and along the staircases. He strode past them swiftly, slipping a bit on the stone steps in the smooth-soled sandals. But at a side entrance to the immense stable at the ground level of the barbican tower he saw in the light of a torch Père Malachi and Nichol, the armorer. He stopped and the priest came forward and blessed him in simple words, while the gray-headed English armorer shook his hand until it ached and said, "Go with good fortune, Sir Jean."

Baignault was keenly touched. The chaplain had given him nearly all his education, and in the tilting yard Nichol had taught him the use of the sword, the mace, the lance and bow. He saluted, abruptly speechless with emotion, before he went on into the sally-port space.

Sir Guillaume Prunel stood in front of the narrow-arched gate. The constable was alone, and must be on special duty, Baignault realized. This post was usually kept by the officer of the guard. "Pass on outside," Sir Guillaume told him in a low, rapid voice. "The others wait for you there. Not even in El Kerak do we know who might be a spy. But fare you well."

Baignault gave a short nod. Sir Guillaume had opened the sally gate and beyond was thick, misty darkness. Entering it, Baignault had the impression that he had suddenly gone blind. His hand reached beneath the cape and grasped the sword hilt. Then he felt the desire to laugh. At the end of the drawbridge Mustaf tapped him on the shoulder and said softly, "The Templar's right behind me. Come on."

The Templar appeared almost wraithlike in the mist. Baignault made him out as small and slight as his eyes adjusted and he stared at the man. But the other did not waste time. "Sir Jean Baignault?" he said.

"That is right," Baignault said. "And you must be Sir Gerard Louvic. Good morning."

"Maybe not a very good morning," Louvic said. "Still, it will help us. Give your sword to the sergeant, please. He can put it in the same bale with mine."

"Yes, sir," Mustaf said, the words grunted, and Baignault grinned. Louvic was letting Mustaf know right at the beginning who was in command. And to take the big sword and put it inside a goods bale under such conditions was a pretty fair test of Mustaf's ingenuity. Six animals were clumped together at the head of the trail, held by their halters and reins. Baignault walked to them and saw that two were stocky horses of desert strain, the rest mules, three carrying packs and the fourth a saddle. Mustaf cursed as he loosened a pack lashing and thrust the sword inside. "Me," he told Baignault, "who rode a horse before I was weaned! They give me a fat-rumped garrison mule. And have you noticed?" he pointed to himself.

"I could not help it," Baignault said, the laughter plucking his throat cords. Mustaf was dressed in a dirty Arab abba, wore a floppy headcloth and sandals that were so loose they slapped the ground with each step he took. "But we have to go on the Roman road. You're too well known. If you did not wear something like that, you'd be recognized. Look at me. I am supposed to be a Pisan clerk."

"So," Mustaf said. "You're funny too."

But Louvic was beside them and his voice had a sharp edge. "We must get down into the valley before the sun takes the mist. The trail is off to the right from here. Start with your mount and the pack animals, Sergeant. Sir Jean and I will follow you."

"Yes, sir," Mustaf said. He blew his nose loudly with his thumb and forefinger. "Go slow behind me, though. This isn't easy in broad daylight. If the mules break their necks, don't blame me."

The trail was one seldom used because of its steep, torturous course and the danger of loose shale and rocks underfoot. But Mustaf's pride had been aroused and the mules were well chosen, sure in all their movements. Mustaf knew this thoroughly, Baignault thought; still he had admiration for the way the little turcopole guided them down around the curves, past the edge of a gorge into the valley. They came out there just before sunrise while the mist still hung low over the fields and the Roman road was empty.

"Nicely done, Sergeant," Louvic said.

Mustaf shrugged. "I could ha' done better on a horse. We'd ha' been down here ten minutes ago."

But Louvic said nothing in answer. He dropped back beside Baignault, sitting at ease in the saddle, his gloved hands lax on the reins. When the sun lifted over the ridges and spilled across the valley Baignault took the time to study him with care. There was no henna left in the curling hair, but maybe the gloves were worn to hide painted fingernails. Even in his role of a Pisan merchant who had come to *Outremer* to make his fortune Louvic was elegant.

There were seed pearls stitched to his cap. His doublet was of rich velvet, and his hose were of ribbed silk, his boots fashioned from fine-quality suede. A gold chain hung around his neck, and another around his waist. Rings were on his fingers over his gloves, and the hilt of his poniard, the only weapon he carried, was worked in silver filigree. A real dandy, this Templar, and strikingly handsome, with features to match those of an old Greek statue.

But the Sieur Amboise had warned him, Baignault remembered, that Louvic had a real combat record, although right now it was hard to believe. He'd find out more about the man along the road, and soon. It was important that he did. Louvic studied him too, he saw. The hooded eyes were intent upon his face.

"How much do you know of Italian?" Louvic said.

"Very little," Baignault said.

"Then let us begin," the Templar told him. "Repeat these

words after me. I will correct your accent and also tell you the meanings. And Italian is a pretty tongue."

"So I have heard," Baignault said with just the flicker of a smile.

They met all kinds of people from the complex, polyglot Levantine world upon the road as they moved north, and the lesson continued hour after hour. There was a steady succession of camel caravans, and mendicant gray friars, Arab tinsmiths who were really gypsies, and Italian merchants, most of them mounted on splendid Spanish jennies, their tough men-at-arms with lances lifted. Then peasants passed, and Jews in wide black hats, and shepherds from the hills with their flutes and flocks.

Jean Baignault was reminded that the road was the main route from Persia and Asia Minor to both Arabia and Egypt. But Aleppo in the north had never been held by the Crusaders, nor Damascus. So *Outremer* was like a leaky kettle that without warning might blow up and cause serious damage. It was very good, he told himself again, to be taking part in something that might stop that.

Louvic halted outside an inn in the late afternoon sunlight and made a sign to him and Mustaf that they would enter to spend the night. "See that the animals are fed and watered and well bedded," he told Mustaf. Then he dismounted and with Baignault started through the crowd at the main door.

A single knight without obvious affiliation, whose armor was dumped at his feet and whose eyes were reddened with wine, tried to block Louvic from the door. "No more room," he said. "The owner put me out and he'll do the same for you. But you merchants are lousy rich. Give me a dozen bezants and I'll fix the matter for us."

"Take your hand off my arm," Louvic said.

"What?" The knight stood straight, no longer staggering.

"Take your hand off my arm," Louvic said. He moved before Jean Baignault could, yet it seemed slow and without effort. His left leg went behind the knight, and with his left hand he freed the knight's hand from his arm. With his right hand, he pushed the much bigger man in the chest.

The knight vaulted backward into the roadway as if hauled by an invisible block and tackle. He landed on the flat of his back, spanking up dust, groaned and was still. "Such as that," Louvic said, "give Christianity a bad name."

41

"But I don't think he will again," Baignault said. "You have broken a good deal of his crockery."

"Take him from your mind," Louvic said. "Come in and join me in some wine. This has been a thirsty day."

"Yes, sir," Baignault said, then cleared a way for Louvic at the door. He was impressed. The dapper, slender Templar had enormous strength. Here was the proof he'd been looking for; now he could understand why Louvic had been picked to lead the mission.

They were drinking their second cup of wine when Mustaf came in from the corral. Baignault could tell from the turcopole's unconsciously swaggering manner that he also had seen the knight's rise and fall. Mustaf was obviously proud to serve under a man like Louvic. He touched his fingers to his forehead before the Templar. "Sir, the beasts have been watered and fed. They'll be ready at dawn. But can I have your permission to swap a mule for a horse?"

"What kind of a horse?" Louvic said.

"A pretty fair fifteen-hand Arabian, sir," Mustaf said. "It belonged to the man who just broke his leg in the road. When I got him out of there, I explained to him that he wouldn't do too good with a horse. A mule, though, he can ride, and maybe he can sell that junk he calls armor to the gypsies and work as a tinsmith."

Louvic smiled slowly at Mustaf. "I did not break his leg."

"Just lamed it," Mustaf said. "But I took care of that once I hauled him over into the corral. So he got around to thinking he might swap the horse."

"Permission granted," Louvic said. "Tell the innkeeper you're to have a flagon of wine with your supper. But keep sober."

"He doesn't drink much," Jean Baignault said quickly. "You need not worry. He will be all right."

Louvic turned his level, steady glance to Baignault. "Please remember," he said softly, "that you are my clerk. You must speak with me in Italian unless we're alone. And you must have a name. Attilio, that's good, isn't it?"

"Si, signor," Baignault said. This was important, he knew. Any carelessness might betray them.

They rode from the inn at dawn, Mustaf mounted on his new horse, and four days later they crossed the stony, turbid river that was called Nahr El Kelb, the River of the

42

Dog. It was inland from Antioch and marked the unrecognized frontier. North of it, the Saracens roamed at will, checked only by the Mongol patrols many marches beyond. But Louvic had ridden the country before and Mustaf had lived in it in his youth. "We have fast mounts," Louvic said. "Fifteen days should put us at the Iron Gate, the pass this side of the Samarkand Road. Then we are in the Mongols' hands and safe, because they hold the pass."

Jean Baignault recalled the maps he had gone over in the library at El Kerak. Those for this region were poor, indistinct. He hadn't got much from them. But he knew that the Saracens watched every trail. If they rode by day for fifteen days, it was quite certain that a Saracen *rezzia* would catch up with them.

"We could ride by night," he said to Louvic, "and sleep by day. Of course we make more speed in daylight. But there is a greater chance of being seen."

"The Saracens are out at night too," Louvic said. "They could find us then. I know that we meet danger either way. But day is best. We can ride faster, save time, get out of the region much more quickly."

"Very well, sir," Baignault said. "Then we ride by day."

Louvic swung his mount at once and for the first time rode out alone in front. He kept a continuous lope, erect in the saddle to inspect each ridge and gully. "A good man to follow," Baignault told Mustaf. "We'll have tired animals, though, when we get to the pass."

"Before," Mustaf said. He was smacking the mules into line. "I don't like this country. I never did."

There were few caravans on the trails they rode, then none at all. The big khans, the barnlike stone structures put up for the use of travelers, were deserted, the hearthstones cold, the horse and camel corrals empty. Farms were burned or abandoned, fields fallow, and the people they met upon the way either lepers or demented, the miserable and the terrible of the hinterland.

They were twelve days past the River of the Dog when Louvic caught sight of a huge Saracen war party on a ridge to the east. They cut down into a dry wadi where the sand muffled the animals' hoof sounds and rode at the full gallop and doubled back twice before Louvic was content that they weren't pursued. Then they continued roughly parallel to the trail, keeping to the hills and every fold of the ground, and that night when they bivouacked they ate cold food, kermess and corn cake, jerked meat and raisins, and made no fire.

But at dawn when Louvic climbed to the top of the ridge ahead with Baignault there were armed men at each point of the compass. They were Saracen warriors and they had good horses, were obviously under unified command. Louvic slowly stroked his horse's neck. He squinted in the sunlight reflected from the flints of the short, arid plain beyond the ridge. "I was wrong," he said. "We should have moved by night."

"I don't believe that, sir," Baignault said. "We were forced to take the chance. But do you think that we might have been betrayed?"

"No," Louvic said. "If so, we would have been attacked back inside the border. There was plenty of opportunity along the Roman road or in some inn where we stayed for a night. This country is big enough for escape, and with luck we would be quite safe. The Saracens are such, however, that they'll go for anybody. We look promising to them—bales of goods, horses, mules and the gold any merchant must carry to keep in business."

The Templar had drawn off his gloves and put them inside his doublet and Baignault could see the red flecks of paint that still adhered to the fingernails. Louvic was getting ready to fight, he realized. This was the sign. "I count twenty-two of them," Baignault said. "But we still might ride wide. We could get out before they bunched on us."

"Then you agree with me," Louvic said quietly, "that there's no more reason to pretend that we are unarmed. Let us go down, Sir Jean, and equip ourselves to fight."

Mustaf had already unhitched the bale and put it on the ground. They opened it and took out their body armor and their swords and Mustaf's tulwar and bow and quiver. But Baignault saw that Louvic also had a bow of his own, a long Norman weapon of magnificent workmanship, and a quiver of arrows of exceptional length. "My pleasure has been gazelle hunting," Louvic said. "I have been known to knock down a beast at a range of over two hundred yards. This is not to boast, though. I want to propose a definite plan of action."

He squatted and with Baignault and Mustaf beside him described a curving line on the sand. "If we tried to ride to-

44

gether at any part of their line," he said, "they would shift men like this to meet us." He moved his finger along the curve from right to left and left to right. "They could double up and catch us between them. Man would replace man and the circle would pull in close."

"You mean," Baignault said, "that one of us should go ahead and draw their fire, pull them from their positions by himself. Then the other two would be able to ride through."

"More," Louvic said. "If I ride up on them I can break the formation with my bow before they know how much range it has. It will make a hole that we can use. Sergeant, do you think the Saracens have ever been against a bow like this?"

"No, sir," Mustaf said. "But they're pretty fair with their own. I'd like to try yours myself. Shoot the bastards bow-legged."

"Another time," Louvic said, a smile at the corners of his mouth. "You would have to start with gazelle to get used to it."

"But you are our chief," Jean Baignault said. "You shouldn't expose yourself like that. We can still move together. There must be a place where we can break through and keep on going."

Louvic had put a finger to the string of his bow. It twanged with a high, vibrant note. His eyes gleamed as he said, "We are too few for such a thing to work. I shan't expose myself unduly, though, Sir Jean. I will take the mules along. They will not serve us any other purpose now I'm no longer a merchant. For me and my horse, they will be a shield. Take the packs off them, Sergeant."

"Whip 'em hard enough," Mustaf said, "and they'll run as fast as a horse for a while."

But Jean Baignault said, "You are taking too great a chance, Sir Gerard. Let me do this. Or Mustaf."

"Obey me, please," Louvic said harshly. "Wait until I am over the ridge. Then ride past me. With my fire, you will be able to go quite a distance. But I will meet you on the next ridge—that one there, straight north. *Au revoir*."

Louvic was in the saddle. He loosened his bow string just a bit, then tightened it. Reaching around, he took the halter rope of the lead mule from Mustaf. The other two bumped close on their ropes, nervous and side-kicking at

45

his horse. He spoke gently to them, and they fell back in line. He spoke to his horse and started up the ridge, his hand momentarily on his cruciform sword hilt to free the weapon in the scabbard.

Jean Baignault watched him with a mixture of admiration and anxiety and envy. This had to be, he realized. Louvic took only what was a most necessary risk. Still, he wished that he could ride in his place. He wished also that he owned the bow and could use it as Louvic must. But if the Templar were wounded or killed, he'd be forced to continue the mission and command it himself. That knowledge made Baignault turn to Mustaf. "Come on," he told him, "we go and fight."

The ridge was formed of shale and their horses spurned the stuff and labored, could not come rapidly to the gallop. When they were over it and out in the plain Louvic was more than a hundred yards past them and the Saracens had ridden as he had predicted to intercept him. Louvic halted his horse. He gentled the mules and they gathered, one on his right side, one on the other and the third in front.

Jean Baignault sat very still in the saddle for an instant, a surge of rage reaching his brain. He recognized these men who passed cantering around Louvic. They were Saracens in the broad Crusader meaning of the term, but they were also Bedouins of the famous, restless and savage Wahabi tribe from the desert beyond Jordan. He had fought their emir and bested him in single combat and the fellow was here now and glaring narrow-eyed and beginning to shout: "You remember, *roumi?* I told you that we would meet again!"

"I remember," Baignault bawled back. "But this time we are better met, Ibn Aud Aghaf. There will be no mercy shown."

"You use a nice word." The swarthy, wiry Wahabi laughed and swung up his scimitar in a whirling arc. "For two years, I've waited. We found your track back across the border and followed you. The vultures will say your prayers for you tonight. What holds you? Must your leader fight alone?"

The Wahabi warriors, Aghaf a bit closer than the rest, kept to their circle, but he urged them inward and they bunched up, several men within yards of each other, and shot at Louvic with their bows. He had disregarded the shouts between Baignault and the emir, and he did not fire, and their arrows slanted short. He only shot at them when they drew quite near to him, and then he stood up at his full height in the stirrups.

Baignault could see the sunlight glint upon Louvic's knuckles, white against the skin of the hand that pulled the bow string. The arrow took flat flight and it made a humming sound in the air, with an impact that was like a hammer blow but tore flesh, then bone. Striking a warrior in the chest, the arrow came out his back and he was knocked from the saddle, flopping legs-high onto the ground.

Louvic missed with his second shot. It flailed a warrior's neck and caught a horse behind him. The horse staggered, neighed, rolled down over his rider, rose and ran across the plain to topple dead. *"Dieu nous protège,"* Baignault whispered. Eight warriors led by Aghaf had turned inward from the circle toward Louvic. Four of them had enough sense to rein in and attempt to answer with the arrow instead of the lance or scimitar. "Those are for us," Baignault told Mustaf. "We will take them off him. Leave the emir for me. Ride, man, and fast."

Mustaf had his own bow strained taut. He fired and cursed. "Yes, sir," he said. He slung the bow and drew the tulwar. "This for me is better than watching."

Baignault hardly heard the words. The pressure of his blood made his ears ring and his eyes were dimmed with sweat. He had taken his sword from the scabbard and he raised it and yelled his battle cry, "Baignault, Baignault!" and now the horse was really running and the man he wanted, Ibn Aud Aghaf, was almost close enough.

It had been two years ago in February that they had first met. That was on the road from Antioch, when Baignault was spent from the bouts of Candlemas celebration with his cousins in the old, walled city. He rode home to Beth-Haggan as usual, more careless than he should have been, drowsy with wine yet forcing his horse. The country through which he rode wasn't safe for a lone Christian at night. Moslem marauders often moved across the region and they boasted that after dark the road belonged to them.

The boast had fact behind it, he learned when his horse threw a shoe, then began to limp. He was down from the saddle and examining the bruised hoof as the Wahabis surrounded him. He counted six of them, all young men and well armed. They took no trouble to hide from the moonlight and his sword was in the scabbard attached to the saddle.

He gave them the customary greeting of the countryside, "*Salaam aleikum*"—"Peace be with you." But he was lowering the horse's hoof and straightening to grasp his sword.

"Listen to the colt," their leader said. He thrust back the folds of his gold-trimmed burnous, jumped to the ground. "We're given talk of peace, and in our own language."

The word "colt" in Syrian slang was an insult, applied only to a man of mixed blood. Baignault did not hesitate. His heavy leather gauntlets were inside his belt and he yanked the pair and pitched them spanking into the Wahabi's face. "Jean Baignault is the name," he said. "Of Beth-Haggan, at the foot of El Kerak. My blood is pure. But yours must be mucked from the streets of a dozen captured cities."

"So?" the warrior said. "So, *roumi?* I am Ibn Aud Aghaf of the Wahabi, and my people have served the Prophet from the beginning. Take your sword. Stand up to me. I wouldn't like it told that I killed even you without a fair fight."

"And the others?" Baignault said, his fingers tight on the sword.

"They obey me. Guard yourself."

The fight raged back and forth across the road while surprised frogs beeped in the ditches, the horses rolled their eyes and the mounted Wahabi warriors leaned down grim and silent in the moonlight. For Baignault, it was not very difficult. He had been trained to fight against the scimitar, and his weapon was heavier, his reach superior. Ibn Aud Aghaf attacked quite well, but was lacking in defense; the scimitar was knocked from his hand when he tried a head-high parry.

Jean Baignault might have killed him then. But instead he stamped upon the scimitar blade and snapped it. "Return to your horse," he told the Wahabi. "I do not need your life, and I give you pardon. There's nothing to fear from you. My people are the masters of this land."

The Wahabi emir stood trembling, his hands extended rigidly from his sides, his eyes incandescent and a bit insane with frustrated rage. Jean Baignault had brief understanding of how much the people who had once owned all this country hated Christians. He almost felt pity. But the

48

other kept control of the rage; he made no attempt to draw his dagger, but swung around and went to his horse and mounted without a word. Then, sweat along his chin from the effort at self-control, he stared down at Baignault. "Remember me," he said. "Don't forget this. I will come looking for you."

He called an order to the other warriors then, to ride off along the road. But several of them were not quite so willing to accept defeat; they prodded Baignault's horse with their scimitars, sending the beast into a limping run in front of them. Baignault cursed savagely, but the horse was gone. He walked back to Antioch that night, and at the drawbridge the men-at-arms grinned at him as though he were an urchin who had lost his way or were frightened by ghosts.

Now on this plain where Louvic had chosen to fight alone he tried to get through to the Wahabi emir. A warrior let go an arrow that skipped past the flints past his horse's nigh foreleg. Two more, wheeling their horses in unison, came rushing with their lances lowered. He raised in the stirrups and measured the man who carried the bow, killed him with an overhead slash that crushed the steel cap through the skull to the brows. Mustaf yelled, a thin, yipping cry, and pulled his horse sidewise so that the pair of warriors had to break formation. He overreached a lance point and swiped the tulwar upward; the Wahabi's mouth gaped as the throat was pierced, the dark face convulsed, and then the blood spattered and the eyes blinked with death.

Baignault took the other warrior of the pair, gave him time to make his thrust, then parried with the sword. He sheered the lance shaft cleanly and while the point spun and bounced from his chest, leaned in, struck again, killed. But his battle fury began to subside with the execution of the blows. He was abruptly and acutely aware of who he was, and remembrance of the responsibility that had been given him came back; he glanced down and under the butt of his palm, where he gripped the sword, he saw the emerald.

He would be a fool if he fought any more here. Ibn Aud Aghaf had left the combat, riding away swiftly to avoid personal attack. The emir was no coward, Baignault told himself, and neither was he likely to be a fool. This was not the time nor the place to press the fight. He was quite certain that the Wahabi had some other plan of attack. So Louvic, Mustaf and himself should get out. He turned and shouted to Mustaf, beckoned with his raised sword to Louvic. Mustaf was all right; he was unwounded and there were no Wahabis near him. He responded, moving at the gallop toward Baignault. But Louvic was still engaged.

Louvic sat his horse with the three mules around him in their same triangle. He shot arrows at the Wahabis along the ridge as though they were practice targets. He seemed not to have heard Baignault. The arrows were fitted, fired with a mechanical, almost perfect precision.

Baignault jerked his arm at Mustaf. "We must get him out. Ride around on the other side. At once."

Louvic regarded them with a remote glance when they flanked him. "You should not be here," he said. "You were ordered by me to go to the ridge. I would have followed you, but it was my desire to take all I could of them and stop pursuit."

"Come along with us, sir," Baignault said. "They have lost too many dead to chase us. And they have no liking for your bow. It gives them more than their emir can get them to meet and still fight. The man is known to me from Syria and he's hot for combat. Yet he refuses to close further with us here. Something else must be in his mind. We would do best to leave."

"You could be quite right," Louvic said mildly and put his horse in motion. Mustaf had the mules by the halter ropes and began to lead them, then stopped. One of them had been wounded in the barrel by a lance, was slow and must be abandoned. But off to the west the ridge was open. They rode through and when Baignault turned to look back there was no pursuit.

"A lesson in tactics," Louvic said. He sat lax in his saddle, hands on the pommel, the reins loose and the bow dangling. "You see, Sir Jean, they were forced to bend to us. Not because we are Christians and they heathens. But because we are better fighting men. I should like to halt for a moment now."

"Why?" Baignault said roughly.

Louvic glanced up at him and then down at his thigh. He said, "I am reminded of the single knight we met at the inn. Some of my crockery is broken. It was a lucky shot, obviously—still it found me."

Baignault did not speak. He was staring at the ugly projection of the shattered arrow shaft from Louvic's upper thigh and the flow of arterial blood that had started to clot

50

around it. "Bad," Mustaf said. He was down from his horse to inspect the wound. "You know that, Sir Gerard."

"Yes," Louvic said. "But can you pull the arrow out? It would help me."

"What I do will hurt," Mustaf said.

"Go ahead," Louvic said and clambered out of the saddle and lay prone. But he bit through his underlip while he tried to repress his agony. Mustaf worked with the poniard, then gave that up, his face pale and his hands shaking. "Not for me," he said. "I can't, messires."

Jean Baignault took the weapon from him. He knelt and while Mustaf restrained Louvic dug at the stubborn fragments of the arrow. They were deeply imbedded, and the arrow head had shattered the thigh bone. He could not clear that and in his turn he gave up, only stanched the wound and bandaged it. Louvic had passed into shock; he lay supine, the handsome head aside, the hair soaked with sweat.

"We will put him on a mule," Baignault said. "It will be more comfortable for him than his horse. And we must leave here. The Wahabis aren't through with us. They will have trackers out."

Mustaf pointed, wordless. A Wahabi warrior sat his horse on a ridge to the south in dramatic silhouette, the westering sun on his shield, lance and cap. Louvic's bow power has made him afraid to come any closer, Baignault thought. But there must be more of them behind him. They still believe they can come upon us this side of the pass. Aghaf for certain has not forgotten the insult paid him on the Antioch road. . . .

"Mount and ride," he told Mustaf. "We shan't halt again till the animals ask for it."

They rode through the afternoon into dusk and night, holding to the north by the stars. Then the weary animals complained once more and Baignault knew that they must stop. He and Mustaf lowered Louvic to the ground, wrapped him in a cape, eased him against a saddle. Louvic was partly conscious. He looked around and asked Baignault, "How far have we gone?"

"Some few miles."

"But the Saracens are still with us."

"They are not too close. And let me explain now, sir. They're of the Wahabi tribe, and their emir is known to me. I had a brush with him in Syria two years back, spared his life and then taunted him. He would seen to have borne me ill-will ever since. Somewhere before we crossed the border he discovered that I was in this party, and that is why we have been followed."

"Such is fortune," Louvic said softly. "I don't blame you, nor can Mustaf. All Moslems are our enemies. But you must have stopped here to feed and rest the animals."

"So I did," Baignault said. "Rest, though, please, Sir Gerard. We will need you later."

"There shall not be much more later for me," Louvic said. Then consciousness failed him and he lay still.

"The mule was of no good to him," Mustaf said. "The beast has a hard gait, and the other one too. He'll die if we keep on with him."

"But he cannot be left," Baignault said.

"No," Mustaf said, "not this man."

There was a wide skein of gullies ahead and when they started Mustaf asked to lead the way. He checked against the stars and never seemed in doubt and Baignault knew that this was a skill he didn't own which Mustaf had picked up as a boy riding herd on his father's horses. Mustaf would bring the party out safely, he told himself, and by dawn they should be out of the reach of any Wahabi tracker. Then they would have no more than another day's ride to the Iron Gate.

But Louvic began to moan and writhe under the bonds they had put on him to keep him in the saddle. Baignault got down and gagged the quivering, fever-hot mouth, tied the hands and they rode on. He dozed, able to trust the horse, and awakened to the sound of Louvic's voice. It was a gabble; the man was in delirium.

"Make the gag tight enough and you choke him," Mustaf said. "And he has pulled his hands loose. He's *maboul*—crazy with pain."

"Hold the animals while I do this," Baignault said. He went over to Louvic. The man was in a heavy sweat despite the night chill. He had dragged at the leg bandage, torn it aside. Baignault saw that the wound was inflamed and the leg swollen to the groin.

He braced himself and lifted Louvic's head, and taking a gradual breath, aimed the blow at the jaw. It worked. The impact sent Louvic deep into coma and the babbling yells that might attract the enemy had stopped. But he couldn't repeat this. If he did, it would have its effect upon the heart, and Louvic would only die in a slightly different way.

He was overcome by sorrow, feeling a sense of shame that made him want to weep. Then all the years of his training, the discipline of his entire life sent him to his horse. He got into the saddle and the horse moved. Mustaf was in motion with the other animals and they kept north, the night silent around them and to Baignault weirdly empty.

Louvic was sane, though, at dawn. He hauled himself half upright and looked with an open, understanding glance at Baignault. "I must have made a great lot of noise in the night," he said.

"Not too much," Baignault said. "We are away from them, in any event. Mustaf led us clear."

"How far to the pass now?" Louvic said.

"A day's ride," Baignault said.

"Less, sir," Mustaf said, "if we keep the same pace."

Louvic was looking at his leg. He had looked around, too, at the horses which trembled and stumbled and the mules which panted as though they were spavined. "I shall not go any further," he said. "This animal is not fit to carry me and I would endanger you. I should like my bow and arrows, please, Sir Jean. Then you can leave me."

"That makes no sense," Baignault said. "We can bring you through to the pass. The Mongols must have some sort of surgeon within call. He will tend to you."

"No," Louvic said. "Give me the bow and arrows. I will stay here. Watch, and you will learn that I am right." He gestured at his horse. The beast, the reins slack, had moved to stare to the south. The ears were raised in response to sound; a tremor went through it and it whinnied. Now the other beasts whinnied and their ears were up and they stamped the ground.

"Help me down," Louvic said.

"There are only a few arrows left," Baignault said. "Do come along with us, sir. Stay in the saddle as long as you are able to bear the pain."

Louvic smiled. "I could not ride another mile. The same thing would then happen. You would be delayed. Have no worry about me. Once the arrows are gone, I will still have these." He let his fingertips pass across the hilt of his sword, then the poniard. "Be so good as to help me down."

Jean Baignault and Mustaf lifted him from the saddle

53

and carried him to the crest of a small ridge. They built up a low, wall-like rampart of stones around him and gave him the half-filled water sack although he protested that they should keep that. Then he said, "You have your orders, Sir Jean. I know no more about them than you. Kneel, and let us pray."

They prayed in unison, only Louvic's voice strong. He shook their hands and said, "Ride." His head was turned aside; he had the arrows out of the quiver. He tightened the bow string and gauged the wind and the sunlight. It was as though, Jean Baignault thought, gripped by grief, Louvic had transferred himself to another world where he was alone with the Wahabis.

Baignault ran to his horse. He was tempted to flog it into a gallop. But he restrained himself. Louvic's sacrifice would mean nothing if he failed to reach the pass. Behind him, Mustaf said quietly, "You can't lose it like that. I have tried. The sadness still rides with you."

Baignault drew rein for just a moment, and stared back. Hawks hovered in the sky over Louvic, and a vulture. It was certain that he would be found. There would be first one Wahabi and then several, and they would wait until the arrows were gone. "A real soldier," Baignault whispered.

"He has paid his way with them," Mustaf said. "But, Sir Jean, we must ride."

Another plain lay between them and the sandstone cliffs that walled the Iron Gate. It was barren and rocky, cruelly hot under the mid-day sun. The foundering horses gave out one after the other. Then Baignault and Mustaf rode the mules until those too dropped. But the Wahabis who were following them from the south had fresh mounts, and there must be men from other Moslem tribes among them, Baignault imagined.

Still, his thinking might not be very clear now, he realized. He was so weary that it was agony to breathe, and painfully hungry and thirsty as well. The stones cut his boots. They abraded his hands and his knees when out of weakness he tripped and fell, then pushed himself upright again. Mustaf was in trouble worse than his own. The turcopole went at a stooped, veering stagger, his head low, his back arched and his hands thrust forth like a man beneath a tremendous burden. Then he fell and crawled and could not rise.

Baignault returned to him. "I cannot carry you," he said. "But maybe I can drag you."

"Do that, then," Mustaf said.

They could see the Wahabis, small, neat, white figures distinct upon their horses. Give the lot another quarter of an hour, Baignault thought, give them even less and he would not be forced to haul Mustaf or keep on any further himself. It would be quicker than with Louvic. An arrow licked the air beside him. A second, a third and fourth were very close; the fifth whipped his ear and he cried out in instinctive, animal fear.

But he kept on and he saw that the cliffs at the sides of the pass were a buff color, darkening with magenta shadows that stretched out onto the plain. Cool in the shadow, Baignault told himself. Don't stop moving toward it. He had clutched Mustaf by the hair and there was a smear of bloody spittle at the corner of the turcopole's mouth, but he was unconscious. Baignault stumbled and almost fell and then the shadow was around them.

He stood still, sucking in his breath. The sound he heard, like that of cloth being torn, he made himself. It was his breathing. The sounds of the Wahabi arrows were a drone and a whine, a slap, a chitter along the stones, and then a solid whack as Mustaf was struck. Baignault's eyes were blurred; he could see only that the wound was in the upper body. When he went on, still dragging Mustaf, he did not hear the arrows any more. His breathing was too loud.

At the foot of the pass, he fell and knew that he was unable to rise. He hunkered on his elbows, still with his hand hooked in Mustaf's long hair. But he looked up into the pass and felt a flicker of hope.

People were there. Now they were coming down. They wore hooded robes and the sandaled feet went a lot faster than he could crawl. He saw, though, that they were not Mongols. These were Jebel Druse. He had gone from the Wahabis to the Druse, and they too were his enemies. Down in the burning pit of his chest he started to laugh.

But then he heard the voice. It said, "Stop. Nobody will give you harm. Let your comrade be. We will take care of him."

The laughter went out of Baignault. He did not move, and only stared upward. A woman stood in front of him. Her voice was young and she gave orders. When he could laugh again, that would be funny. Now he was too tired. He said, "Thank you," and the last of his energy was spent. He rolled over inert beside Mustaf.

CHAPTER FIVE

It was cool and quiet and he wasn't near death any longer. Jean Baignault sensed that in the depths of the pain. He slept again and the pain returned to wake him. But he was able to look around, for the pain, after the sleep, was less.

He was in a tent of finely made camel's hair. It was dyed black in the Druse fashion, and gradually he remembered that Druse warriors had come to him and Mustaf at the foot of the Iron Gate. They had kept off the Wahabis, stopped the pursuit. But there had been a woman too, and she had given orders to the warriors. Impossible, Baignault thought. A woman of their tribe was never a leader. It was foolish stuff, he told himself out of confused, blurred memory.

Then he lifted his head and studied the tent in detail. He lay on a pile of exquisite Cashmere robes. His pillow was a broad camel saddle covered with them. There was a beaked brass pot on a brazier beside him and beyond it an ivory-inlaid chess set and an arms rack that was empty. A warrior of some rank had occupied the tent or owned it, and he had been brought here only because he was wounded.

Baignault got slowly to his feet. He was dressed, he saw, in a short cotton shift, and beneath that, across his back and over his ribs, were bandages on his wounds. But they couldn't be serious, he knew. He had received them near the end of the march while he was in delirium and he hadn't even felt them. Mustaf must be much worse off, and he wondered where Mustaf was, and how he could find out about his condition.

The teapot made him aware of his great thirst and he forgot Mustaf and went toward it. The tea was cold; he poured it into one of the little porcelain cups, and drank until there was no more. It was laced with mint, rich with sugar, and he felt better and moved in the dim light toward his armor heaped in a corner.

The steel mesh of his shirt was ripped, punctured and

bloody. But he paid little attention to it. He was looking for his sword. He flung aside the armor, groped in increasing, frantic haste across the rug-strewn floor. His motions were clumsy and he knocked the teapot from the brazier.

There was immediate response to the sound. The rug that covered the tent doorway was raised. A big Nubian slave who carried a scimitar and wore padded leather body armor stood staring at him. "I don't mean to make trouble," Baignault said in Arabic, "yet I would like my sword."

The slave stepped back and dropped the door rug behind him. Baignault began to curse. He must have the sword. It was his cherished possession and it bore the Tree of Life emerald. Then the anger that gripped him drained away into dull shock. Without the emerald the mission was hopeless. There was no reason for his going on if he did not have it.

He had been able to take Louvic's death; he had seen other men die in action. Their loss had been accepted and their comrades had kept on fighting and won. Even he himself, if Mustaf were to be killed, would still hold onto some hope and carry through the mission alone. But the emerald was his passport, the talisman he needed to take him to Karakoram and the Il-Khan's court and thence to Rome. Without it, the whole, long, dangerous and mysterious way would be blocked.

He told himself that he should never have been assigned to the mission. The Sieur Amboise and the Hospitaler and Templar leaders and King Henry had been wrong about him. He was not enough of a soldier, and his knighthood was nothing but a stupid mockery. He should have remained an esquire; yet with this failure on his record he could not even return to El Kerak and serve as that.

Baignault put his puffed, raw hands to his aching head. He felt the impulse both to revile himself and to laugh at his lack of skill. Then the door rug was pulled aside. He looked up, the sun against his eyes.

A woman stood in the entrance to the tent, her body in a wedge of sunlight. It traveled from her head slantwise down over her hair and face veil to her velvet, gold-worked jacket, her thin woolen trousers and her red gazelle-hide slippers. He remembered her, although she had been differently dressed. She had been at the pass when he arrived there dragging Mustaf.

"How are you?" she said in Arabic.

57

"I do not do too badly," he answered, his voice harsh. He still stared at her, uncertain of himself and how he should act. But when she let the rug drop and crossed the tent and seated herself on a saddle he became aware of the oddness of his appearance. He tried to tug the shift over his gashed knees. The effort made the pain jerk through him and he gasped.

"Sit down," she said. "The Saracens made a fair target of you. That wound in the ribs is not good."

He nodded and shuffled over to where he had slept and sat down and drew a robe over his legs. He pushed the thought of the sword from his mind for a moment and asked, "How is the man who was with me? He is dead?"

"No, he will live. He is in the tent next to this. But he is severely wounded."

"What tribe is the owner of this camp?"

"It belongs to a clan of the Jebel Druse."

Baignault felt irritation, then anger. She was too calm and too sure of herself. "The Druse come from the region around Sueida and the Lebanon," he said. "This is far from there."

"The matter should not concern you," she said. "Only the fact that we saved you and your men from the Saracens. You are lucky."

He sat wordless, his thinking distracted. For she had lifted the veil and he stared hard at her. There were no tribal tattoos on her face. It was strong-boned, the nose straight, quite prominent, with wide nostrils, and the mouth was full-lipped, the chin short and round. Her eyes were gray-green, but they appeared light against her tanned skin. He realized that she must not believe much in the Moslem tradition that women should go veiled. Her skin was so tan that she must have spent many days in the open without one, and the shape and strength of her hands suggested that she might handle a hunting bow with ease. Then he remembered that the Druse were a proud and independent people who usually kept to their Lebanese mountains and had never joined in alliance with the confederation of Arab tribes that had come to be called Saracens.

She was also studying him steadily, her eyes fixed on his. "What might you be named?" she said.

"Attilio," he said; the name he and Louvic had agreed upon weeks back.

58

"How is it that you and the turcopole came to the pass?"

"My master was a Pisan merchant. We were attacked by a *rezzia* of Saracens—rightly, they were Wahabis—and he was killed. I worked as his clerk. The turcopole was our guide. We were on our way to trade with the Golden Horde. I am grateful that your people saved us, and let me now thank you. Could it be that I might talk with your sheik?"

He had decided to keep silent about the sword until he knew more about this woman. The matter was too important for him to risk disclosure by some impetuous, angry demand. It was also the Arab fashion to be guarded in any contact with a stranger and he must carefully follow their ways.

"My brother is the chief of this clan," she said. "He was wounded in combat a week ago, so I have taken his place." She smiled slightly, and her eyes were warm and bright, and Baignault recognized suddenly that she was a handsome woman, not plumply pretty like the Syrian's wife who had attracted him in *Outremer*. She let a little silence fall, then added, "I do not usually enter much into the affairs of men."

"*Kismet*," Baignault said, "so be it. Then perhaps you would not mind telling me your name."

She laughed without restraint, her head back. "I am named Subeyla," she said. "My brother has the name of Akhu-et-T'ib. That of course means Brother of the Wolf. But do not be frightened by it. My teeth are the same size as any other woman's in the clan; I eat only what is told me by the Koran."

"I feel no fear," Baignault said, then laughed with her. "I have heard the name before. Your father was a famous sheik. He was named Ibn el Elash. No more than three years ago, he was killed while at the hunt. His horse tripped and he was thrown and his neck broken by the fall."

"For a clerk who is a *roumi*," she said, "you know a good deal about us. And you have told me that you come from far away."

"I have spent some time in Syria," he said, "also in the Lebanon. That is one of the reasons why my master hired me."

"But it is not why, when we found you, you were wearing Crusader body armor. At the pass, some of our men who know the tongue heard you talking with the turcopole

59

in French. They have traveled in *Outremer* and could not be mistaken. Explain to me too, if you would, how you, a clerk, got such a sword."

Jean Baignault kept still. Some part of his newly developed sense of caution warned him. He stared levelly into her eyes, his face impassive as he considered his answer. She was no older than he, he realized, and probably younger, yet she was ready to push him into the trap he made with his own talk. He should be very careful. This Subeyla with her unveiled face, her smile, her laughter and her open, direct manner could be too much for him. To be safe, he should distrust her. There was no clan of the Druse that lived on terms of friendship with the Crusader forces in *Outremer*. All the Druse clans had kept to the tradition of rejecting outside authority and living fiercely alone.

But it was time he spoke. Silence could also be a trap if maintained too long. She would be able to find other shrewd questions to ask him. "What took your people out of Lebanon?" he said.

She smiled again. "I give you an easy answer. We were in possession of a fine herd of camels we wished to sell. So we brought them here in order to deal with the Mongols for their sale. But the Mongol force that is usually stationed at the pass was called off. Our understanding is that they have been sent on some special service near the western border. A Saracen *rezzia* of as many as a hundred lances came in after them and fought against us for our camels. My brother was wounded in the combat. I make this clear to you?"

"You do," Jean Baignault said slowly. Then he paused for a moment and listened. He could hear from outside the sounds of a large, active camp. Warriors who relieved each other at guard duty called and were answered. A low, nasal whinnying came from camels being saddled and mounted and yanked into formation. He saw by the change of light in the tent that it was dusk. Cooking fires were starting up; he smelled mutton on spits over the flames.

"I bought the armor and the sword," he told her. "They were sold to me in Aleppo by a single knight whose luck was out. My master paid for them from my wages."

"Then he paid a good amount," she said without expression. "But you are no doubt worth it. Our scouts searched the plain after you were brought in from below the pass.

60

They found your master and he was dead and he had six Saracens around him. There were others further back you must have killed. And you worked most stubbornly to save the turcopole."

"Why do you remind me of this?" Jean Baignault said.

"For the reason that we are of the Ruada clan," she said. "Honor is of importance among us. The Saracens when they tried to take our camels made themselves our enemies. You fought them in your turn, and so we accept you here."

"I thank you most deeply," Baignault said. "Do bear my thanks to your brother. But it was a *rezzia* of Wahabi warriors which we fought, and I would believe that they followed us from across the southern border."

"No matter," she said. "They have joined with the other Saracens who attacked us. And they are still in the region." Her voice slowed; she was looking at his hands which although he gripped them tightly on his knees were shivering with nervous tension. "Did you think that by telling me about the Wahabis you might cozen me into giving you back your sword?"

"Yes," he said hoarsely, "somehow, I did."

"Then you made a mistake. We will hold your sword and the turcopole's weapons also until we are fully certain of you both. It is not for me to return them to you. When my brother has gained his strength he will talk with you. Then perhaps he will give them back."

"I hope that is soon," Jean Baignault said. But she had risen to go to the tent door and clap her hands. She told the slave, "Bring tea and food. See that the man here is served well." The slave touched his forehead to her and bowed, and then she went past him, on outside.

Baignault felt breath rush into his lungs. He almost rose to go after her, compelled by his need for the sword. But he realized that would be wrong. Once again, he must wait. So he sat unmoving while the slave asked him, would he like mutton and rice, and he answered that, yes, he would, and took care to thank the man. He was not a prisoner here yet, neither was he free. For him, it was good sense to be polite even with a slave.

The food and the tea relaxed him and he fell asleep after he had finished the meal. He had meant to get up and try to see Mustaf, but instead he flopped beside the camel saddle on the softness of the robes and it was the intonation of the *azan*, the evening call to prayer, that forced him awake.

The words were familiar; he had heard them many times in the Arab villages where he had ridden on patrol. Yet tonight they profoundly disturbed him. He was very aware of the strength of this clan; he knew that it was only an extremely small fragment of the immense and implacable power of the Moslem world which menaced his people. He felt alien and weak, and almost willing to surrender to them.

The words beat in at him:

Allah is great.
I testify that there is no god but Allah.
I have no power nor strength but from Allah most
High and Great.
Allah willeth what will be be: what he willeth not
Will not be.
There is no god but Allah.

But from the secret places of his mind Baignault found determination to answer back. He recalled the stories his grandfather had told of the early Baignaults in *Outremer*, and he remembered vividly the way the Sieur Amboise gave proof that true Crusader glory still existed. That tradition was his own; he was part of it, would die for it. He said softly yet clearly the absolution for his moment of weakness, *"Ego te absolvo a peccatibus tuis in nomine Patris et Filii, et Spiritu Sancti!"*

He stood erect, and as though he held his sword, he extended the blade point down in formal, ritualistic Crusader fashion. Placing his right hand over what would be the cruciform hilt, he repeated his knightly oath. "I do swear to carry out all my duties." Then he added, "As long as I draw breath, I will go forward to Karakoram and from there to Rome. The work I have been given will be done."

He felt instantly better. This was hard, he thought, and yet he would get through it, and right now he must understand that along the way he was going to follow there might be much worse. He walked to the doorway and lifted the rug. The slave on guard had been changed, but the new man did not stop him as he left the tent.

There were as many as twenty tents pitched inside the pass. Some were simple structures, the sort a war party would take with it as shelter for a campaign. But three or four were larger than the one he occupied, with double flies and tall cypress poles that glinted silver in the star-

62

shine. The largest must belong to Akhu-et-T'ib, the sheik, and the tent beside it probably belonged to Subeyla. Beyond the encampment were rope-and-stake corrals holding both camels and horses. If the Ruada clan had come here to deal with the Mongols as Subeyla had said, they were prepared for quite a stay.

Warriors passed from tent to tent, but none gave him more than a quick glance. They all knew who he was, he supposed, and he wouldn't be able to go very far barefoot and in this cotton shift. There were also mounted sentries out at the perimeter of the camp who surely could check any attempt at flight. He turned toward the tent next to his own, rapped on the ridgepole and entered after a man answered him.

The tent was lit by a number of brass lamps that burned wicks soaked in oil. Mustaf was stretched out on a pile of rugs; he was in coma and the man who stooped over him wore the green turban of a Meccan pilgrim. The fellow was not a surgeon, Baignault thought, but what the Arabs called a mediciner, and obviously a veteran at the treating of wounds.

"How is he, sir?" Baignault said.

"He took an arrow through the upper back," the old Druse warrior said, then straightened to look around. "I thought that the lung was punctured, but I find that I was wrong. He will live, and he will ride and fight again. You are in fact both lucky."

"That I know," Baignault said, and touched Mustaf's cheek. "He has been my friend for quite a time. I am very grateful, sir, for what you have done for him. And for myself as well."

"*Inch' Allah.*" The warrior held forth his hand to Baignault and touched palms in the usual Arab gesture of greeting. "My name is Ibn Rahim. I serve the clan as mediciner." He smiled faintly, gathering his medical instruments and bandages and ointments. "It is my work since I have been told that I am too old to ride in combat."

Here was a man, Jean Baignault thought, who might supply him with a good amount of information. A mediciner moved around a camp, had knowledge of nearly everything that happened. He told Rahim, "I understand that your sheik has been wounded. What sort of wound has he? Is it worse than my comrade's?"

"Considerably so," Rahim said. "The sheik met in per-

63

sonal fight with the Saracen chief. He killed the man, surely, and yet for it he took a lance point that pierced close over the heart. He will not ride again for some time to come."

"Then his sister is charged with his duties?" Baignault said. "She is in command of the clan?"

"It would seem as much," Rahim said.

Baignault heard a sound at the doorway. It was Subeyla standing motionless while she looked in at them. Then she beckoned to Baignault. "Come along, *roumi*. You have seen your friend and have been told about his condition. I would like to talk to you."

Baignault saluted her almost as he would a superior officer of the Hospitalers, but with a trace of mockery in the gesture. "At once," he said.

A slave waited for her outside and walked behind them as she accompanied Baignault to his tent. "Go in," she said, "and the slave will help you. He has brought clothing. We cannot have you around in such as this."

"You would say I embarrass you," Baignault said. But she said nothing, and stopped outside the tent. Baignault entered and with the slave's aid changed clothing. The new garments, he found, were of the best quality and very nearly his exact measurement, but they were all of Druse style from headcloth to long white robe, burnous and sandals. He had no mirror, yet he could imagine how he appeared, and he was both amused and perplexed. If he looked like a Druse, he told himself, then, next, he might well begin to act like one. He remembered his moment of weakness while listening to the evening prayer, and he stood in a stiff, antagonistic posture when the slave left the tent and Subeyla entered.

Her swift glance told him that she was curious about how he would look, and he was pleased when she grinned. "You are too big and too fair, *roumi*, ever to resemble one of us. But neither do you have the air of a merchant's clerk when you wear that armor and are carrying your sword."

"I have explained to you how I came to have them," he said. He bowed to her with calculated exaggeration. "If this is my tent, then you are my guest. Make yourself comfortable. I am unhappy that there is no more tea."

She flushed slightly. "Whenever you wish anything," she said, "call the slave from the door. It is not our idea to treat you as though you were a prisoner."

"Still, you will not let me keep my sword."

"No, not as yet," she said. "I have talked shortly with my brother about you. He has told me that if you give your word of honor not to attempt escape you will be able to move freely in the camp. And once he is fit enough for it, he will listen to your story, and decide whether or not you should be allowed to leave us."

She stood almost in profile to him, and he carefully marked each line of her body. Her long, strong, yet slender legs were visible from the thighs downward through her loose and flimsy trousers. He was aware of a desire to run his hands over them, to caress her breasts beneath the jacket, to kiss the wide, full lips until she panted for breath. It was too long since he had been with a woman and she made him acutely conscious of the fact. And, logically no doubt, that was probably her purpose—to excite him to the degree where he would lose his wits and tell her everything.

A strange one, this Subeyla. She was moody, subject to whims, regardless of what her orders were. He could not yet understand her beyond knowing that he must be wary with her. It might very well be true that her brother was seriously wounded and couldn't talk with him. But there was always in a force of such size a group of senior warriors to take over decisions, at least give advice. Doubtless it was the senior warriors who had told her to bring him the clothing and lead him into a conversation that might reveal his real purpose.

"When shall the sheik be able to see me?" Baignault said.

"I am not certain," she said. "His condition will tell. It might be another week or two."

Baignault let his glance swerve upward to her eyes. "Then I am caught here," he said. "My word of honor is seemingly worthless to you. But—" he smiled wryly—"I have no vows to give, such as would a noble or a knight."

"We will take your vow as a clerk." Scorn was in Subeyla's voice. "My brother has asked me to keep personal watch on you. I shall be here again in the morning. Good night."

"But I haven't yet given you my vow," Baignault said. But she was gone, without looking back. There was one thing left for him to do, he realized. That was to get all the sleep possible. He needed it, and he could never leave this place until his wounds were healed.

Subeyla was at the tent door an hour after dawn. She called in at him while he sat at his breakfast. "Are you ready, *roumi?*"

"For what?" he said, a piece of dough cake in his hand.

She peered under the door rug and he saw that she wore simple clothing fit for riding and soft, light boots. She said, "I will show you the camels before the heat of the day makes them evil-tempered. Then maybe you will understand why the Saracens wanted the lot. They are worth a great amount to us."

Her mood had changed again, he thought, or if not her mood, her manner. He advanced toward her warning himself to be careful. She had begun to attract his fancy, and his experience with women was not great. He had, indeed, never met one in any way like her. The ancient warning had been given him at El Kerak—to be careful of women who might trick him—and she could well be among them. . . .

He stepped forth into the sunshine beside her and said gravely, "I tried to make it known to you last night as you were leaving, but you failed to hear me. I am willing, Subeyla, to give you my word that I will not escape."

"Good," she said. "Life will be less irksome for both of us. I would like to be able to trust you." She wore no veil today, and her eyes were squinted in the sun brilliance as she stared at him. The light put prominence on her high cheekbones, raised a luster on her hair and, oddly, darkened her eyes. She walked with a short but rolling stride, her weight forward on the balls of her feet. He thought, there are no Syrian women like her. They are broad in the butt and soon fat; they eat too many sweetmeats and sit all day in their houses over sugared tea. She is no less feminine than they, but beneath her curves are muscles and trained strength.

"Tell me," she said suddenly. "What is the full truth about you?"

He laughed, and yet he had been startled. "Even if I wished," he said, "I could not." He shrugged a shoulder toward the group of bearded, silent and motionless men who sat beneath the fly of one of the largest tents and sharply watched him. "You would have to take what I told you to the senior warriors and them I do not trust."

66

Subeyla held a carved camel stick in her hand. She slapped it against the skirt of her short robe and there was anger in the gesture. "I will wait," she said. "I too can be stubborn."

But by the time they reached the camel line she was smiling. It seemed to please her very much to explain to him the various fine points of the beasts, the intelligence exhibited in the head shapes, the power in the long, slender necks, the smooth-coated bodies and the thin but extremely muscular legs. Most of these animals, she said, were of ten remembered sires and dams and would bring a top price in any market from Mecca to Samarkand.

Baignault knew little about camels and at first grudgingly, then eagerly, as he became fascinated with the subject, asked her questions. His training had been with horses alone; an inflexible theory of warfare had persisted at El Kerak and he had been taught as an esquire to fight in armor, while the animal he rode was also encased in steel from muzzle to rump. He was not surprised when at the end of his questioning she said, "There is no need for your people to fight as you do. Those metal suits you wear act like ovens to broil you. So you can only wage combat in early morning or late afternoon. What if your enemies refuse to wait for you?"

"We take them whenever we are ready," he said. His pride had again been touched. "No camel force can stand up to mounted knights. Or any other."

She grimaced, her face suddenly bleak and her eyes remote. "What does it matter?" she said. "We of the Jebel Druse stand aside and watch you kill the Saracens and the Saracens kill you. The only answer is that you weaken each other. In time, unless you stop, we will become stronger than either side just because of your weakness. There is no glory in war. It is terrible, a waste, a madness. But you will excuse me. I do not mean to make you angry, so I will leave you for a while."

She had already beckoned to one of the slaves on the camel line. While Baignault stood speechless, his throat tight with rage, the slave led forward a magnificent dun animal. He was aware, as he watched its leg action and grace of movement, that this was a very valuable mount. He noticed the saddle too, of an intricate design worked in Nejd leather, the housings pieced and inlaid in various colors,

67

decorated with plaited fringes and nets embroidered with metal tissues.

He asked, "Subeyla, what is the animal named?"

"An Najm," she said.

That meant, The Star. She was preparing to mount. The Star, he thought, and Subeyla. They make a marvelous spectacle.

As she swung into the saddle, there was a flash of white above the boot tops and the browned calves of her legs. He drew his breath. If he hadn't acted stupidly a moment before, he told himself, he might be riding out with her. The sight of the eager, superb animal pawing the ground, whinnying and stretching to run and the lithe, confident and handsome woman in the deep saddle aroused him. He said, almost unaware of the words, "Where might you ride?"

"Out to hunt," she said. "Some of the scouts have found gazelle over to the east. We will bring back a few and you will have meat for your dinner. Really, if you wished, you could accompany me."

But he was on his guard once more, and he realized that this was not the time for him to ride. His wounds wouldn't bother him much in a deep, soft saddle like that. She would keep a slow pace, too, and stay at his side, and ask him one question after another until at last, when he was sufficiently relaxed or charmed, get her answer and find out about the mission. He grinned, and waved his hand at her. "I will wait till I'm fit to mount a horse," he said. "Good hunting."

He turned back toward the camp, knowing he should not stand here and watch her ride away. His desire to go with her was sure to be seen in his face. Along the ground, the beast's hoofbeats came to him. There was the trot. Now the canter. Now the gallop, and the strides lengthening until the camel was at top speed.

Baignault swung around at the edge of the camp and stared in the direction she had taken. She swerved the camel down into a depression beside the road. It was filled with thorn bushes, studded with boulders, and she rode among them without slowing the animal's stride. The light there was russet-shaded and not very clear. She burst up out of it into a dazzle of sunlight, the blue scarf around her neck flaring like a pennon, her hair shining loose in the wind.

Baignault whispered her name, "Subeyla, Subeyla . . ." Then to himself, "It is good that you are not a Moslem.

Women like her a warrior is supposed to see in Paradise, once he has been killed in combat. And you would do it. You would follow such as her and die for her."

He walked slowly to his tent, entered and sat down, clasping his head between his hands. Fear was in him, fear of Subeyla. Her charm, he knew, was working steadily on him. He dozed fitfully in the day's heat, awoke troubled by flies, to hear her voice at the tent doorway. "May I come in, *roumi?*" she said.

"Do, please," he said. It was better, he thought, to test his wits against her than to lie here like this. "How was the hunt?"

"Fine," she said. "We came upon four gazelle within a league or so. You will not be forced to eat mutton tonight."

"For that I'm glad," he said. He saw that she had changed from her riding costume, again wore the short velvet jacket, the thin silk blouse that exposed the shape of her breasts and the loose trousers that hid very little of her legs. The Syrian merchant's wife could not be compared with her. He rose and indicated a pile of rugs where she might sit. Then caution prompted him to ask, "Why do you give so much of your time to me?"

"I thought," she said, "that you and I might play some chess." She pointed to an elaborate ivory set on a table near her. "You must know the game."

"I play badly," he said.

She grinned at him. "Almost every good player whom I have met tells me that he is bad at the game. Do sit down and let us play. There is no cause for you to be frightened of me."

A slight edge of sharpness in the words fired his anger and he stood unmoving. "Why do the warriors stay away from me?" he said. "There must be a chess player among them. Or a man who can cozen more information out of me than you have."

"There is not a warrior in this camp," she said, "who will talk with you. Not even old Ibn Rahim, and he is gentle and generous. The entire lot of them are convinced that secretly you are our enemy."

"For the single reason that I have refused to tell you what you think should be told."

"Yes. True. And after we saved you from the Saracens."

"Whom you call your enemies although you profess that

your people have no liking for war. But this is wasted talk. All I want is to be allowed to leave here with my comrade. Soon, very soon."

"With your weapons, and without telling us what your purpose is in this country. Remember if you would that we must protect ourselves. If we do not, we are lost. It is the only fashion in which we can keep our freedom."

Baignault's hands were clenched into fists. He walked close to Subeyla, gazed down at her at the low table. But she did not look up. She was busy arranging the chess pieces. "Very well," he said; her calm had quieted him. "Then let us play. I warn you, though, that I am bad. About that I am wholly honest."

"No doubt," she said, "I might be wrong; still, some of what you say I believe."

They played several games in a row and Subeyla beat him each time. Baignault laughed ruefully and pushed the table aside. "You were given warning," he said.

"But I will be back tomorrow," she said. "You are a lot more skillful than you make out, and better than I had hoped."

He bowed to her wordlessly as she left the tent. He was bemused by the sudden realization that she was attracted to him. He could sense it, feel it in his nerve centers, along his veins and in his groin. So, let her return and play chess. Perhaps, while he learned the game, he might find out from her something that would help him and Mustaf on the Karakoram road.

He played with Subeyla regularly for a week after that and at the end of it he beat her. His wounds were nearly healed and he had been to see Mustaf in the morning, to find the turcopole conscious and beginning to recover rapidly; so in the afternoon's game with Subeyla he was sharp, eager. "I will make you a wager," he said as they started. "Should I win today, you will give me a horse to ride. I am fit enough now for it. Should I lose, I will stay here without further complaint of any sort."

"Taken," she said, and smiled. "Make a move, *roumi*."

She showed no surprise when he won, only told him in what had become her usual fashion, "I shall see you in the morning." But with the next dawn when he went to the doorway there was a horse held by a slave outside and she sat beyond on a fine bay mare. He went out and mounted, pushed his feet into the short stirrups and went over and thanked her.

"But you cannot go past the sentry lines," she said. "Some of the senior warriors are not too content with this. I was forced to go to my brother before permission was given."

"I understand," Baignault said. Then he urged his mount and she rode beside him watching each movement he made. He was almost too big for the mount, but he was quick to handle it, put it through its gaits and jump it over bushes and a pile of corral stakes. "You ride almost as well as a Ruada," she said. There was a glint of laughter in her eyes and, he thought, a bit of admiration. "Tell me. Where you were taught your horsemanship? Did they ever play at mall?"

"You mean the Saracen style of polo," he said. Again he warned himself to be careful. It was known throughout *Outremer* that the young knights had been recently trained in the game to rid them of the rigid habits of European warfare. He had been taught polo in the tilting yard at El Kerak. But it was hardly a sport that a Pisan merchant's clerk would know how to play.

Subeyla let her smile broaden. She said, "I own the horse you ride. Beat me at mall and you may ride it out of here when you leave. Bearing with you my best wishes."

"But you are too generous," Baignault said. "I have nothing to wager against you."

"You do not worry me," Subeyla said. "Should I lose, I can always win it back at chess. Are you ready?"

"Yes, I am," he said, and now he smiled in return.

She clapped her hands for a slave and told the man to bring a pair of mallets and a ball. Then she sat quietly in her saddle, stroking her horse's mane although a number of the senior warriors, hearing her call to the slave, had moved out from under their tent flies. They would make quite an audience, Baignault thought, and every one of them was sure Subeyla would win. That only meant he couldn't spare himself or the horse. He had seen enough of her skill to realize her chances of beating him.

Old Ibn Rahim came out onto the open space between the tent rows as the slave appeared with the mallets and ball. "This, at the corner of the tent," he said, "is a goal. The other goal is directly opposite. Ride to the center, and

71

I will toss in the ball for you. There are no rules except that the ball must be kept in play on the field."

Subeyla leaned far down from the saddle, went fast-breaking when the soft, hide-covered ball·was tossed. She struck it cleanly, lifting it, and wheeled her mount to gallop and stroke it on the bounce. But Baignault stood up in the stirrups and, grasping the supple mallet handle tight, blocked the ball in flight. Subeyla rode straight at him; she almost lunged her mount into his.

Baignault dragged her horse aside and she had the ball. She rode with it at a tearing gallop, keeping it alongside her horse's fore nigh leg. She was about fifteen yards from the tent corner that was the goal when Baignault caught up with her. He swung his mallet full circle in a backhander and felt the force of the impact up his arm to his ribs and shoulder. Pain clamped down on him, but he disregarded it. He gave his horse short rein, rearing the beast into a turn, then urging to the gallop.

Subeyla sprinted with him the full length of the field to where his shot was beginning to roll to a stop. She reached the ball first and was set to strike. Only his greater reach allowed him to stroke the ball away from her. He tapped once, centered the mallet and whipped through the goal shot.

A couple of the watching warriors muttered what sounded to Baignault like "very good." But the slave had picked up the ball and started back toward the middle of the field with it. Ibn Rahim took it in his hands and Subeyla asked him, "How many more goals?"

"None," Rahim said, "if you would listen to a mediciner." He let go of the ball and walked to Baignault and touched his shirt. Blood came off on Rahim's fingertips. "That backhander was a fine shot, *roumi*, but you have opened your rib wound. You should not play further. If you do, it might have grave consequences for you."

"But there is not much pain," Baignault said. "I would like to go on."

"Then you are a fool," Subeyla said in a flat voice. "You have won this." She dropped her mallet to the ground. "Let the mediciner tend to you. We have no wish to keep you here forever."

"Thank you very much," Baignault said. But she had swung her horse around and Ibn Rahim was leading his away by the bridle.

He slept for hours after Rahim fixed the wound. When he awoke he rose and nervously paced the tent. He was thinking of Subeyla, and suddenly she was at the doorway. "You must want to win your horse back," he told her. "Come in, please. I can still play chess. What would you like, one game, or three out of five?"

"One only," she said. "Rahim has told me that you are not to tire yourself over much."

They played in silence, but she was distracted and careless, and he won easily from her. She sat back at the end of the game, half-reclining against a saddle. She supported her chin with her right hand and with the other absently picked up and put down the chess pieces. Baignault sat still, waiting for some explanation of her mood.

She had picked up a pawn from the table and was turning it in her fingers. "Did you ever hear of the enchanted Castle of Carbonek?"

"Yes." He was both startled and cautious. "That is where the Holy Grail is supposed to have been found."

"Then you must be in search of it," Subeyla said. "Nothing else could be so important to you. If you seek money, stay with us. We make it by trade with several tribes. Very soon, we shall return to the Lebanon. You and your companion would be given safe passage there by us."

Baignault nearly stretched out his hand to caress her arm and let her know the intense emotion she stirred in him. She was honest in this moment, he sensed. There was nothing hidden or prearranged in what she had just said. Thousands of men like him had given up their knightly vows and become renegades for Moslem women. It would be a good life with her. She was the sheik's sister, and later, when he had proved himself, he might even lead the clan. That would demand hard work, bitter fighting and riding, but it would be better than the incredibly long road which he had vowed to follow.

"Let me think on it," he said. "I cannot tell you now, Subeyla."

Her teeth had closed on her lower lip and left sharp marks. Anger or hurt pride had sent a flush of color up into her cheeks, staining the skin under the eyes. "It must be now," she said. Her fingers contracted on the fragile chess piece and the ivory shattered, flying in fragments across the tent.

He stood up and stepped away from her. "If I could—"

he trod one of the fragments under his foot— "I would not wait. Nor would I ask you to do so."

"You make it quite clear," she said. She stood erect. "My brother's condition is such that you can see him tomorrow. The slave will call you early in the morning. Enjoy your dinner, and sleep well."

He bowed to her, wanting to say that he was sorry, and almost ready to tell her that he was in love with her. But he said instead, "I am grateful. This would have been another dull afternoon without you."

After dinner he sat in front of the tent while the dusk gathered lilac over the low hills to the North of the Iron Gate and the senior warriors left their vantage and the camp settled for the night. It would not be long now, he thought. The senior warriors wouldn't have to watch him much more. These people were realizing that they gained nothing by holding him and Mustaf.

Darkness climbed the sky and then, over high cloud, the full moon broke. Its brilliance lay like a silver film upon the tents, the tossing, narrow heads of the camels and horses in their corrals, the sentries where they rested beyond. Lakes of light quivered along the ground between the tents and Baignault was unable to remain still. He walked quickly across to the camel corral. The beasts made a magnificent sight; their eyes shone, and An Najm moved rhythmically back and forth like a figure lifted from a dream.

"She brings to my mind sometimes," Subeyla's voice said, "the statues fashioned by the ancient Greek people. I have seen such work. There are pieces of it out in the lost cities in the desert. But she is too alive ever to be a statue."

"You are right," Baignault said. Entranced by the camels he had not heard Subeyla approach. Now he moved slowly from her, as if to go back to his tent.

"Stay, *roumi*," Subeyla said. "The night is too fine. And, if you wish, we can go forth on a ride. There are saddles here. We will take An Najm and the other, the big, white animal. Would you like that?"

"Very much indeed," he said. "But what about the sentries?"

"I shall be able to get us past them without trouble."

He was abruptly aware, staring at her in this moment, of the only woman he knew who was at all like her. His mother. His mother had none of the softness of the other

74

women of *Outremer*. She tended her garden, yes, and quietly ran the household at Beth-Haggan, on the surface seeming to be no more than the complaisant if intelligent wife of the Sieur Amboise. But she could ride like the wind and often did. She was easier with the handling of the horses she rode than the Sieur Amboise, too; and she could outdistance him across country—jump walls, run orchards, stony fields and broken ground and be home long before him. She could, further, sit with her husband late at night and reason through some knotty, involved question of Hospitaler policy; something she had learned young among her father's people in the troubled palace at Antioch.

Jean Baignault stood bemused. He wanted to tell Subeyla what was in his mind, but some inner sense warned him that he should wait. The two camels were bridled, saddled. Subeyla was about to mount. "You are ready?" she said.

"Yes," he said. "I only hope that I am not pitched off on my head."

"Follow me and you will have no trouble," she said. "A man who can ride a horse with your skill can stay astride a camel. Just make certain to remember that you have instead of reins a single head rope." She had chosen a pair of long camel sticks from the pile of gear beside the corral gate and she handed him one. Then she mounted from the kneeling position, clucked to An Najm and began to ride.

Her passage out the corral gate and down the slope was a streak of flickering silver. Baignault cursed. He couldn't ride like that, not without years of experience with these beasts. He mounted his animal, slid down into the comfortable saddle with its crosspieces at pommel and cantle, set his right leg around the pommel, eased the head rope a bit and tapped very lightly with the stick.

His beast wanted to keep the pace An Najm had taken. But Baignault reined in on the rope. That could wait for later, he thought. He would never make it to Karakoram and back with a broken neck. He kept to a conservative lope until he reached Subeyla waiting beside the nearest sentry. "Give the animal its head," she said. "Let us get out into the night."

"But if—" the sentry said.

"Be silent!" she told him. "Ride, merchant's clerk, ride. Here are no ball and mallet—just the moonlight."

She stroked An Najm with the carved stick so hard that the beast almost leaped in the perpendicular. Then the splay hooves caught the ground. The arch of the neck extended, the legs stretched, flexed, fluttered in motion too fast for the eye to record, and woman and camel were gone plunging into the moonlight.

"Allah give me help," the sentry said to Baignault. "If the officer of the guards find you are gone it will be a beating with his scimitar blade for me. She should not ride that way. It's mad."

"That is something I will try to tell her," Baignault said, and hit his animal a lick and slackened the head rope. But he couldn't overtake her. She was like an arrow loosed from some tremendous bow string. She flung An Najm over ridges, through depressions, across boulder-strewn patches where the beast's knees grazed rock on each side. Baignault felt fierce anger as he rode after her, but part of that, he knew, might well be jealousy. If he were a better rider, things would be different.

On the crest of a high ridge to the north, An Najm slowed to a stop as Subeyla tugged the head rope. They poised there in silhouette, woman and animal almost motionless, her hand out to beckon Baignault forward. Something, however, severely startled An Najm. The camel screamed and reared. It rose up, up, the fore hooves striking the air, came down toppling, over and backward, and Subeyla was beneath.

Baignault went up the slope hitting his animal with strokes of the stick that almost snapped it. He leaped while the animal still ran at the gallop. His momentum tumbled him flat, his hands spread to break the fall, and it was as he started to rise that he heard the hissing.

He knew at once from his desert years. That sound came from a nest of vipers. An Najm had stepped close to or into one here, perhaps had been bitten. "Take care," he heard Subeyla call. "There are snakes."

"I know," he said. "I will tend to them."

He slid his hand down the sturdy camel stick so that he held it by the end and had maximum reach. Then he picked up a heavy, jagged piece of rock and stepped toward the nest. The nodding, evil, brown-gray shapes writhed and the eyes were mica-bright, spelling death. He smashed them with the rock, hurling it down; but two escaped and darted at him and he was forced to jump back and strike with the camel stick before they were still.

76

The hissing ceased. He had killed the lot. But his stomach muscles quivered yet, and like a school boy with his first snake, he stamped into the ground the heads and bodies of the pair he had killed outside the nest. Then he turned to look at Subeyla and An Najm. Subeyla had been thrown on her side, backward out of the saddle, and her clothing and her right arm were pinned by the weight of the animal so that she could not move.

"Do not bother with me," she said. "It is An Najm who needs your help. Very probably, she was bitten."

Baignault knelt down and gentled the shocked, shivering animal. But he could find no marks of a sting, and there was a severed, hoof-stamped viper near her off hind leg. An Najm had saved herself and Subéyla too, and only afterward had reared and fallen.

"How is she?" Subeyla said.

"No more than stunned," he said. "But for a time she should rest quietly. I shall tend to you."

"I saw you kill them in the nest," she said. "You do very well—" she was trying to make her voice light—"for a merchant's clerk."

"And you," Baignault said, hard-voiced, "you ride like a demented woman." He walked over and stood looking down at her. She lay asprawl, arms and legs spread, and if she moved, he realized, she would hurt the arm pinned beneath the camel. Her robe and underrobe were pulled well above her waist and she wore nothing else. He studied her body with a passionate curiosity he couldn't control and saw that she gazed back at him with unashamed, defiant interest.

"Now I am your prisoner," she said.

"No," he said. "Even a merchant's clerk does not take such advantage." He went around and grasped An Najm by the head rope, urging the sluggish, half-comatose animal to move. Subeyla sat up, her arm free. She massaged it from the elbow to the shoulder and groaned, then grinned. "I am lucky to be alive."

"Indeed you are," he said.

She sat with her back against An Najm and he lowered himself beside her. "Let me do that," he told her. He began to massage the arm from the wrist upward, his broad, thick fingers working the skin and releasing the tension of the muscles. It was too much, he knew, the moment he touched

77

her. She couldn't take this, nor could he. She moved suddenly against him with a sound that was part cry of desire, part agony.

"But you must be careful," he whispered. Her body was hard against his; she was straining to return his kiss. "Do not hurt yourself."

She laughed, the moonlight in her eyes where she lay. "I am fine," she said. "Nothing can possibly hurt me. I am too much in love."

He drew away from her only when An Najm struggled to his feet and stamped. It was nearly dawn. They had lain here for hours. He looked down at her narrow-eyed where she lay on their heaped clothing. "The entire camp will know," he said.

"Then let them," she said. "I am my own woman and I answer only to my brother and with him I talk in freedom. Now I would like to talk to you. But with more clothes than I now wear." Trembling with delight and the dawn chill, she now pulled her robes over her head and arranged them.

"Let me ask the first question." He knelt beside her and took her hands. "What forces you to hate me at one moment, then, in the next, show affection?"

"That is no more so," she said. "I am not like that any longer. For all I do is love you. . . . Still, it was as you say. I was attracted to you and then I thrust myself from you. A strange thing. You will not make mock of me if I explain why that was?"

"You have told me that you love me." Jean Baignault traced a fingertip along her eyebrows. "So do I love you, Subeyla. Never will I mock you. Whatever that was, it must have been of great importance in your life."

"Very great," she said. "It happened when I was a quite young girl. Understand that my mother died in childbirth, bearing me. She was beloved by my father and his favorite wife. And the midwife who brought me up was considered to be extremely wise, have the power of second sight. She made a prophesy concerning me. She said that because of the manner of my mother's death I would never marry in our clan or tribe. If I married at all, it would be an outsider, a stranger."

"But that was simply superstitious talk and you should not have believed it."

She stared at him, her eyes deeply thoughtful. "You have no superstitions among the *roumi* folk?"

"Of course," he said, "many people among us believe in weerwolves and goblins and devils and a lot more too. You, though, who know so much, surprise me."

"But what I have told you weighs heavily," she said. "I have carried it in my head since I was a small girl. Then, when I met you and came to know that I might fall in love with you, I was afraid. But that is behind us now. We can talk with each other about anything we wish."

Jean Baignault shook his head. He picked up a handful of sand and pitched it, watched the grains fall in the greenish dawn light. "Not about everything, Subeyla," he said. "Not about where I am going and why. I tell you this straight off, so that you will not ask me again."

"You would hurt my pride," she said. "But I will not let you. Act in the same fashion. Listen patiently while I tell you that war is not all that you think it is. For you, chivalry is the end of all effort, the great goal, the true meaning of your life, and that should not be so. Life can be lived without war. There is honor also in peace."

"Subeyla, you cannot change me. Nor can I tell you what the purpose of my life is. If you were to know, then you might want to become a part of it and you would end in being very unhappy. You are far happier here with your own clan, your own people. And you should not be in love with me."

"Then you refuse me." Subeyla's face and lips were pale. She was on her feet, sweeping back her tousled hair, moving to snatch up a camel stick.

"For the present," Jean Baignault said, "I must."

"Then this." She let him have the notched stick hard across the jaw. "You are the first man to lay with me. I am bitterly ashamed that I did not take one of my own kind."

"Get on your camel," Jean Baignault said quietly. "I am not in the habit of being slapped. Get on that camel or I will break the stick over your behind."

She whispered, "The clerk would give an order to the sister of a sheik. But it is the last." Then she had An Najm by the head rope, was up and in the saddle, rushing at the gallop down into the gully that led toward the camp. Baignault rode after her at the canter. Let her go, he thought. There was nothing else he could do if he were to keep his vows.

No one approached him when he re-entered the camp. He left his animal at the corral, noting that An Najm was already there, entered his tent and fell at once into a deep sleep. A slave calling from the doorway awakened him. He turned on his side and the man told him that he was wanted by Akhu-et-T'ib, the sheik.

"I shall join him at once," Baignault said. But he took time to wash himself, eat some of the fruit and cold meat from a bowl on the table. When he left the tent, he noticed that the camp was deserted except for a few sentries. Most of the fast camels were gone from the corral, and he sensed that a combat might be about to start. That could be the reason why the sheik had sent for him, or it might be because of his conduct with Akhu-et-T'ib's sister last night. But remembering that Subeyla had told him that her brother would see him today, his tension lessened, and he had full control of himself when the slave announced him at the doorway of the big, black tent.

Akhu-et-T'ib sat straight-backed in the center of it. He was no more than a few years older than his sister, Baignault thought, and they bore marked family resemblance. But the effects of his wound had thinned Akhu's face. It was almost skeletal and very pale, the bridge of the nose accentuated and the eyes set deep within the discolored sockets. He wore a silk-embroidered headcloth with a double row of scarlet cord wound around it. His hands were clasped on a ceremonial dagger with a gold hilt and as Baignault salaamed to him he lifted the right and said, "Welcome to you here. Sit down."

Baignault sat with his legs under him in Arab style and tried to relate this man to what he had learned from Subeyla. The appearance of the tent would lead him to think that Akhu devoted himself to little beside the chase and warfare. A watch cockerel was on its perch behind him. Stretched panting in the morning heat, a big greyhound raised bloodshot eyes, then subsided again in his corner. An African oryx and an ibex with long, curved horns were held by silver chains to a rear tent post and snuffled in chorus. But there was a beautifully illustrated Koranic scroll at Akhu's knee, and the inlaid bowls and tables and the Bokhara rugs showed exquisite taste.

The sheik lives in luxury even away from home, Baignault thought. This costs a good deal of money; the Mongols must pay well for their camels. Then he saw that Akhu had lifted from among the pile of rugs that supported him the sword with the emerald in the hilt. "This is yours?" he asked Baignault.

"Yes, it is," Baignault said, his mouth dry and nerves pulling in his throat.

"My sister has told me," Akhu said, "that you bought it from some single knight in Aleppo. I do not believe that. But the fact of the matter does not have much importance to me. Subeyla holds much more interest in you than I." The pale, gaunt man stopped speaking to inspect the sword. He touched the emerald, tracing the design, then tested the blade and looked up abruptly at Baignault. "Exactly, *roumi*, what is your purpose here?"

Baignault stared calmly back. "I have already given my explanation," he said. "Your sister was told it days ago. She gave me to think that she would tell it to you."

Lines formed between Akhu's eyes. He sat very still. "My people," he said, "are not in the habit of calling a man of supposed honor a liar. But your story does not sound right. If your master is dead, why do you wish to go over the Samarkand road? It would be much better for you to make the return safely with us to *Outremer*."

"I keep a promise to my master," Baignault said. "He had dealings with the Mongols that I would finish. There are two caravans of Cathay silks that I should pick up at Samarkand. They have been paid for and I should take them home to Pisa."

"Not a bad story," Akhu said. "But an impossible trip for a man like you whose companion is still badly wounded. He will not be fit to ride or fight as he should for weeks to come. And the Mongols do not let every stranger travel their roads."

"I will have no serious trouble," Jean Baignault said in a quiet voice. "I can make myself known to the Mongols. The road cannot hold too much danger for me. Until my companion has his strength I will ride no more than a few miles a day."

Akhu hefted the sword and described a blow, and Baignault could realize his strength. "Then take your sword and your guide and leave us," Akhu said. "You have stayed here long enough."

"I thank you, sir," Baignault said. He had begun to move forward to take the sword.

"But there will be a small price for that," Akhu said.

"Let us call it something shared by you and the clan. The Mongols will not be back here at the pass for another day. My scouts are now out and have met with them. They will ride in their company and not alone, as the Saracens are still in the region. The *rezzia* that attacked my people has been reinforced. The men who joined it are Wahabis, of the tribe which attacked you. The road beyond here has been cut by them and they sit tight on it."

"Then I would not be able to ride on toward Samarkand." The words came slowly from Baignault. His body and his hands were tense. He kept staring steadily into Akhu's eyes.

"Not unless we helped you," Akhu said.

"Tell me how," Baignault said.

"You and your companion would have to ride into a trap," Akhu said. "A trap devised by us. We would make it seem as if you were to pass along the road by yourselves. And we would give you a string of animals and load them with packs of goods. You are not forgotten by the Saracens. They will, I believe, come swiftly after you. The Wahabis will very probably be in the van of their attack. But before they strike you, it will be our turn. We will move against the *rezzia* in that same moment."

Jean Baignault coughed to release the tightness in his throat. But he forced himself to smile. This was, he knew, repayment for what had gone on with Subeyla. The sheik took his price in his own way. "You offer something, sheik, that demands a great deal of trust on my part. What assurance have I that you will not leave us to the Saracens? Were we to be killed, the trap would still serve its purpose for you."

"I can only give you my word of honor," Akhu said. He was expressionless, his glance lowered to the sword. "But this is much too fine a sword for a Wahabi to own, or any Saracen. We will take the utmost care to keep you alive to wear it. Here, catch!"

Akhu flipped the heavy-bladed weapon with his hand balanced at the exact center. Baignault caught it without having to move. "I am convinced," he said. "You have my word. I am ready to serve my part. Still, I must talk to the turcopole. He might not be so willing."

"That is for you," Akhu said. "Settle it in your own way." Fatigue had suddenly roughened his voice; his eyes were no longer bright or keen. "Go to him now, then afterward meet with Rahim. You should be on the road, though, before dawn."

"And as for Subeyla?" Baignault said. He wouldn't leave here until he knew more about her and her feeling for him. "She has been the one with whom I have talked in the past, not Rahim."

"I have sent my sister away from the camp," Akhu said, his voice low. "She is now out with the scouts and will not be back for several days. There will be no chance for you to see her again. All that interests her is to clear the Saracens from our way so that we may return home."

"She is wise," Baignault said. "Although I thought that she was a great believer in peace."

"The circumstance does not permit her to be," Akhu said. "Go with God, *roumi*. And good luck to you."

Baignault gave a low salaam. He backed wordless from the tent. Talk would do no good, he thought, not any more. This had come to an end here. He wouldn't see Subeyla again, and there was no reason why he should.

But her image was vivid in his mind and he heard echoes of her voice while he walked to Mustaf's tent. The turcopole was sitting and drinking broth from a bowl and Rahim was with him. Baignault was conscious of the way Mustaf stared at the sword.

"Maybe I don't feel too well," Mustaf said. "Maybe, despite all that this man has done for me, my eyes still play tricks. But, if you have your sword, then we will get out of here."

Baignault nodded smiling. "The sheik will let us go. At his price."

"Tell me," Mustaf said. He glanced over the tilted bowl at Baignault and winked.

Nothing he would say would surprise Rahim, Baignault knew. The mediciner was here for a definite purpose and at Akhu's orders. Time was short for Akhu as well as for them. "Stop blowing soup between your teeth," Baignault told Mustaf, "and I will explain it to you." Then, as Mustaf put the bowl down, he spoke fast.

Mustaf squinted while he listened. He opened and shut his stub-fingered, square hands. When Baignault was finished he stared at Rahim. "I'm a simple man," he said softly. "Nobody who's worked as long for hire as me can be very smart. But I do not think that the sheik had the mediciner patch me for a target to be used in Saracen lance practice. I will go with you. I will take the chance."

Baignault stooped down silently to take his hand. Rahim had gone out the door, on the way to make a report to Akhu, Baignault knew. But that didn't matter; not now. The road to Karakoram was open again, if only a little bit. He signed to Mustaf, and side by side, heads bowed, they began to pray.

CHAPTER SIX

There was rain at dawn, and then mist. But the senior warrior who came with Rahim to give Baignault his instructions said that was good. "It should help you reach the road and move forth into the open country. But be sure that you do not ride beyond the stone marker at the ruins of the old Roman camp."

"May I ask why?" Baignault said. He stood beside the horse he had won from Subeyla, rain dripping from the hood of his burnous, and Mustaf was in back of him, already mounted. He could hear Mustaf's teeth chatter from the cold and wet, and he knew that in today's combat he must fight alone.

"You can find cover behind the ruins until we join you," the warrior said. "The worst danger for you will be the Saracen arrows. But, once those have been delivered, we will be on our way to take part. Stay close to the ground until we arrive. Make no move except for safety."

"You would tell me," Baignault said, "that you will do all the fighting?"

"Ecomil is right," Ibn Rahim said, short-voiced. "What might one man like you and a wounded man do against fifty or sixty?"

"Not much," Baignault said. His hand went to his sword belt and he swung the blade a bit more to the left. Then he adjusted the poniard that had just been given him and looked aside at his horse. There were a Druse bow-and-arrow quiver attached to the saddle thongs and the slave who stood at the horse's head held a lance for him. Mustaf had his own tulwar too, he realized, and a bow and quiver,

84

yet those had been given only as a token to stop Mustaf's protests about being unarmed.

"Then mount and ride," the warrior named Ecomil said. "You will see the road as the mist begins to lift. But do not leave it, and do not go beyond the marker. We will come in from both the north and the south when we are ready to attack."

"Just be sure that's not too long," Mustaf said, his voice squeaky with fever.

But Ecomil had moved away toward the corral gate and Rahim had started to follow him. "A minute, please, mediciner," Baignault said. "I would like to know—"

The old man stepped back to his side. "You must go," he said. "But if it is your desire to learn about Subeyla, she is still away with the scout force. Should we win today, you will quite probably see her."

"Then she has been told about this," Baignault said.

"She had a hand," Rahim said harshly, "in the planning of it. But her duty was to reach the Mongols. There may be need of them in the combat. If you do not ride out now, though, nothing will be accomplished other than getting yourself killed."

Baignault nodded. "You have been good to us. Again, I thank you."

He rode first at the walk as he left the camp, letting Mustaf go ahead so that he could be free to maneuver the string of pack animals. There were five of those and they were an added burden, but he remembered how well Louvic had made use of animals like them and he felt better. His horse was fresh, full of energy, and they moved quickly down the slope that gave to the north from the pass.

The mist had lifted with the sunrise. Baignault could clearly see the road, rutted by the passage of caravans that for centuries had used the Iron Gate. Small yellow flowers shimmered with moisture, the thorn bushes were glossy, and the grass swayed knee-high under a sweep of breeze. It could be a good day, he thought, a very good day if he met Ibn Aud Aghaf. He wanted one more chance with the Wahabi to settle the account. But, looking aside, he found that Mustaf already slouched in the saddle. Mustaf caught his glance and called, "We haven't a chance, Sir Jean. The Wahabis might well have cut our throats, back the other side of the pass. This promises to be no good."

"Be still," Baignault said. "Straighten up and ride."

But across the rolling spread of country beyond, at each crest and ridge, he could see mounted Saracens. He had been given an accurate report by Akhu; the *rezzia* certainly sat tight upon the road. At least forty Saracen warriors were out there, and about half from their dress were Wahabis, and more were gathering all the time to join the crescent-shaped formation. They moved in without hurry, as though fully prepared for him and Mustaf. If this was a trap, it would be sprung by them, not by the Druse.

He thought for a moment of turning back, releasing the pack animals and making a run with Mustaf for the Druse camp. Then he saw that the points of the Saracen formation had closed in upon the road behind. It was too late for retreat. The Saracens would barely have to move to bring them within easy bow range.

Off among the yellow flowers, a lark sang to the sun. Baignault thought, that will be gone later. There will be vultures instead. And, tonight, when the vultures are through, jackals will have their turn. Then, on the smooth stretch of plain ahead he saw the stone road marker and tumbled, lichen-covered walls of what had once been a Roman garrison post.

He kicked his horse into a lope, pulling the pack beasts along and taking Mustaf's reins. From the way the Saracens started toward them, he realized that their leaders also understood that the ruins were the only place where a defense could be made. He eased the sword in the scabbard just a bit, to have the feel of the blade, then took the bow in his hands. It was a powerful enough weapon. He could use it to make a small score against the Wahabis as soon as he and Mustaf were at the ruins.

He could both see and hear Aghaf now, and the Wahabi emir must have asked special permission, because the men of his tribe were closest to the ruins. They were drawing bow at Aghaf's order and beginning to fire. An arrow clipped Mustaf's horse in the neck and it bucked and kicked and frightened the pack animals. Baignault let them run off while he struggled to keep Mustaf mounted. He rode in front of the sergeant, protecting him with his body, and drove both horses at the full gallop.

If he lived, he promised himself, he would remember this. The Wahabis were poor bowmen. They must have sent something like a score of shafts at him and only one had come close to target. But they were riding in, straight down

86

the road, and they had their lances seated and their scimitars drawn. Baignault hauled Mustaf's horse around, then his own, and sent the beasts stumbling in among the ruins.

He placed Mustaf flat on his back against a fallen door cornice. He brushed a green-eyed lizard off a stone fragment beside it and kneeling drew the bow, notched an arrow and began to shoot. His aim was better than that of the Wahabis, but he did not hold them back for long. The horses he wounded were let go, and their riders advanced on foot. He took satisfaction from a shot that ripped Aghaf's shoulder with such force that the emir was knocked around in the saddle, then pitched out of it by his excited horse onto the roadway.

All of the frustration that Baignault had felt and all of his eagerness for action were translated into hatred for Aghaf. He would go out to the road now, he told himself, and finish the man. It was the third time they had come to combat and the last. He dropped the bow, took the sword in his hand and moved forward. But, before he was fully upright, a Wahabi arrow point chipped stone dust into his eyes.

He could not see. He stared blindly forth at the road, hearing the Wahabis, the sounds their boot soles made on the ruts, then Aghaf as he shouted to them. "The big *roumi* is mine. Leave him to me. I will chop him down like a rotten tree. His ears will make me an amulet."

"Get out of here," Baignault said to Mustaf. "Do not stay here because of me. I'm blinded. Even to run is impossible."

Mustaf bumped into him, grunting and cursing. The sergeant was trying to draw his bow, Baignault realized. "No luck, Sir Jean. I lack the strength. Maybe, though, you can run."

"Not yet," Baignault said. His senses were made more acute by his blindness and he heard somewhere out there in the darkness the rush and thud and thin, tense nickering of camels. There were many. They came from the north and from the south, and now they screamed as their riders yelled. He stood up and yelled back, gripping the sword.

Arrows cleared the air, but they were Druse, not Saracen. He heard the men on the road; some of them were running, and it was like the sound of giant, frightened rabbits. He laughed and swiped his hand across his eyes, then dimly saw the road.

Aghaf still stood there, staring backward at the attacking Druse. They came at almost incredible speed. The Saracens who guarded the rear must have become careless. They had been struck hard and turned, because they were being driven down toward their fellows on the road. The Wahabis, all but Aghaf and a few others, rode or ran to form some sort of solid defense. The Saracen leader, erect on a splendid chestnut horse, his banner bearer beside him, called orders in a firm and strong voice.

But Baignault's concern was Aghaf. He went after the Wahabi with the sword slanted shoulder-high in his hand. "Baignault," he called, "Baignault! You know me from the Antioch road. You know me from the combat where my leader killed your fellows like pigeons too fat to fly. Fight now, Wahabi. Do not turn and run."

"The big, blond colt," Aghaf said. "The loud-mouth whose talk is better than his swordwork. Come here to me, *roumi*. Right here . . ."

But Aghaf did not wait. He sprang for Baignault with the scimitar whipping over his head. Baignault parried slowly, just able to see the blade. He must be faster, he knew, or this man would kill him. His eyes were not yet clear; Aghaf was a grayish, obscure shape before him, and the scimitar blade was just a tremor of light. He parried again, and the blade slipped past, slit into his right forearm. The pain was instantaneous, adding to his rage and his power. He swung aside, and back, then in, and he brought both hands to bear on the sword with all the strength he owned.

Aghaf had time to parry the blow, was ready to make a counterthrust. But he flung up the scimitar with only partial effect, and the weapon was knocked from his hand. Baignault had forgotten Aghaf's wounded shoulder, had expected the blow to be heavily blocked. He spun on, carried by the momentum of his own blow, and staggered to his knees in the roadway.

Aghaf was at him at once, stabbing with a poniard. Baignault smashed him in the mouth with his sword hilt, kneed him in the groin, and rolled clear enough to get his own poniard out and raised. He was insane with fury, no longer even remembering that this man had called him a colt, and also had been responsible for Louvic's death.

They rolled and kicked and tumbled and strained back and forth over the roadway stones, blade locked to blade, flailing and clawing each other with their free hands. Then, with his left hand, Baignault found Aghaf's throat, and he closed his grip until the other screamed. "Drop the poniard," Baignault told him. "Drop it! You hear me?"

Aghaf let the weapon drop with a small clatter. The strength was nearly out of him. Sweat dribbled from his face and his heart thumped so hard that Baignault could feel the beat. He reached over for the other's poniard and broke the weapon against the stones. Then he rose erect above the Wahabi and got ready to kill, his blow aimed for the dimly seen throat.

But the Druse camels were too close. They came thundering down the slope off the hill through the Saracen ranks. Baignault stared around in the moment that was left to him. The camels ran at a pace no horse could keep. The long, bump-kneed legs were right in front of him in a blur of angular movement. Foam splattered from the thick lips, and he looked up at lance points and over the curve of the long necks and saw both Rahim and Ecomil. The old man was yelling as if demented, and Baignault knew what he meant. He ducked low and put his arms around his head and stayed very still.

The camels hurdled him, sprang galvanically to miss both him and Aghaf. They were like horses, Baignault remembered, afraid to step upon a man. But a thick, splay hoof had smashed his poniard into fragments, and as the attack passed Aghaf was up, running, and Baignault lacked the speed to overtake him. "Come back!" he yelled. "Finish it with me!" They were fool's words, he realized, and came from his pain and shock. Aghaf had found a horse; he was in the saddle, galloping toward the ridge where, beyond the center of the combat, there were a few other Wahabis.

Baignault laughed harshly as he picked up his sword. He wouldn't have been able to see that ridge, he realized, if his eyesight had not returned. Let Aghaf go. Their lives were such that they were all but certain to meet again. And he had more than one enemy. Here were plenty of Saracens to fight.

Many of the Saracens had been knocked from their saddles by the heavier animals. But they still fought dismounted; they flung arrows into the camel ranks, then charged and with the scimitar and poniard hacked at the beasts' legs. The Saracen leader in his fine mesh armor was among them, carrying the stub of a scimitar whose blade had been broken at the guard. A lance hit him and he went down and as he rolled dying, he stabbed the camel above him in the belly.

Baignault winced as if he had taken the blow himself. He hefted the sword and went in among the Saracens. These men should die. All of them.

But in the clash of blows and the death cries he heard Mustaf shouting, then the insistent drum. Mustaf called his name, and memory told him that the drum sound was made by the nakers, the huge brass kettle drums the Mongols brought with them into battle. He listened carefully, beginning to emerge from battle frenzy and becoming conscious of what his purpose was, and what he must do. Next came the braying of the *kourrouns*. The Sieur Amboise had described them to him as a boy; the horns were seven feet long and sent their call for miles.

The Mongols were quite near, though. A detachment rode at a sharp gallop on sweaty, dusty horses along the road from the east. He recognized again from the Sieur Amboise's description the high-crowned white felt hats, the coat-robes of dressed horsehide with the wide flaps at the shoulders, the light, curved swords and round shields. He stepped onto the road walking drunkenly, the combat reaction heavy in him. Stand straight, he told himself. Hold up the sword for their commander to see.

He was straddle-legged, the sword raised to head height as he saw Subeyla. She rode at the Mongol commander's side and she wore a burnous, carried a lance, a scimitar and a shield. But she had just shucked the hood back from her head; her hair slid about her face and she pushed at it with a quick, characteristic gesture. "The clerk," she said. "Here is your man, *ming-bashi*."

That term meant leader of a thousand troops, Baignault recalled. He saluted the *ming-bashi*, the sword hilt against his chin, and the emerald clear and bright, the sun refracting from it to make him blink his eyes. Subeyla was down from her horse. She almost ran to Baignault.

Her hand gripped his hands on the sword and she pulled it aside. Then with a corner of her burnous she swiped the blood from his face. "I have something for you," she said. "Perhaps not so much as you will be given by the Golden Horde, but take it there with you." She stretched up, and with her arms embracing him, her body very close, kissed him until they both reeled.

90

The Mongol officer had, dismounted when Baignault looked around. But that was not, Baignault realized, because of what Subeyla had done. The *ming-bashi* stared for just an instant after Subeyla as she walked along the road to the spot where the last of the Saracens had fought. "You have done very well," he said in Arabic. "No wonder that she is pleased."

Baignault watched the man's hard, thin face and realized that the Mongol had noticed the emerald. He grounded his sword, then turned. There were no Saracens left alive. Even the wounded had been killed, and the bodies were being stripped. The only survivors were Ibn Aud Aghaf and the few Wahabi tribesmen who had withdrawn early and found mounts to take them to safety.

Subeyla was now talking with Rahim. The old warrior held a camel for her while she mounted. Then she rode on toward the Iron Gate. She will take the word to her brother, Baignault thought, both about what happened here and about the Mongols. He should be pleased; his trap had opened the road wide.

"You will excuse me," the *ming-bashi* said to Baignault. "But you are not from this tribe, or from the others. You come from—far away. The sword too is your own?"

"Yes," Baignault said. "But while the sword is mine, the jewel it bears is the property of my father. That was a gift to him from the Il-Khan."

"I understand," the *ming-bashi* said. "My orders are to find you. Then to travel east in your company."

"A turcopole who has served my father as sergeant is with me," Baignault said. "He stands there, across the road. A third man was with us, but he was killed in combat with the Saracens some days back."

Baignault stared back toward the pass as he spoke. The road was empty; Subeyla was gone. The kiss had been her farewell. It had meant, too, that he and Mustaf were free. "We are ready," he said to the *ming-bashi*, "to leave whenever you might wish."

The Mongol bowed to him and gravely smiled. "I must pay my respects to the sheik. There is business also about the purchase of camels that I have to transact. You have no desire to spend the night in the Druse camp?"

"None." Baignault's voice was flat. "I would prefer to stay here with the sergeant. All my farewells have been made. If you would give us a few soldiers as a guard, we will spend the time in sleep. Karakoram, I have been told, is a great distance away."

"You are right," the *ming-bashi* said, "and I envy you the chance to rest. I shall be with you early in the morning. Then we will start east."

·

CHAPTER SEVEN

If a man kept going toward the east long enough, Jean Baignault recalled from the stories of his early boyhood, he would reach the home of the sun. That was a pretty fantasy told for a child, but as he went over the Samarkand road from the Iron Gate he began to think it might make sense. The road was so old, so endless. The Romans had marched it on the way to India, and Darius and Alexander, and now it was his turn, his and Mustaf's. And behind him he had left Subeyla.

He spent hours at a time in thought of her. There was more to it than just that night of passion on the hillside where he had killed the vipers. She had let him know the true strength of her feeling for him when she had kissed him in front of the *ming-bashi* and in the presence of Rahim and the other Druse warriors. She really loved him.

Perhaps he had been mistaken not to have told her of his mission, not to have asked her to come along as his woman. Her sense of logic would have been helpful, and her knowledge and her ability to deal with people. Then of course there was the powerful physical attraction she held for him. Loose in the saddle, eyes shut against the strong sunlight of the Persian highlands, he imagined her in his arms, in his tent at night, awakening him with a kiss at dawn, riding at his side through the day. Why not? he asked himself repeatedly. Why not, Jean?

Still, all he had to do was open his eyes to recognize that it would have been impossible to bring her along. At his side, and never leaving it during the daylight hours, was the Mongol officer he had met just short of the Iron Gate. The man's name was Khotel, and he was young, less than thirty, hard, lean, quiet-spoken and canny, with contemplative and

92

yet always watchful eyes. Khotel spoke more than half a dozen languages with ease; his Arabic was better than Baignault's and his turcopole dialect equally as good as that Mustaf spoke. Dismounted, he looked misshapen, almost dwarfed, his legs hooplike from years in the saddle practically from birth, the upper body thick with compact muscle, the arms of such length that he could touch his knees when erect.

Khotel rode in a cloth-of-gold saddle. His reins were heavy with silver and there many jewels in his sword hilt. He wore pendant from his neck by a thick chain a stamped silver-gilt plate that was not only his sign of rank but showed he was on the Il-Khan's personal business and should be so respected. It carried the inscription: "By the strength of the great God, and of the great grace which He hath accorded our Emperor, be the name of the Khan blessed; and let such as disobey him be slain and destroyed."

Baignault was greatly impressed by Khotel. Here was a man who represented the immensely powerful and to him quite unknown world ahead. Khotel talked freely with him. It was his obvious intention to be friendly and gracious in every way he could. But, Baignault told himself, Khotel also wanted to pick his brains of every bit of knowledge he owned.

That realization sharpened Baignault's thinking. He compared himself to Khotel, and in the comparison he lost. The Mongol was much better informed. Khotel not only had a thorough knowledge of the Mongol empire; he had a very good understanding of the countries outside it.

Baignault was aware that until he had left *Outremer* it had pretty much been his world, with Asia and Europe somewhere vaguely outside, and Rome of course the center of civilization. Subeyla had started his doubt about the importance of Rome. But Khotel made him realize that *Outremer* would be a pebble dropped into the space of the Mongol empire, and Europe the size of a child's playground alongside it. The land of the Mongols stretched from the Mediterranean at the Straits of the Bosporus, east to that other and far vaster sea past Cathay.

But Khotel talked quietly, quite casually, of the fact that he had left Karakoram less than four months ago. He described without boasting the route they would follow over more than seven thousand miles. Their daily life on the road bore out all he said. The rest houses where the column halted at night were clean, well built; a man was always in attendance to start the fires, draw water and supply forage for the animals. There must be places like these throughout the empire, Baignault knew, as well as huge road maintenance crews and patrols who constantly guarded them. Each town or village of any size had a garrison in close touch with the next. But the royal couriers riding with dispatches to and from Karakoram were to Baignault the real proof of Mongol power.

The couriers passed along the road in daylight, darkness and every kind of weather. Standing with Khotel at the doorway of a rest house a few days out, Baignault watched a courier approach. He did not need Khotel to tell him that in Christendom there was nothing to match what he saw. The courier rode crouched low to his horse's withers. His eyelids were caked with dust and his boots with the mud of some river bottom. The facial lines drew deeply down toward the jaws, and the eyes stared straight at the road ahead.

Khotel was given no more than a very quick sidewise glance, then a flipped salute. The horse did not slow in its stride. The small, roweled spurs the courier wore gashed its flanks. The whip with its steel pellets imbedded in the leather was used without mercy. Pieces of dirt from the hooves pattered on the roadway and a dip of valley land beyond hid the courier. But on the horizon to the east there was another figure, crouched and sending his straining horse this way.

"They cover a regular distance of two hundred miles a day," Khotel said. "Some of our best horsemen are in that service."

"But who pays for it?" Baignault said. He felt no shame nor sense of embarrassment at the question. He must learn, he realized. Khotel had already become aware of the degree of his ignorance, but this time the lean-faced *ming-bashi* stared at him with open surprise.

"Trade does, Sir Jean," he said. "Trade keeps the empire together. More than twenty caravans a day come into Karakoram. The Il-Khan takes his tithe from each and the merchants and the caravaneers are glad to pay it. So the roads are kept in shape, and the army sees that there's peace and no brigands. But in Christendom you must—"

"I know very little about Christendom," Baignault said,

the words slow and forced from him. "I am in my way a legal bastard, a European in name and blood only, born and bred in *Outremer*."

Khotel gazed off toward the horizon for an instant, then back at Baignault. "You are an honest man, Sir Jean," he said, "and no fool. There must be many others like you in *Outremer*. Else it would have been impossible for you to hold off the Saracens for generations while they have outnumbered you thirty and more to each of your people."

"We can fight," Baignault said, his voice as quiet as Khotel's. "Never forget that about us. . . ."

The days of the march seemed to Baignault to roll rapidly into weeks. The column had passed the Persian highlands and entered a region bounded by mountains where, Khotel said, unless they forced themselves they would find snow. "The city of Abaku is beyond the mountains," Khotel told Baignault and Mustaf. "Once we reach it, we shall be in pleasant country, on the broad Tartar steppes. We will take time to rest in Abaku. But meanwhile we will ride as long as daylight lasts."

"We will keep any pace that you set for us," Baignault said. He sat with Mustaf inside their white-felt, dome-shaped tent, ready to crawl into his sleeping bag for the night. Khotel stood at the doorway, fresh from guard inspection. "I have great respect for both of you as horsemen," Khotel said. "Sleep well, and good night."

"There is a man I like," Mustaf said when Khotel was gone. "A *ming-bashi*, a commander of a thousand troops, and he talks to us straight out, tells us squarely of what's ahead. This place he spoke about, Abaku, I know of it. Pretty women and cheap wine and palm trees. A sea is there too, called the Caspian."

"But snow in the mountains before we come to it," Baignault said. He had crawled into his sleeping bag, reached to snuff the wick of the sheep fat lamp. "Khotel would like to make sure of us. He would find if we are ready for the truly difficult marches we must make. These until now have not been hard. But get to sleep, and do not let it worry you."

But then as sleep closed in Baignault imagined the steep, snow-filled mountains. He had seen very little of snow in his life; he must not fail up there ahead.

It was piercingly cold and shrill with wind in the mountain passes. Baignault suffered intense pain. He rode numbly, head down against the wind, and during the first day Mustaf had to instruct him how to treat frostbite. After that, he massaged his wrists and face regularly with snow, and held his horse in place in the column, halting only when Khotel halted.

Then they were out of the mountains. He looked with delight across the plain below. He had learned one thing, he told himself. This for him had been a personal triumph. If he could get through the mountains, nothing that he met further along the road would defeat him. The Caspian lay blue-shining below and he smiled and sang a verse from a roundelay and both Mustaf and Khotel looked around at him in surprise.

Abaku disappointed him. He found it shabby and dusty and filled with the motley of tribesmen who served the Il-Khan. He studied the troops with care. He recognized Copts and Syrians and Armenians and Georgians, tribes from half of Asia. Crossing a wide square flanked by a barracks he saw blond Turks, swarthy, gaunt Kirghiz, Uigurs and Afghans and Turkomen.

Khotel watched him, his glance oblique. "They all fight well, Sir Jean," he said.

"So I would guess," Baignault said. Then he saw the long, low building ahead where an honor guard was drawn up and an enormous blue banner flew. The guard wore dark bronze breastplates and enameled helmets. Their horse harness was polished until it gleamed; along the ranks horse and yak-tail standards were lowered in salute.

This was for him and in honor of his people, Baignault knew. He was profoundly pleased, and proud. He rode very straight and whirled the sword upward in the return salute with a sweeping motion that made the blade flash.

But he was surprised, then angered, when he entered the governor's palace with Khotel. The governor sat on a silver chair in the long reception hall. His courtiers stood impassively in front of him and the governor had a face like a falcon, bony, beaked, the eyes hooded. His voice had the sound of metal upon stone when he answered Baignault's formal greeting in Arabic with Talmuk, the general Mongol language. Khotel translated:

"I have heard of your business. You are to proceed at once. Nothing is to halt you on the road. The *ming-bashi* will care for all your needs until you meet the Il-Khan. You are dismissed."

Baignault gave another salaam, lower than the one when

96

he had entered. There was nothing to say, he thought, except that this was rather rude treatment for an ally. But he should hold onto his temper and leave. He was as expressionless as the courtiers when he backed away from the silver chair.

Khotel joined him outside the reception hall. "A meal is ready for us in the next chamber," he said. "Come and eat, Sir Jean."

"I would have no liking for any food served here," Baignault said. "The governor made me feel that I am not welcome. We would do best if we were to get back onto the road."

"Then I shall not argue," Khotel said. "But allow me to explain. You should remember that you are not the first Christian to come here and attempt to deal with us. Kublai Khan gave all manner of honors to Niccolo and Maffeo and Marco Polo. They made him the solemn promise that they would carry his message of friendship back to the Pope when they left. Yet nothing came of that, and Kublai Khan was not pleased. He is now dead of course, but the Il-Khan has not forgotten. The other merchant, Bendosi, also made promises that have since gone unhonored. The governor here has a long memory. He is aware that any man can make a promise. To keep them, that is another matter."

"You would tell me," Baignault said, "that the Polos were not sincere and that neither was Bendosi. Maybe you are right. But let us go. Our next meal can be in camp tonight."

"As you wish," Khotel said, and side by side, while the guards stiffly saluted them, they stepped forth into the sun-white square where Mustaf waited with the horses.

The column camped that night on the shore of the Caspian. Riders had been sent out from the city, at Khotel's request, bringing special food. Fermented mare's milk, spiced meats and caviar and then orange sherbet and tea were served as the evening meal. "How do you like it?" Khotel asked.

"The stuff is strange," Baignault said, watching Mustaf take another dish of sherbet. "But so are many things I have come upon inside your borders. Tell me if you would about the journey ahead."

Khotel pointed at the Caspian. "We cross that by boat tomorrow, animals and all. Then we come to a river called the Volga and another called the Don. They are wide; we will again need boats to cross them. Beyond are rivers called the Syr and the Sarya and the Ob. Those are in what is known as The Land of Shadows." Khotel's voice dropped; he sat staring at the quiet and gentle Caspian where small waves rustled and birds softly called. "The Land of Shadows holds a great deal of danger."

"Why?" Baignault said.

"Night lasts there for six months of the year," Khotel said. "Men freeze in the saddle from the cold. The snow, the wolves, the wind, just the space itself are to be feared."

Baignault felt the grip of nervous tension. He noticed that Mustaf had stopped gobbling sherbet. Like himself, Mustaf knew that Khotel was a man who was not easily made afraid. "Then through this Land of Shadows," Baignault said, "must be the shortest route to Karakoram. Else we would not follow it."

"You have the answer," Khotel said. "South of it are great mountains that border upon India. We dare not enter them at this time of year; the passes cannot be used. But from The Land of Shadows we enter lesser mountains, then come out upon the Gobi."

"The Gobi is the vast desert upon which Karakoram lies," Baignault said, trying to see the spaces in his head, trying to visualize how they would be crossed. "Past the Gobi on the east is Cathay, and it is a huge country and the Il-Khan rules there too. So he has put Karakoram where the caravans from east and west can meet."

"You are right again," Khotel said.

"Then we should sleep before Mustaf makes himself sick on the sherbet," Baignault said. "Truly, we have only begun to march."

"I will need a little fat on my bones," Mustaf said and rose grunting. "My tail is worn thin by the saddle. Never have I ridden so long, or hard. But there will be rest and women and maybe a little wine for us in Karakoram, *mingbashi?*"

"All that you wish," Khotel said smiling, but he had already started to turn away toward his own tent.

The land they traversed after they left the Caspian was so vast that often Baignault believed that he was suspended in dream. His mind was lulled. It seemed that he had been seated forever in this saddle, listening to the leather creak and sigh, staring at his horse's ears or at his companions and their mounts, all so familiar to him that he could identify them with his eyes shut.

Here the road stretched arrow-straight across the steppe. It reached on and on, slightly undulant, dun-shaded, covered with the grass that was the only source of forage for the horses. Man was very small in such a region, Baignault told himself. There were no towns or villages or houses. Nobody lived in this immensity except the bands of roving nomads who tended the herds of half-wild and shaggy horses and stayed in shy solitude, not coming near the road.

A morose mood settled on Baignault. He was saddle-weary; his body ached day and night, and at dawn he had difficulty with Mustaf. The turcopole did not want to get back into the saddle. "What's the sense of this, Sir Jean?" he asked. "The road is endless. And even if it isn't, the wolves will take care of us when come into The Land of Shadows. I have heard of them. They grow as big as horses; one bite of their jaws and a man is snapped in half."

"You are too old to have listened to such stupid bazaar stories," Baignault told him. "Dress yourself. Go out to the fire and eat. Then you will be ready to ride."

"I am too old for that too," Mustaf said, but he struggled up and dressed, helped Khotel's soldiers with the packing of the tent, then mounted and rode.

But, slowly, the days had begun to change. Sunlight was shorter. The cold increased, and Baignault could tell by the tight, grave faces of the troopers that the column was about to enter into The Land of Shadows. Soon, there would be no more day, and six months of night. . . .

Massive gray wolves, almost as big as Mustaf had described, drew in around the column. Khotel sent men out who were expert with the bow and a number were shot and the road was clear while the rest tore at the carcasses. But there were thirty and forty at a time to replace those which had been slain. They made concerted attacks. It was necessary to fight with the lance, then at dangerously close quarters.

Mustaf missed a tulwar blow and a froth-jawed wolf tore the throat from his horse and he was flung from the saddle. Baignault was right behind him and decapitated the wolf with a single stroke of the sword. But he still had to lift the turcopole from the ground, and it took the help of Khotel and six troopers who formed a ring around them to beat back the attack.

Mustaf was numb with shock. Coma claimed him, and

99

Baignault told Khotel that a fire should be started, camp made. "I cannot afford to lose this man," he said.

"Nor can we," Khotel said. "Each one of us is needed. And he is a good soldier." Khotel's face was pale in the darkness and his voice rough with emotion as he called to his senior noncom to pitch camp.

The men assigned to picket duty when a fire had been built and tents pitched were unwilling to ride alone. Khotel sent them out in pairs and he ordered them to sing and shout to scare off the wolves, to slap themselves and move constantly in the saddle to keep from sleep and fatal frostbite. The wind moaned and gobbled; the sounds the pickets made were lost in it as Baignault sat by the fire with Mustaf. Snow was beginning to fall. It built an impenetrable wall that moved in from the darkness and doubled his sense of dread.

The only solace was the fire. Men crouched shoulder touching shoulder around the little yellow sputter. They shared both heat and companionship, but their talk was of demons. Baignault listened in surprise. The demons were supposed to capture the human spirit and devour it; they were insatiable, and they had teeth longer than wolves' fangs and talons instead of hands.

Four of the troops went insane despite anything that Khotel could do to save them. One frothed at the mouth and proclaimed himself a demon. His eyes rolled, his face contorted and he clawed at his companions until they beat him away in horror and he stumbled out into the snow to die. Another just sat where he was, dully, his gaze fixed on the darkness. Life slipped from him and he toppled forward into the fire. The other two were afflicted suddenly with the idea that they were possessed by demons. They rose and fought the wind gusts and staggered in the snow and then, howling, fell convulsed.

Khotel chafed their wrists, faces, throats. He talked to them and pleaded that they act like men. But they died face down in the snow. None of the remaining troopers would touch those who had died. Khotel and some of his junior officers had to drag the bodies off and bury them in drifts.

Khotel came back to the fire sweaty-faced. It was impossible for him to keep his hands still. They trembled even though he gripped them around his scimitar belt. He sat spent, careless of how he must look, and at a loud gust of wind he ducked his head as if menaced by an actual blow.

The *ming-bashi* was afraid, Baignault realized. He took comfort from the knowledge. It eased some of his own fear; Khotel had been here before, was supposed to be strong-willed, a real leader. But Baignault had begun to see demons of his own. They pranced in at him and showed their fangs and claws; their hot slobber splashed his face. He shuddered and almost screamed. Then, in terror, he looked to Mustaf for support.

Mustaf was conscious. He sat hunkered and gropingly made the sign of the cross. His eyes were shut. He was alone, deep at the bottom of an abyss of fear. Mustaf could do him no good, Baignault realized. Nobody could but himself. Pray, he thought. He was a Christian and must pray for his salvation.

He prayed, but the wind broke the words in his throat. His mind refused him; memory was still. He felt the demon fangs. They were tearing at his throat. In a moment now, he would be devoured. Pray, he told himself. Pray in the name of God. If he did not, he would be gone. Recite the Creed. . . .

The words were frail against the wind. But he uttered them: "I believe in one God the Father Almighty, Maker of heaven and earth, and of all things visible and invisible."

His eyes were open; he stared forth to see the demons. They swirled before him, beckoning, reaching. Fear tugged his throat. Instead of the words of the Creed, he wanted to scream. But he said the words: "And in one Lord Jesus Christ, the only-begotten Son of God, begotten of His Father before all worlds; God of Light; Light of Light; Very God of God; Begotten, not made; Being of one substance with the Father, by Whom all things are made; Who for us men, and for our salvation, came down from heaven."

He stopped. Strength was in him. He had found some well of faith within his spirit and now he was unafraid. Subeyla had shaken his faith. Khotel had shaken it. But he believed, and he was saved. Not that it was the only faith. Not that it hadn't been misused by the corrupt, by the greedy. But with it to sustain him he could go on. After all, every man had to die in his time, and death was not to be feared, only how a man lived, whether in honor or in shame.

He rose to his feet. The demons he had seen, he realized,

were spectral shapes formed by the snow. Their voices were the wind, and the hot slobber he had imagined was frostbite. He walked to Khotel's side and shook him by the shoulder. "We should ride, *ming-bashi*," he said calmly. "This is no place for us to stay and the men are without rest."

"You speak sense," Khotel said. His eyes were sane, and he tried to match the calmness of Baignault's voice. Then he stood up and went from man to man and told them to get up and saddle and mount. But when Baignault had lifted Mustaf into a saddle and was ready to mount, Khotel nodded to him.

Khotel meant, Baignault realized, that he was to take over and lead the column. It was Khotel's way of expressing his respect to him. The Mongol was too proud to speak.

Baignault smiled as he stared into the snow and calculated from the wind direction how the column should move. Mustaf rode next to him, shoulders bowed, snow in a crusted mask over his face. Baignault gave him a broad-handed whack across the back. "You are fit to ride by yourself?"

"Yes, Sir Jean. I might fall out of the saddle. But I will get back."

"Then take a brand from the fire. We will need it for light and for fire at the next camp."

Mustaf scrubbed the snow from his brows and eyelids. He looked back at Khotel about a half-dozen paces behind them. "So you are in command."

"For a time, yes. The *ming-bashi* has accorded me the honor. He would make me believe that I deserve it."

"If you put the column back in the saddle, then you do," Mustaf said. "But I will go for the brand. Holding it will make me a little warmer."

"Give thanks to God for that," Baignault said. "Pray to Him for your deliverance."

"He helped you?"

"He helped us all."

"Then," Mustaf said, "I will pray from here to Karakoram."

There were many more awful weeks before they were across the Siberian steppe and came forth into the sunlit regions to the south near the Gobi. But Khotel was once more in sure control of himself. He had taken over the column from Baignault a few hours after it had left the encampment where the men had died, and never by any other sign permitted Baignault to recognize his gratitude.

Baignault was content. He was carried forward by a sense of constant eagerness. The scenes he met fascinated him. He would be, he knew, among the first four or five men of his race and religion to visit Karakoram.

The Gobi was to be crossed, though, before the column reached Karakoram. The Gobi was like bleached bone. Sun blazed over it. The awful dazzle inflamed the eyes; skin shrank or distended in raw blisters. The camels that had been sent from Karakoram for the use of the column were thin, nasty-tempered and unruly.

Khotel, with his fine skill, was almost thrown off the first animal he mounted. The young major in command of the camels beat at it with his stick. The camel whirled savagely and snapped an orange-shaped bite through his forearm. He dropped the stick and stanched the blood and looked up in silence at Khotel.

"Very well," Khotel said. "I do not hold any blame against you. But go and have that cleaned. Then you must find us other mounts."

Baignault stood off a bit to one side. He was back at his habitual practice of watching Khotel. The camels presented a problem, and he wanted to see how Khotel would solve it. But Khotel stared at him. He seemed to penetrate his thought. "Your turn, Sir Jean. Take an animal and mount. You should be able to ride a camel."

"If I cannot," Baignault said, "I will finish the march on foot. But I was given instruction in the riding of camels back at the Iron Gate."

Khotel's eyes narrowed. "You should, then, have no trouble," he said.

CHAPTER EIGHT

It seemed like a mirage, caught in the desert shimmer, but Baignault knew that it was real. Here at last was Karakoram, after all the trial, the suffering, the fighting and marching. Elation leaped in him and yet he felt solemn.

He came to this place a changed man, he thought. He was greatly different, if not so much wiser. His awareness of this fact made him solemn; back in *Outremer*, he had been so inexperienced that he had not even considered what the journey might do to him.

He rode steadily forward, his camel kept at a sharp canter. But he told himself, take care. He had no idea of what he would meet here. These people might readily outwit him. They might be clever enough to twist him around into serving them. Almost all that he knew about them had been picked up from Khotel, and it was certain that as the Il-Khan's trusted officer Khotel had given him only the best side of the story.

His own duty, he remembered, was really simple. He was to stay out of politics, have nothing to do with religion or trade. His single purpose was the mission—to take Chagan to Rome, bring the young prince back safely again to Karakoram and then arrange for the treaty between his people and the Mongols. When the time arrived for the treaty negotiations, he would leave them to men like his father and stand well aside. He was no politician or ambassador, and the success of the mission would satisfy any ambition that he held.

Baignault urged his camel to the gallop. His mind was clear; he felt sure of the welcome that was ahead. He rode the final few miles with Khotel one pace behind him on his right, Mustaf three paces behind on his left. But he did not turn to look at them.

Karakoram was a loose, low collection of buildings within the tremendous sweep of the Gobi. It lay among sandy barrens, and wind hummed over the huts, the corrals and tents which lay at its perimeter. He saw past the black domes of the yurts the minarets of stone mosques, then Buddhist temples and small wooden Nestorian churches. Khotel had told him of these. All kinds of religions were permitted here as long as the basic Mongol law was obeyed.

Fires burned between the edge of the desert and the first huts. Baignault recognized their purpose: they were set in welcome. And Khotel called to him, "Be sure to ride between them, Sir Jean."

"I will," Baignault said. He pulled his camel around and, striking with the riding stick, went at the fast gallop. The pair of fires was built of piles of thornwood but they were

104

huge and cast intense heat and high flame. Baignault remembered what Khotel had told him about them while the camel pranced in approach to the narrow gap. It was old Mongol superstition that if a man went between the fires and there was deviltry in him it would be brought out. Back at El Kerak they would say that this was shriving.

The camel skittered past the flare of the fires and then out into a wide street. Dogs, children, goats and a couple of half-grown colts scampered about the street and he laughed at the sight. But there was no scorn in the laughter. He knew that the Mongols called Karakoram an *ordu*—a camp. They had no need of the formal elegance Europeans believed was necessary for a capital. He had seen a great deal of their country, and he could imagine the immensity of their wealth from the amount of land they let lie fallow. And with a million warriors to ride for him, the Il-Khan could afford to live in any fashion he wished.

Baignault could see ahead now the Il-Khan's own pavilion. It was easy to recognize from Khotel's description, and he reined the camel to a slow trot. He sensed that he could count to quite a considerable extent, also, on what Khotel had told him about the court. Khotel was a noble and had served as a courtier, and had passed on to him details about imperial policies, of the rivalry and intrigue, and even the names and looks of the Il-Khan's favorite wives.

But Baignault understood also that Mustaf was the one man he could completely trust. He would have to rely on the sergeant if anything went wrong here. Yet Mustaf was just a rough soldier, and the difficult work must be for him, Jean Baignault, alone. Nobody could help him in extremity except himself.

Baignault tapped the camel and made it step smartly ahead. The Il-Khan's pavilion was resplendent under the afternoon sun. Wealth wasn't spared here. The structure was long, high and wide, reared out of white felt and lined with scarlet silk, visible in the tunnel-like side entrances and the great main portal. It faced to the south and before it was arrayed the honor guard. These were picked warriors and the officer who commanded them was a *tuman-bashi*, a leader of ten thousand. His order to the guard started Baignault's camel twitching and kicking.

Then the cymbals clashed. The nakers boomed as the mounted drummers hit left, hit right, and the seven-foot

105

horns threw out their tremendous braying. Baignault drew his sword. He let the camel sway as he saluted and rode down the line in review with the *tuman-bashi*.

A huge crowd jammed the dusty space opposite the portal of the pavilion. He stared at brown, yellow and black faces and into slanted, curious eyes. He was on inspection before half the tribes of Asia, he thought, and sat the camel gracefully, making the beast obey every pressure of the head rope. His hands were taut; a nervous constriction took his body. Buddhist priests in mustard-yellow robes watched him. Behind them were bearded and shabby Nestorians whose sect had broken centuries ago from the main stream of Christian dogma. Then, on one side, keeping to themselves, were the Moslem holy men. Their angular faces were shaded by their headcloths and their eyes contained a calm that irritated him. It might be scorn, he thought, but they weren't that much interested in him. It was just a cold and measured lack of respect. For them, he was simply another outlander who had come to Karakoram to pay tribute to the Il-Khan or ask some favor. Yeah and verily, Baignault, a Crusader did not bother those fellows a lot. Mohammed was very great, that was the reason, and Mohammed controlled the world and most of its peoples. . . .

But a sergeant was in front of Baignault and saluted him and reached for the camel's head rope. The *kourrouns* were still. An order had been passed to the honor guard and they stood at parade rest. Baignault returned the sergeant's salute and swung down to the ground before the portal.

Carpets covered it. Files of bowmen flanked it at rigid attention. The *tuman-bashi* was at his left side as he stepped forward. Then, he looked quickly back. Khotel was behind them, and within four short paces, Mustaf.

Baignault almost laughed aloud. The shrew old turcopole bastard, he thought. He should have told Mustaf to stay outside. But Mustaf had made the journey too, and had the right to a look at what was in here; he had earned it.

Baignault stared into the pavilion. He was conscious that he wore the same kind of headdress and robe and yak-hide boots as Khotel and that his face was burned dark tan by the sun and wind. Only his sword showed his identity. He carried himself stiffly erect, his stride slow and even, in rhythm with that of the *tuman-bashi*. The palm of his left hand rested on the sword hilt, but did not cover the emerald. That he wished to be seen.

There was an immense silver table just inside the portal. It bore mare's milk and fruit and meat. Any man who served the Il-Khan was supposed to go there when he chose and eat. The thought came to Baignault that he was hungry. He served the Il-Khan too, in his fashion, and would savor some of that food. But he swept the thought aside as he studied the men beyond the table.

The nobles attached to the court stood in ranks formed toward the center of the pavilion. Baignault saw that they wore regular undress uniform, ankle-length padded coats, girdles whose ends were heavy with silver bullion, and up-tilted white felt hats. His glance traveled past them to the center of the pavilion where the traditional fire of thorn-wood and dung burned.

It gave a ruddy light. Smoke from it made him squint. Now the *tuman-bashi* had halted, and Khotel too, and Mus-taf. He moved forward alone and in front of him on the dais at the end of the pavilion, on a low bench, his favorite wife seated below him on his left-hand side, was the Il-Khan Arghun, the Master of Thrones and Crowns.

Baignault stretched out prostrate. At last, he thought. Here before him was the man who had begun this. And he must say to the Il-Khan the words he had pondered so many times. He took a slow breath and then another, to ease his tension. Khotel had taught him the Talmuk language on the road and he spoke strong-voiced:

"Sire, I am Sir Jean Baignault. I greet you in the name of my father, the Sieur Amboise Baignault, and in the name of my masters, the rulers of Christendom. I bring with me to you the jewel which you had the goodness—"

The Il-Khan said, "Rise, Sir Jean. Come to my side. Your father and I fought so when we were young men. Thus you are my friend."

Baignault rose up and looked fully into the Il-Khan's face. A narrow mustache drooped over the sensuous mouth. The eyes were dark beneath protruding brows, and the nose beaked. He was a short man, thin and sallow. He wore sables and silk. There were superb jewels pendant from his throat and on his fingers. His hand grip as he took Baignault's was extremely strong.

"I present you to my Queen, Tudin-La," he said. Then, as Baignault salaamed to the small, silent woman, "This is my son, the Prince Chagan."

Baignault was already staring at Chagan. He was young,

107

in his early twenties. No older than I am, Baignault thought, and a good amount more handsome. Chagan had his father's features and full-lipped mouth, but his skin was clear and he was clean-shaven. Baignault bowed deeply to him. This was the convert to Christianity, the man he would take to Rome.

"It is a great pleasure." Chagan smiled. "We have waited quite a time for you, Sir Jean. I began to doubt that you existed."

"A few times out on the steppe," Baignault said, "I shared the idea. But we made the best possible speed, Your Highness."

"You shall call me only by my name," Chagan said. "The title is for others. We must be able to know each other well."

"Thank you," Baignault said. He liked Chagan, and sensed that there would be no trouble between them. But the nobles had begun to move forward and Baignault was forced to turn away from the prince. He salaamed and bowed and repeated formal phrases of greeting again and again, then answered questions about the journey.

The Il-Khan relieved him as a noble with a well-greased mustache went into a long, involved interrogation about the strength of the Saracen armies. "No more talk at this moment, Sir Jean," the Il-Khan said. "You must be tired, and later you will meet with my councilors in audience. I put you in Chagan's hands. Take him off, Chagan."

Baignault salaamed. "I must ask a question, though, sire. What happened to the man who brought this to the Sieur Amboise?" Baignault touched the Tree of Life emerald.

"He did not return." A rough note was in the Il-Khan's voice. His eyes drew almost shut. "Somewhere beyond the Ob River, he disappeared. But my officers had already been in talk with him. They had knowledge of his message. Come back here to me within two hours, Sir Jean. Be ready then to talk to the council."

"As you command, sire," Baignault said.

He moved away from the dais beside Chagan. The young prince had taken him lightly by the arm and they went slowly through the groups of courtiers. Baignault took care to notice that Mustaf stood in a far corner and seemed sober, and that Khotel was near and watched them with an intent, thoughtful glance. "It would be pleasant," he said, "if the *ming-bashi*, Khotel, were to join us. He has some fine stories of what went on along the road."

108

"You tell them to me," Chagan said.

"But I do not speak your language very well."

Chagan laughed. He stood before Baignault, a gay and attractive figure in his sables and jauntily peaked white hat. "Let us talk with Khotel later. I understand you. But if the Talmuk makes trouble for you, we can talk in Arabic. I have been studying that."

"The journey to Rome, then, must mean very much to you," Baignault said quietly.

"Very much indeed," Chagan said. "For months, I have thought of it and how it can be accomplished, what may arise from it."

He and Baignault had crossed the pavilion to a side table where a servant stood. Meats and fruits were spread there on trays, and alongside them stood bowls of kermess and flagons of European wines. Baignault checked his surprise. The wine was a special tribute to him, he realized, and obviously Chagan had arranged for it. He should relax, he told himself; there had been enough of tension, and with Chagan he could be at his ease.

"Would you like some of the wine?" Chagan said. "If we are to go to Rome together, I imagine I must learn to drink the stuff. The Il-Khan at my request had this brought in last week from the Byzantine border. The merchant who sold it has a good name."

"I hope he keeps it," Baignault said laughing. "There are two things which I haven't fully mastered yet—your language and the liking for kermess. We drink in *Outremer* and Europe either wine or cider."

Chagan spoke to the servant and a flagon stopper popped. "So," he said, "I instruct you in language and you in turn teach me wine-bibbing. But my sister has not advanced far yet with her Arabic. We will be forced to take time out on the road in order that she may learn it."

Baignault drew a slow breath and then asked himself, what sister? Khotel had told him nothing about such a person. Still, Chagan had just spoken as though she would be along on the journey to Rome. Small beads of sweat rose on the backs of Baignault's hands. He had to act with care as he took a wine goblet from Chagan. A woman crossing the Gobi, then the mountains, then The Land of Shadows, a woman who was a princess and the Il-Khan's daughter . . .

"Khotel might well have told me," he said hoarsely. "I was not aware that you had a sister, Prince Chagan."

109

"Khotel has been absent from the court for months," Chagan said. "There was no way for him to find out that the Il-Khan has decided to send my sister with me to Rome. Her name is Litei, and she is one of my father's daughters by another marriage. She was brought up in Cathay, where her mother was born. But she is of the Buddhist faith and the Il-Khan is not overly pleased with that."

Baignault looked down thoughtfully at his goblet, then brought himself to smile. "In my country and in Europe we wish each other luck when we drink. Here is a toast to a good journey out and back to Rome. I am deeply honored that the Il-Khan has decided to send the Princess Litei to Rome with us. But I must tell you that some of the marching may be very hard for her."

"She is younger than I," Chagan said as he nodded to the servant and the goblets were refilled. "Still, she is a most accomplished rider. She has often accepted wagers from me and Khotel when we have ridden after game in the desert with falcons." Chagan sipped his wine and grimaced. "The greater part of those she won, and came in ahead of us at the prize. You should meet her. Accompany me now; there will be time before you are to talk with the council."

"I would be delighted," Baignault said. But he was silent as he left the main pavilion beside Chagan. Perhaps, he told himself, he had lost his ability to carry wine. The stuff he had drunk stirred through his veins and thumped in his head. He hardly noticed that Chagan led him through a covered and carpeted passage and that, suddenly, they were at the end of it. Chagan looked at him with a slight frown. "Has the wine stolen your wits?"

"Somewhat," Baignault said. "But I am in possession of myself, and quite eager to meet the princess."

"You are not alone," Chagan said without expression. "So are many men." He had picked up a padded stick that hung next to a gong and tapped a resonant note from the embossed brass. A woman servant in a long Chinese robe answered the gong. She bowed to them and stepped back and lifted the door hanging for them to enter.

They went forward into a chamber that was hung completely in silk. It smelled of crushed roses and faintly of incense. Baignault breathed faster; he felt his nostrils flare, and his eyes and his hands grow hot. Never, he thought, had he been in such a setting. It made him feel that he had been brought up in a monkish existence.

110

The furniture was done in black lacquer; delicate bird designs covered the embroidery. Chinese and Mongol women servants, all of them handsome, moved to light tall candles in silver candelabra. He sensed their sidewise glances at him and was pleased. It was good, after the rough, bitter months of the journey, to be made aware that he was attractive to women. But then he glanced at the woman in the center of the room.

She sat alone on a low divan. Her eyes were raised for his glance and he saw that she was lovely. The impact of her sexual appeal started a warmth through his thighs to his groin. He had never had a woman like this, never. . . . There had been delirious passion in Subeyla's arms, and over and over he had repeated that he loved her. But Litei was like an animal who was yet a woman, and she had eyes that burned his brain.

Then he was aware of Chagan presenting him to the princess, and he made a low salaam. Litei held forth her right hand. The nails were long and were shellacked an orange shade, and the hand was so delicate that it was hidden within his own. He stared at his hand, brown and thick and weather-coarsened, and he was tempted almost beyond control to run it up her wrist, over the arm curves to the curves of the motionless body. She was conscious of her power to excite him, he realized. He was not the first man she had touched with fire.

Litei smiled at him. The smooth, oval face was radiant with delight. Her eyes, dark brown, with large pupils and greenish gold irises, were speculative, though, and the provocation of the lips was deliberate. He took his glance from them before she would understand how close he had come to putting his hands on her body. She wore a brocaded crimson jacket. Nothing lay beneath it but the thinnest gauze. He could make out the tender nipples of her breasts. Her skirt was of the same material as the blouse, though beneath it she wore a tight, short undergarment of black velvet.

"Sir Jean, the Crusader," she said. "Do sit down."

"Thank you, Your Highness." He moved back with a wide stride.

"Sit down also, Chagan," she said. "I would hear from the Crusader about the journey. They have told you, Sir Jean, that I will accompany you to Rome?"

Baignault answered slowly, his mind tormented by erotic images. He had this woman stripped of her clothing—he was on the divan alone with her. . . . "Yes, Your Highness," he said. "Chagan made that known to me in the moment."

"You are not perhaps afraid that my presence shall cause you trouble?"

"No, Your Highness. I have no such fear."

She provocatively crossed and uncrossed her legs. "Address me as Litei," she said. "Titles are not for us. I hope that Chagan has also told you that."

"I waited for you to do it," Chagan said. He sat somber but amused. He gazed at his sister as though inspecting some piece of voluptuous statuary that did not quite suit his taste. Chagan wished to warn him about Litei, Baignault realized. If he were to become infatuated with her there would certainly be trouble. He should remember steadfastly that Subeyla was his woman. There was reason for him to love Subeyla, while Litei seemed to be half lynx, half houri.

"So, Sir Jean, let us hear of your Rome and the road to it," Litei said.

"I know little of Rome, but more of the road," Baignault said. "There you will find thirst and heat, then bitter cold and weeks of absolute darkness. I am not too certain, Your Highness, that you shall be happy on the journey."

Litei drew back her lips and showed her small, even teeth in a mocking grin. "You are as big and brown as a bear," she said. "But you do not frighten me. I am determined to go to Rome, and the Il-Khan has given his permission. Now, please, tell me—and Chagan—the true story of the dangers of the road."

"As you wish, Litei," Baignault said, quietly. He felt no anger or doubt. Let her hear, he thought. It could not do any harm. And, *Dieu damme* and *Dieu garde*, he would keep on looking at her, even if it did him harm. . . .

CHAPTER NINE

Baignault was alone with her when Khotel came to take him to the council. Chagan had left them more than half an hour before and Litei had ordered her servants to retire behind screens at a corner of the chamber. Baignault talked, and she sat half-reclining as she listened.

He drew closer to describe the rugged Crusader jousts and tourneys. But his thought was not on what he said. He was still erotically aroused by her. He was aware that she clearly sensed his passion, and yet he could not control himself. His eyes constantly searched and probed her body, and within the shield of his words he embraced her.

Khotel's arrival startled him. His passion ebbed, and he felt weak and almost sick. He resented Khotel; he was instinctively jealous of him. If she had such an effect upon him, then she must provoke much the same reaction in Khotel. He stared across the room at the *ming-bashi*.

Khotel stood at attention just inside the door, his manner curt, very correct. But do not count too much on that, Baignault thought. Khotel was a handsome man, and strong and tough; he had his own need for a woman. There was a peculiar fixity in Khotel's eyes. His voice was harsh as he said, "You would pardon me, Your Highness? The Il-Khan has sent me to bring Sir Jean before the councilors."

Litei made a quick gesture of dismissal. "Then take him," she said.

But, Baignault thought, this formality is simply for my benefit. From what Chagan had told him, Khotel knew Litei very well. He had been smart enough, on the road, to say nothing about her. But it was quite possible that the young and ambitious *ming-bashi* had been in bed with her, or gone beyond that and fallen in love.

"You will excuse me, Litei?" Baignault said, and salaamed to her.

"Should you come back later, yes," Litei said. Her right arm was raised behind her head, the jacket loose from her body. "There is more about the outside world that I must hear."

"But the *ming-bashi* might tell you equally well," Baignault said. He watched Khotel and saw the man's face flush and slightly tighten.

"I have already heard the stories Khotel has to tell," she said. "While yours are new to me. Join me here again this evening."

"The Il-Khan has other plans for Sir Jean," Khotel said. "Tonight a banquet will be held in his honor."

A flick of malice was in Litei's voice as she said, "Thank you, *ming-bashi*. But you need not worry about Sir Jean."

This, Baignault thought swiftly, had become dangerous ground and he had better leave it. Khotel was a man whose

113

friendship he needed while he was in Karakoram. Later, too, on the road he must be able to trust him.

"I am very tired," he said to Litei. "Once I am finished with the councilors, I will ask to be excused from the banquet. I shall go straight to bed."

Litei did not pretend to answer; she rose and turned her back on both of them. Baignault moved across the room to Khotel. He took the other man's arm as they left and he could feel Khotel's tension. "If I could," he murmured, "I would like to make the Il-Khan and the council wait."

"That will not be necessary," Khotel said.

They walked the carpeted corridor without speech. Baignault felt a sudden sense of relief and confidence. He had just won back there, he knew. He had saved himself from a difficult situation. He was smarter than when he had started on the road here. Each day taught him a little more. Still, he should move slowly, look constantly around him. The road ahead was very long.

His confidence wavered with that realization, remembering once more the immense extent of Mongol power.

Khotel stared curiously at him. "I must leave you here," he said. "A meeting of the council is on too high a level for a *ming-bashi*. That is for the great nobles, the generals and the Il-Khan. Let me wish you good luck with them."

"I might very well need some," Baignault said. His confidence had faded. He was aware again that he was young, untrained. The members of the council could easily overwhelm him with their brilliance. He represented a few hundred thousand people and a narrow strip of land with the sea on one side, the desert and the Saracens on the other, while the Il-Khan's councilors had behind them nearly half the world.

But the sentries at the entrance of the audience hall had just swung their iron maces to him in the present arms. He saluted, then stepped past them stiff-legged toward the dais where Arghun sat. The mink and sable and silk and jewels worn by the men gathered in the chamber were lustrous in the candelabra light. Their eyes searched his face and he stared back. He should show them that he was not afraid, he thought, for if he became so he was finished.

The Il-Khan introduced him in formal fashion to each member of the council. He salaamed as the names were said, but stared straight at each man. He saw that there were blonds among them, and men so swarthy he was sure they came from Afghan or Indian tribes, and there were several who must be Chinese. He recalled that Khotel had explained they belonged to a corps of engineers; they handled the *pao-yu*, the artillery that used gunpowder to fire iron shot, which was still a mystery to the best military minds in Europe.

But he was impressed by the fact that none of the council offered him a sign of friendship. They stayed deliberately aloof inside the barriers of their rank, waiting for the Il-Khan to set the pattern of their behavior. Then, with the last introduction, the Il-Khan smiled. He said, "I hope that you feel rested, Sir Jean."

"Somewhat, sire," Baignault said. "It was a pleasure to talk with Prince Chagan and meet Princess Litei."

"Your words please me," Arghun said. "Now, these men and I would discuss the journey with you. We would like to learn from you that it is not too dangerous, particularly for my daughter. Rome is far from here. I ask you to remember also the warning my messenger gave to the Sieur Amboise about safe return."

There was only one answer, Baignault thought, looking around at the bearded, hard faces and the watchful eyes, and these men knew it. Their engineers, their guard officers and couriers went over the road daily to the Iron Gate. But he should be cautious and show deference to Khotel.

"The *ming-bashi* who commanded the detachment that brought me here," he said, "must have already made his report to you, sire. The road is open and well maintained. But the region known as The Land of Shadows should be avoided by the Princess Litei. It would prove difficult enough to Prince Chagan."

"The *ming-bashi* Khotel has reported." It was a gray-headed general who spoke. He was a powerful-looking man with an arm crippled by some severe wound, and a scar from his chin to the corner of his left eye. His name was Gelim as Baignault had heard it and he was obviously of high rank.

"Then the dangers are understood by you, sir," Baignault said.

"They are," Gelim said. "There is, however, another route that does not lead through The Land of Shadows. That is to the south, through the Pamir Mountains, along the border of India and by way of Afghanistan. The Polo brothers and their young nephew made use of it some few years ago."

115

"Thank you, sir." Baignault turned his glance from Gelim to the Il-Khan. "Allow me to inquire about the princess. When your messenger spoke with my father, nothing was said of her. Only the prince was supposed to accompany me to Rome and be returned home."

"A great number of my people are of the Buddhist faith," the Il-Khan explained, "although every religion is permitted among us. Were my daughter to return from Rome a fervent Christian, she would be of much help here. She could convert those of her former faith."

Baignault thought, a thrill of excitement along his nerves, this man had spoken truly. The Il-Khan did not attempt to hide the existence of religious dissension among the tribes of the Golden Horde. The awful scene of madness at the camp in The Land of Shadows returned to Baignault. Four of the Mongol troopers had lost their minds and died claimed by superstitious demons. The Mongol empire must be a vast jumble of religions into which everything had been tossed.

If the people could be drawn together by a common faith and worship Christianity, a great, an almost incalculable victory would be gained. "Allow me to ask it, sire," he said. "But you have Moslems among your people as well as Buddhists and Nestorians and other cults. Some are the enemies of my kind. Would they not resent Christianity?"

The old general, Gelim, grunted and said, "Tell the Christian. Have him to understand, sire, what Kublai Khan had to say to such a question. I heard it; it was said right here in this hall."

The Il-Khan leaned forward on the dais. He propped his arms in their loose-flowing sleeves on his knees and his dark, keen eyes studied Baignault. "Kublai Khan once told Christian emissaries who came to him, 'You inhabitants of the West believe that you are the only Christians, and despise others. But how do you know on whom God may bestow His favor? We adore God, and in His strength will overwhelm the whole earth from the East to the West. But if we were not strengthened by God, what could we do?'"

That was fine language, Baignault thought. The Mongols hadn't yet overwhelmed the world, though, and if it were that easy, the messenger would not have been sent to the Sieur Amboise. *Outremer* was still needed as an ally. . . .

He salaamed and said carefully, "A most wise statement, sire."

The vast hall was silent. The Il-Khan sat with his eyes almost shut. Gelim stood ruffling his fingers through his beard, his eyes filled with pride. The other councilors stood motionless and inscrutable. They reminded Baignault of pieces of ornate marble that some sculptor had designed for a hidden, secret palace. He realized that they waited for the Il-Khan; they had nothing they wished or dared to say.

The Il-Khan was rising from his bench. "You should now understand us better, Sir Jean. Religion is our own matter and is settled in our own fashion. You will take both my son and my daughter to Rome by the route that General Gelim has chosen. And you will see that they return safely home again. Do we have your word to that?"

"You do, sire." Baignault let his voice ring through the hall. These men respected strength and he was strong. "I give you my vow as a sworn knight. Let none of you doubt me. The Prince Chagan and the Princess Litei will be guarded by my life between here and Rome."

He gave a sword salute instead of a salaam as he finished. He took the blade slicking out of the scabbard, presented it in a shining blaze, the hilt against his chin. The Il-Khan's eyes were bright at the sight, and Gelim's, and Baignault did not bother to look around at the rest. These, he knew, were the two who counted.

"We are agreed, Sir Jean." The Il-Khan had stepped down from the dais. "You are dismissed. It is time; you must be bone-weary. Tomorrow, though, we will talk again of the journey."

"Gladly, sire," Baignault said. He backed away bowing to the councilors. But reaction had begun to set in. He almost reeled with fatigue. It had been a day like none other in his life, he thought. First Chagan. Then Litei. Finally this ordeal. And any part of it would have been enough. . . .

A young officer of the guard stepped in front of him, as he reached the end of the hall. "Sir, I have been assigned to accompany you to your quarters. There is something that you wish? I can have brought you whatever might be your fancy." The officer's voice lowered a bit. "My orders are also to supply you with a woman, should you like."

"Some food and drink," Baignault said, and laughed. "But not a woman, not tonight. I have only sufficient energy to take off my boots. Tell me, where is the *ming-bashi* Khotel? And my sergeant, the turcopole?"

"Both asleep already, sir," the lieutenant said. "The

ming-bashi was so gone in sleep that I was forced to carry him from the table where he dined. Your sergeant when I last saw him had slipped away from the noncommissioned mess."

"With a wine flagon in his hand, no doubt," Baignault said.

"No doubt at all, sir," the lieutenant said.

"He would and he should," Baignault said. "Now take me to the food and the wine."

When Baignault had finished his meal and was conducted to the quarters reserved for him he found Mustaf snoring under wolfskin robes. "We believed, sir," the lieutenant said, "that you would like to have him close to you."

"This man, always," Baignault said. Only Mustaf's bushy eyebrows and the end of his nose, blistered by the Gobi, showed above the robes and he snored with a roaring sound. But Baignault was reassured by his presence. Mustaf was the single remaining link to the past and home. As long as he was with Mustaf, the connection existed.

The young lieutenant stood alert in the doorway to the quarters. "I shall be outside through the night, sir," he said. "I command a special guard of twenty men. The *ming-bashi* Khotel is in the quarters next to these, should you have any need to reach him."

"Thank you," Baignault said. "Tell the officer who relieves you that I will sleep for a long while, possibly until mid-day."

He fumbled off his boots, then tossed aside his robe and hat and got inside the sheepskins that lined the wolfskin-covered bed. Stretching to snuff the lamp wick, he saw that Mustaf had his tulwar with him. The hilt of the weapon protruded from the robes beside the neck of an empty wine flagon.

The old bastard, Baignault thought, both vexed and amused. That was not the way for a stranger to pass the first night among new allies. As sleep surged over him in vast, rolling waves, he thought he smelled the perfume Litei used. His nerves quivered in longing; he saw in imagination the sharp breasts with the rounded, powdered nipples, and his hands set as if he stroked them. . . .

He slept throughout most of the next day and only roused enough to see that Mustaf had barely moved. Hunger made him get up finally, and he prodded Mustaf with his foot.

"It is time to eat," he said. "Let sleep be. You have had enough and more."

Mustaf blinked and yawned and blew his nose and groaned. When he got up he tripped over the wine flagon and kicked it spinning. "You gave it greater care last night when it was full," Khotel said. He stood at the door in his undershirt and drawers, a towel over his arm. "But there is a steam bath made ready for us, and we shall all feel better afterward."

Mustaf looked refreshed, Baignault thought; his manner was relaxed and his voice naturally gay. "I might well wear some new clothes," Baignault told him. "So might Mustaf. The stuff we have suffered quite severely on the road."

"The court steward waits at the bath to find just what garments you need," Khotel said. "And there is also a barber to shave you and cut your hair."

"Very fine," Baignault said. "But by now it must be mid-afternoon. Does the Il-Khan expect me?"

Khotel grinned. "He was here some while ago and looked in upon you. When he was aware of how you slept, he decided that you should not be disturbed. So he has gone out into the *ordu* for the inspection of some troops. Prince Chagan would like to talk with you, though, and Princess Litei. The princess in particular."

"Then you won't need me, sir," Mustaf said. He had been busy scratching himself, but he stopped to squint at Khotel. "Maybe the *ming-bashi* might tell me how I can find a woman here. It's so long since I've seen one that—"

"Be still!" Baignault told him, rough-voiced. "You cannot talk like that. If a servant were to hear you, we would be in trouble. It would be believed that we are a very poor sort of Christians."

"Peace upon both of you," Khotel said. "I shall give you several names, Mustaf. Then you will be able to go down to the bazaars and try your luck. Take money with you, however. The bazaar women have accepted too many promises from sergeants in the past."

Laughter broke from Baignault. Mustaf had begun to twist his mustache points in hurt pride. "I will give you money," Baignault said. "Then, when I am free, I shall be happy to join you in a walk. Now let us get to the bath. I am not sure of you, *ming-bashi,* but I am aware that I stink fulsomely of camel sweat."

119

The bath was in a special tent where water was poured by servants over heated stones. There were jars of unguents on a shelf and Baignault massaged himself after he was scrubbed. His body glowed and tingled in response. Thought of Litei rose in his mind; he was coupled with her in a straining embrace. But he must get away from such reflections, he told himself. The Mongols were a proud people, and Litei a princess of the royal blood. Should he enter into any sort of dalliance with her the mission would be wrecked. The Mongols would turn upon him in hatred, accuse him, and rightly so, of having betrayed them.

He went to the jars filled with cold water and poured several of them over his body. Then he dressed in the new clothing brought him by the steward and stepped outside the tent. His nerves were quiet when Khotel and Mustaf joined him. He smiled and laughed and joked as he sat with them and ate a meal with great relish.

Khotel left him at the end of the meal to put Mustaf on the way to the bazaars. But the young lieutenant who had been in command of the guard last night was waiting for Baignault. "Prince Chagan wishes to see you, sir," he said. "He would have you come to his quarters."

Chagan sat playing with a fine gerfalcon. "Welcome, Sir Jean," he said. "I am glad to have a moment with you. Let me warn you, though, that my sister is most impatient. She has the conviction that any of your time away from the Il-Khan should be spent with her."

"I cannot agree," Baignault said bluntly. "Any number of men must be eager to occupy their time with the princess. She does not have to call upon me."

"Still," Chagan said, "she has chosen you." Chagan slid the leather hood over the falcon's head, returned the bird to the perch and secured the chain that held it. Then, lithe and nervous and quick, he paced back and forth across the weapon-strewn apartment. "May I ask, how much did you find out about Litei yesterday?"

"Enough to understand that for a man who has just come from the Gobi and long months of marching she holds tremendous fascination. I all but lost my wits to her."

"Do not, Sir Jean."

"Have no fear that I will. I watch myself, carefully."

"Then you begin to understand about her. She is no bawd. She is much too smart, too jealous of her charms to be that. Yet she has enormous ambition. She would like to rule the world, and thinks that only men can make her empress of it."

"I am most grateful to you. But why do you tell me this?"

"I wish to trust you," Chagan said, "and have the belief that you like to have similar trust in me."

"Thank you," Baignault said, "for your honesty."

"I must act so," Chagan said. "It will someday be my task to rule the Golden Horde. My sister—in truth, my half-sister—with her Chinese guile and appeal to men must not get between me and the throne. If you had not given me clearly just now your purpose I would have gone to the Il-Khan and told him that I no longer wished to make the journey to Rome. You should be my friend, Sir Jean, and my ally, not Litei's love-struck dupe."

This was passing strange, Baignault thought, beneath the surface of great power to come upon such enmity and family bitterness. But he should make sure that his own cause was not lost because of it. "Let me speak to you," he said, "with the same frankness, Chagan. There is a woman I deeply love. She is a Druse, and to come here I was forced to leave her back at the Iron Gate. Khotel has met her; he knows the degree of my love for her. Should you doubt me, then talk with him and he will inform you. But it is she I love, not your sister."

"Then, with that known to me," Chagan said, "let us visit my sister now. You shan't be troubled?"

"No," Baignault said, and laughed. "My woman is at the Iron Gate or has returned to her home in Syria. But in any event she is far enough away so that I may take delight in looking at Litei."

Chagan's eyes were sharp. "You Crusaders are a peculiar lot."

"Then let me tell you," Baignault said, "without vexing you, that I was about to make a like remark about you, the Mongols."

He walked shoulder to shoulder with Chagan along the passage to Litei's quarters, and their conversation was gay. But the gaiety was forced, Baignault knew. Both of them, more than they were willing to admit, were worried about Litei.

Her greeting was subdued. She wore a long brocaded gown that stretched to her ankles and a lute player sat before her and played tunes in soft minors. But the gown, Baignault saw when she moved, was slashed on one side as

121

high as the thigh. Then the lute player left and was replaced by girl dancers. Strong, spiced wine was served. Baignault drank sparingly of it and watched her instead of the dancers who were naked to the waists.

"You slept well?" she said.

"Very well, thank you," he said.

Her red, full mouth tightened a bit and she could not keep all of the dislike out of her eyes. "You appear bored," she said. "I am aware that my brother thinks nothing of the dancers. He would sleep with them on occasion, and that is all."

"Litei, you had me tell you yesterday of my world," Baignault said in a slow voice. "It would be pleasant that if today you told me about Cathay."

"So." Litei clapped her hands. The dancers halted and stared and then scampered toward the doorway. "Cathay is vast. It has many palaces and temples and beautiful women. The women are given both respect and honor. They are not scorned by dolts. That is the end of the lesson for today, Sir Jean, except that I have given my word to the Il-Khan that I would make the journey to Rome in your company."

Baignault looked across at Chagan and then stood erect. They bowed in unison to her. "I regret your displeasure," he said.

"But your stupidity concerns you, not me," Litei said. "Make an effort to rid yourself of it before we leave. At present, to me you are only an extremely dull person."

Chagan kept silent until he and Baignault were out in the corridor. Then he spoke, harsh-voiced with anger. "The sly vixen," he said. "She should have stayed with the rest of her mother's litter in Cathay. It took all of my will in the moment to hold back from slapping her full in the mouth."

"Yet I asked for what she gave me," Baignault said. "We sought to escape from there and she became aware of it. That means I must return tomorrow and be pleasant with her and work once more into her good graces."

Chagan stared at him. "Why?"

"If I did not," Baignault said, "she might create a great amount of harm during the journey. That is a risk we cannot take. The journey will be immensely hard in itself."

"Litei called you a big brown bear yesterday," Chagan said. He smiled and slapped Baignault on the shoulder. "But, though you do look like one, your thinking is different. For you right now thought very fast, and remembered all that you should. I leave her to you. She is your charge and you are to handle her."

"I am not too sure that I can," Baignault said.

"Still, you must try," Chagan said.

"That of course I will do. And I wish greatly that we may leave here soon."

"In only a few more days we shall be ready," Chagan said. "The Il-Khan must talk with you again, and then, when the route is chosen, the mounts will be picked. Put aside your impatience for your Druse."

Baignault gave him a somber glance. "I am not too sure of her either," he said. "I do not even know that I will ever see her again."

Baignault spent the hours of the late afternoon and evening with the Il-Khan, the court astrologer and the chief geographer. They discussed in great detail the journey to Rome. Despite his previous knowledge of Mongol thoroughness, he was amazed by the amount of information these men had amassed about huge areas. They had maps on wide parchment rolls that marked each major village between the eastern borders of Cathay and the Iron Gate. All that he had ever seen in his days at El Kerak had been the silver-sheet map made by the Greek geographer, Idrissa, and Père Malachi had been inordinately proud of that.

Time and again, too, as he sat here at the council table, he was given reports that came from merchants. A certain man seeking ivory had been in this region; another had bought spices in a little-known valley, and one whose business was gold dust had been at a mountain pass down into the plains of India. The Mongols might lack a unifying religion, Baignault thought, but trade drew a tight net through the empire, held the parts in place with Karakoram at the center.

There was nothing like this in Christendom. Europe was a motley of duchies and principalities and loosely organized kingdoms. A traveler often had trouble going from one valley to the next and risked his life because of local feuds and petty wars. The nobles kept to their castles, left them only to loot or pillage, and in extreme cases to respond to the call of some crusade. They held most of the land, and the Church the rest. Merchants lived on sufferance, paid enormous taxes to the nobles, and the serfs were considered little better than animals. It was the same in *Outremer* where the

123

Knights Templars owned one part of the land and the Knights Hospitalers another, while they fought for the levies to be taken from the pilgrims.

He looked up and found that the Il-Khan stared at him across the table spread with maps. "When would you wish to leave?" he asked.

"After a week, sire." He still felt fatigue, and Mustaf needed more rest, even if he sought it among the bazaar whores. There was also the matter to be straightened with Litei; he must get back on good terms with her before they left for Rome. And he wanted to move around in the bazaars, study these merchants and caravaneers who poured so much wealth into Karakoram.

"Granted," the Il-Khan said and motioned to his geographer and astrologer. The maps were rolled and taken from the table; the astrologer picked up his globe and then the two men backed away with low salaams past the ceremonial fire. "That is all there is between us," the Il-Khan said, "except for the warning given your father by my messenger."

Baignault sat tense. "What of it, sire?"

"No disaster can happen on the road," the Il-Khan said. "Nor can the mission fail. So I have decided to send General Gelim with you, and also Khotel. The route to be followed is well known to both of them. You should be able to reach Rome without serious difficulty."

"I have no doubt of that." Baignault's voice was quiet. He sat with his hands on the table edge and he was relaxed. It would be good to have those men along. "You honor me when you send General Gelim. And as you know I have true respect for Khotel."

"Still," the Il-Khan said, "the main burden will rest with you. The prince and princess will come fully under your protection once they have gone outside my borders. Should they be harmed, no excuse will help you. My own feelings would not matter. This country would move at once to attack yours and without mercy."

"You make yourself very clear, sire," Baignault said. His head had begun to ache; his eyes burned and blinked. He had taken enough of this, he thought. But he kept his glance steadily on the Il-Khan, and his voice was level. "You offer a hard bargain that I can only accept. Let me, though assure you that my people want peace. They have no desire

124

for war, and certainly not against you and your people."

"Then give proof of it on the journey." The Il-Khan gestured; the audience was finished. "Take the rest that you need meanwhile, and pray to your God for good luck along the road."

"Yes, sire." Baignault salaamed when he stood from the table and he thought that his brains would press through his skull. He walked numbly out of the audience hall. When he reached his quarters, Mustaf was there, and he laughed at the sight of the turcopole and the fatigue and the tension were lifted from him.

Mustaf sat cross-legged with a wine flagon between his knees. He was drunk, but his eyes were clear.

Baignault picked up the flagon and took a long drink. "How did it go for you at the bazaars?"

"Very fine, very fine," Mustaf said. "I found me a woman right off. The nice and quiet kind. She's the widow of a Uigur juggler. When I go back tomorrow, she will show me some of his tricks. But I'll need money, more than I had today. Nothing for nothing is what she says. She wants to be paid every time. Sir Jean, I must be getting old. I was given plenty of credit back in *Outremer*."

Baignault drank again from the flagon. "You may have need of some juggler's tricks before we are home. I will go to the bazaars with you tomorrow. Those I must see myself. Now come over here beside me while we pray."

"Yes, Sir Jean," Mustaf said, and his voice was sober. Then he knelt beside Baignault, head bowed and eyes shut.

Baignault slept deeply that night, untroubled by dream. He was really refreshed, he found, once he had his breakfast and was out in the sunlight. He and Mustaf moved fast into the dusty vastness of the square which was the center for the bazaars.

It was a fabulous place. There were dancers and jugglers and wrestlers and singers, troops off duty and troops just in from the hinterland who guarded the caravans until the final moment of arrival here. He counted seven caravans in the space of an hour. He had let Mustaf go on alone to be instructed by the Uigur widow and he stood unnoticed by a heap of bales dumped from the backs of sweaty, stumbling camels. Those bales contained spices, he knew; he could smell them. They would go all the way from here to Rome, he told himself, then through the other Italian cities, and up

125

through Lombardy into France. That stuff kept the meat from spoiling in the heat of summer, and it was more precious than gold or ivory.

There were gold and ivory aplenty in the booth next to him. And peacock plumes and jade and silk. Buckles would be made out of the ivory, for women's slippers. The peacock plumes would set off their hair. Silk would go into their dresses and undergarments. And the jade—that was for earrings and necklaces. His mother would like a pair of earrings, and Subeyla would adore them. There was yet another woman for whom he should buy a pair. She was Litei. . . .

He walked through the square from booth to booth, haggling, examining, arguing in his fluent Talmuk. Then he came upon a pair of earrings of exquisite design. They were of Chinese manufacture, the merchant said, and done in delicate foliate filigree with a gold base. He took them in his hand before he paid for them and they excited his mind.

Imagination set him in the Chinese city where they had been made. The squint-eyed old man who fashioned them finally put down his tools and sold the pair. The merchant who bought them packed them in a bale. Then they traveled on the backs of porters and camels and yaks and mules across the Chinese trails, till they arrived at Karakoram.

Trade was what counted, Baignault thought. Not swords, or war. There had never been a war fought that affected the world as much as trade. The men of the Polo family and Bendosi had traveled in the name of trade and many more would come after them. He should remember always what Subeyla had told him. She had tried to tell him this and he would not listen; he had been still too much of a soldier.

Standing there in the bazaar, Baignault cursed. The price of the earrings took all his money. He had nothing left with which to buy a gift for Subeyla. But she would understand. Just to have him tell her that she was right and he was wrong would be gift enough for her.

He walked back to the pavilion with the earrings in his hand. Guards saluted him and he vaguely nodded. His thought was on Litei. He wanted to be able to meet her with a clever, assured speech. But he had no more than a jumble of words when he met her. She was outside of her apartment and in riding dress, carrying a whip and wearing spurs on her scarlet boots.

126

He halted deliberately in front of her. His shoulders, he realized, were of more good to him than words; they were broad enough so that she would have to squeeze around him in the passage. She stared at him in anger. "Do I call the guard," she said, "or use this?" She raised the whip.

"Neither," he said. His hand opened and he held out to her the earrings. "I saw these in the bazaar," he said. "They are from Cathay. My belief was that you would take a fancy to them."

"You offer them as tribute to me?" she said.

"I do not."

"Then you attempt to bribe me."

"Again, you are wrong. But you are a beautiful woman and you should wear them. That is my only thought."

"Put them on," she said. She swept back her hair and he leaned close to her. Holes were punctured in her ears, and he slid the loops through and locked them in place. She released her hair, then turned her face to his. "Kiss me."

He kissed her twice.

"We should see a lot of each other on the journey, Crusader."

"We will, Litei." He stood back to let her pass. "You gave me to understand that I should rid myself of my stupidity."

CHAPTER TEN

The ride-out from Karakoram was made in magnificent, barbaric style. For Jean Baignault, it was almost unbelievable. He had seen his share of pomp and splendor at home in *Outremer;* the Crusaders had brought with them from medieval Europe a great sense of pageantry and color and music and to it they had added the flamboyant spirit of display picked up in Byzantium and the Near East. But none of the ceremonies he had ever witnessed could equal this.

Thousands of camel-mounted troops paraded in front of the city as their party left from the pavilion of the Il-Khan. Beyond, across the desert, close rank upon rank to the horizon, were squadrons of cavalry. The time was late afternoon because the Il-Khan had decreed in deference to his daughter that the party should not march far the first day, but camp relatively near in tents already prepared. So the sun in the west sent a carmine brilliance over the desert and drew flame from the lance points and scimitar blades, made the vast banners shimmer, and the bronze body armor, the housings of the camels and the horses. The beasts' eyes shone; the faces of the riders were radiant, held in high relief, and the huge brass tubes of the *kourrouns* flashed while the golden arms of the drummers whirled.

Litei rode beside her father on a dappled, thin-hocked camel, Chagan on his other side, but a pace behind. Litei wore a dress in the Chinese style. It was of gold tissue, tight to the body from the ankles to the throat and with a high collar. Her slippers were brocaded, trimmed with turquoises, pearls and emeralds, and her stockings were silk. The dress hem was slit to allow her movement; her legs, the right hooked easily about the saddle pommel, were visible to the knees. A cape of white wolfskin draped her shoulders and her black hair was thickly plaited under a tilted wolfskin cap.

Jean Baignault could not take his eyes from her. She shocked him somehow, and aroused a latent, savage quality in his nature. He realized that he wanted to fight with her, subdue her, because if he did not she would conquer him. The man who loved Subeyla could give of himself and receive fully in return. Not with Litei, though. A man either possessed the Il-Khan's daughter or he was her slave.

Baignault rode near Khotel and he saw that the *mingbashi* watched her also with a troubled, intense glance and that in the rank ahead old Gelim gazed at her from under lowered lids. Litei cast her spell on any man, Baignault told himself, and looked away at the parade. This he should remember and be able to describe later in Rome and *Outremer*.

Rugs had been spread out into the desert to form an avenue over which they marched. The people had been leaving Karakoram for hours to assemble along it. The yellow-robed Buddhist priests were there, impassive, arms locked within their loose sleeves, and the Moslem holy men and the shabby Nestorians who had made no attempt to communicate with Baignault while he was in the city. He glanced speculatively at them, wondering now if he had been wrong to fail to seek the Nestorians on his own account. But they were a stubborn lot, he remembered, and they hated his kind of Christianity even more than they did the Buddhists or the Moslems. As for the latter, the Il-Khan had told him that they were in complete if silent defiance of the mission. Well, it was the Il-Khan's task to handle them; he was their emperor.

Baignault stroked the neck of the fine riding camel he rode. He slid his body lower into the cushioned leather of the saddle and tossed back from his shoulders the new sable cape which was a gift from the Il-Khan. He should enjoy what he saw, he thought. There would be enough of danger, trouble, hardship between here and Rome.

Dancers moved among the party, and jugglers and wrestlers and clowns. The wild, swart-skinned dancing women swung at times into the packed mass of the crowd, where men snatched at their veils or blouses and got slapped hard. The crowd bellowed at that, and yelled to the clowns in their red horsehair wigs to give a bit of the same to the dancers. But the clowns led leopards on long chains and were busy leaping over them, stumbling and regaining balance in mock fright. The jugglers pitched sharply honed scimitars into the air, caught them by the blades between their teeth. The *kourrouns* and drums gave such tumult that the jugglers could only hear the crowd's applause as a faint ripple, but they could sense the satisfaction from the waved hands, the distended eyes and gaping mouths.

A vast force was here, it seemed to Baignault. The Mongols had swept the tribes of nearly half the world together to work and fight for them. It was a fact that the people of Christendom must understand, then be ready to meet, else they would perish. He felt again his doubt about the ability of the Western people to join as allies on equal ground with the Mongols. Profound loneliness filled him; he was aware that he was a stranger who was incalculably far from home.

The clamor of the military music abruptly ceased. His hand upraised, the Il-Khan had silenced it, and the players who accompanied the dancers were still. The crowd made no noise, and the troops were very quiet, and now the Gobi wind could be heard. Against the wind only the soft breathing and stamping of the animals and the flutter of the banners were audible. The Il-Khan had ridden a sufficient distance from his *ordu* and was about to bid farewell.

He embraced Litei without word, and then Chagan. His brooding, somber eyes passed over Baignault and Gelim and

Khotel, and they saluted, erect in their saddles. There was nothing left for the Il-Khan to say, Baignault knew; it had all been said and he would not forget a word of it. The standard bearers wheeled and began to gallop. The Il-Khan set his mount at the same pace and some of his staff and councilors were forced to use the quirt on their mounts to keep formation. Beside them, no longer silent, but yelling and pushing, the crowd ran. A *tuman-bashi* called an order that was repeated through the squadrons and the troops rode off in column toward Karakoram, a huge and dark mass in the last of the sunlight.

Gelim gave the next order, sending the party and its detachment of cavalry forward at the trot. Jean Baignault looked back once more at the mass of troops. He imagined it on the narrow Syrian plain, between the Mediterranean and the purple hills of home. If those men came as allies, he thought, victory was certain. If they came as enemies, Christendom was lost. His responsibility was a great deal more than any one man should be asked to bear, yet there was no way that he could relinquish it or ease it. There was only one thing for him to do—go on toward Rome.

CHAPTER ELEVEN

They sang as they rode across the desert, even in the parching daytime heat and the night chill, and they were gay and ran races. Chagan had brought along one of his gerfalcons and he and Litei made wagers against Baignault and Khotel that it would knock vultures out of the sky. Gelim unbent at the end of the daily marches and told of old fights when he was young and had fought at the side of Kublai Khan. Then, at Litei's insistence, Baignault described again what he knew of Rome, and Khotel talked of Byzantium where he had been on a mission for the Il-Khan the year before. She insisted, too, that Mustaf be summoned and when he was warmed with a cup of well-sugared tea he performed an imitation of an Aleppo belly dancer that was both lewd and comical.

Now the party was no longer gay. Ahead of them loomed the Pamirs, the famous and dreaded mountains they must traverse. Here was the Suget Pass, through which they must climb at a height of over seventeen thousand feet. Snow banked the grim, fire-colored cliffs. Snow gusts struck in the pass, biting at the stone, sending up an icy spray that would cut to the bone.

Gelim talked with the native guides who had been hired to lead them. He spoke with Baignault and Khotel, then alone with Chagan. When he came back he stared levelly at Litei. He said, "Be so good, Your Highness, as to save your anger from me. But it is the belief of your brother, the prince, that you should not attempt the part of the journey that is ahead of us. You should wait until a more favorable season. Strong, trained mountaineers have been known to be lost in the pass in weather such as this."

Litei was already mounted on the sturdy and thickly coated horse she had chosen for mountain work. She wore the wolfskin cape and cap that had been her father's gifts, and sable mittens, sheepskin-lined boots made of yak hide. She sat motionless in the saddle, one hand loosely holding the reins, the other gripping the cruel Mongol quirt with its lead pellets imbedded in the thongs. "So my brother is against me," she said. "And you, of course, Gelim. But how about the others? Tell me, Crusader, and you, *ming-bashi*. Will you too refuse to carry out the Il-Khan's orders?"

"If you please, Highness," Jean Baignault said slowly and bowed to her from his saddle. "Be patient. Time presses us, but not that much. We will camp and wait for better weather. Then—"

"Then," she broke in upon him, "the General Gelim will send off a courier to Karakoram and ask my father to order me home. And you will go on without me. This much I can guess. But I am able to ride as well as any man and take cold and snow and fatigue. Watch, the whole lot of you, and you will see."

The quirt blow she gave made the horse neigh and leap at a head-down gallop. She struck repeatedly and the advance guard wheeled aside from her and she was on the trail, going up it as fast as the beast could move. Then the huge, reddish boulders hid her from sight.

"Very well," Gelim said, anger in his voice. "She has made our orders for us. Fall in and follow her. You, Sir Jean and Khotel, catch up to her before she breaks her neck."

Baignault and Khotel rode brushing the boulders, straining to keep from being pitched headlong. Anger gripped

Baignault; he forced his horse until it nearly tripped and threw him and from in back Gelim shouted to be more careful. But he was the first to reach Litei. She waited in a little highland meadow beyond the first steep ascent. Grass persisted there at the edge of the snow and her horse cropped it placidly and she seemed very calm. She said, "You may see that you were quite wrong about me."

Baignault kept still; Khotel was also in the meadow, and he let him talk to her. He looked up and saw that the sun had just emerged from steel-shaded cloud and spread light through the pass. Small birds sang. He noticed delicate alpine flowers and the clumps of dwarfed willows from which the pass took its name. Up at the head of the defile, where the trail approached the summit, a prayer flag left by Tibetan caravaneers to invoke the blessing of the gods while they made their passage hung limp.

Khotel seemed embarrassed as he spoke to Litei. "I am not too sure that you should go on, Your Highness. I have been through the pass several times. There is quite immediate danger whenever the wind shifts or rises. I think that we should wait for another day."

"But we can climb to the summit before darkness," Litei said. "The descent down the other side will not be nearly so difficult."

Khotel shifted his glance to the pass, then, obliquely, to Baignault. Baignault had the thought that Khotel was about to ask him to speak. But Khotel knew that this must be settled among the Mongols themselves; no stranger could intercede. Gelim was coming into the meadow, lashing his horse and shouting, and Chagan was ahead of the general, swerving out past the Kirghiz guides in their blue turbans and thick, fur-hemmed coats.

Chagan called to Litei, "Why did you hold up here? The guides tell me the trail can be used. If you will, ride with me. We shan't ever reach Rome this way."

"Wait, please," Khotel said. "Listen to what Gelim has to say. He should give his consent."

But half-brother and half-sister only laughed at Khotel. They raced ahead shunting their horses against each other on the narrowness of the trail. Chagan had to rear his mount to avoid collision at the end of the meadow and Litei led going up into the defile. Baignault swore fervently beneath his breath. He was past anger, and what he felt was a mixture of doubt and dread. This, he told himself, was not the way to reach Rome.

Then Gelim joined them, followed in close formation by the detachment of troopers, herders, servants and pack animals. He asked Khotel, "What has happened?"

As he listened, his facial lines tightened and he spoke sharply to the senior Kirghiz guide. The man shrugged as he answered. If the wind didn't come up, he said, the pass might be used. He wasn't sure. There was a lot of snow above. With this sun upon it, he could only guess.

"Chagan and Litei are already in the pass, sir," Khotel said. His voice was quiet. "If I might suggest it to the general, I do not see how we can now stop them."

"The whole detachment will go forward," Gelim said harshly. "They cannot be left alone. But Chagan should feel a bit of this quirt, and also the Princess Litei." He rose erect in his stirrups and gave a hand signal to the troops to advance. Then he put his horse at the trail, Khotel close behind him. Baignault held back, wanting to talk with Mustaf.

"Stay with the troops," he told Mustaf. "But watch me. I must ride out ahead."

"Take care of yourself," Mustaf said; he was grim-faced. "I have no liking for this. This is no good."

"I will do what is best," Baignault said, then urged his horse. The mount was cat-fast and sure upon the rubble and, afterward, in the slushy snow of the defile. He let it climb most of the way without his guidance, the braided reins slack in his hands. The control he gave was only with the knees, and he sat low, weight forward against the flat pommel, remembering not to look into the awful, jagged chasms below but at the trail.

Litei was still far up ahead when the wind began to blow. He saw her cape billow with the gusts, and it was like a taunt to him. He knew that if she should slip and fall Gelim might very well order the march halted and return to Karakoram. It would end the mission; the Il-Khan, his daughter lost, would not further risk his son. But Chagan rode as though demented, sending his horse at the trot whenever there were a few feet of open space, closing rapidly upon his sister. Some peculiar rivalry existed between them, Baignault realized. He recalled what Chagan had told him of Litei; he must be jealous of his sister and the power she

133

held over their father, and, more, he must be bitterly resentful of the fact that she had been allowed to accompany the mission.

Then blinding snow swept Chagan from sight, and the pass was filled from wall to wall with a silver pelting that stung the skin, clogged breath and blinded vision. Baignault felt his horse slow to a hesitant walk. For the first time he tried to handle the beast with the reins. The snow phantoms tricked him and spun and pranced ahead, and once he felt the horse's right front hoof leave the trail completely, cut out into the void.

His stomach muscles compressed with fear. He shivered, imagining the drop below, the few final seconds of agony. He had the impulse to yell, to release his emotion and possibly make Litei or Chagan hear him. He reached a bend of the trail where a huge boulder formed a lee from the wind, and found Gelim there. The broad-shouldered old general was covered with snow; his horse and saddle were crusted with it and only his eyes showed, small and fierce slits of light. Khotel was beside Gelim, in close conversation. Neither of them turned, and Baignault realized that in the obscurity he was unseen.

A blast of wind recoiling from the cliff behind them carried Khotel's words to him. Khotel was urging Gelim to go on, not halt here. Gelim shouted back, "But it is madness. We may never find them now. They are probably both already lost."

"Then, General, our duty is to make sure."

"You, a *ming-bashi*, tell me so?" Gelim's words beat through the gusts. "I will not move until I can see the trail. Remember that the responsibility for them is mine—not yours."

Baignault moved his horse slowly forward. There was no reason for him to speak or make his presence known to these two men. It was again a problem for the Mongols to decide. His concern was the safety of Litei and Chagan; it was them he had promised to take to Rome.

His horse refused to go any further, however, once he was on the open trail beyond the boulder. Here the wind struck with gale force. It sprang down the pass with a demonic hooting and the snow slashed and strangled. He dismounted and led the horse, moving forward by instinct. Vision could not penetrate the whiteness ahead. Deep in some quiet corner of his brain he told himself that he understood now why the Tibetans had raised a prayer flag to the mountain gods at the summit of the pass.

Then he began to sense motion other than his own. He groped forward along the inner side of the trail, his numbed hands fumbling rock and then a snow-clotted mane and a human body. "I am Jean Baignault," he called. "Who might this be?"

"Litei." Her voice was faint on the wind. "Chagan is also here, and the senior guide. We have come to the decision that we will not attempt to go further."

"That is reasonable," Baignault said. He was shaking with rage and reaction from the climb. Then, as he stepped forward a pace, he bumped into Chagan. "Waste no time with my fool of a sister," Chagan told him. "Stand back, Sir Jean, and save yourself from the wind. The others should be along soon. The guide has told me that the wind cannot keep up like this all night."

Baignault wedged in beside the Kirghiz who stood huddled head down, and hauled his horse in front of him to make a windbreak. He was grateful now for the clothing he wore; it had been specially designed for a climate such as this. He was warm, and with the flow of relaxation through him after the strain of the ascent, he began to feel drowsy. Litei was on his other side, uptrail from the guide, and he crouched shoulder to shoulder with her. He sensed that she was very tense, her body rigid, and that she waited as if to leap or strike, poised for something that was wholly unknown to him.

Then he heard the slur of passage on the trail below, the sound of men and horses dragging upward. The men pulled the horses by the reins, and leaned against the wind, panting, nearly crawling, and through a break in the storm Baignault recognized Khotel and Mustaf approaching. The *ming-bashi* reeled to Litei and propped himself upright against the rock. He stared at her, then turned to Chagan, and his cracked voice was savage. "You are both mad fools," he said.

"Be still!" Litei told him. "We sought to reach the summit before darkness. The guide believed that we could."

Baignault moved away from them. He had listened to enough of such Mongol talk for today. Now he wanted to find out about Mustaf. Mustaf was his friend and the single person here whom he could fully trust. The turcopole squatted doubled over in the snow. He breathed in broken

135

gasps and the snow had made a bizarre, comic mask of his face. "How are you?" Baignault said.

"A bit spavined," Mustaf said, "but not finished. I'll make it to the top. I can still climb." Then he reached out his hand to tug Baignault down level with him. He spoke fast and in French. "Did you happen to see the old general below on the trail?"

"Yes. He stood beside a great boulder with him." Baignault nodded slightly toward Khotel. "They were in some sort of dispute about the climb."

"When I came along," Mustaf said, "the general was gone. But his horse stood beside the boulder, and its reins were broken and the beast was badly frightened. Then as I watched, it slipped and fell over the cliff. Maybe the general went over too."

"Perhaps you are right," Baignault said. "But I cannot be certain. Nor can you. . . ." He stood erect. A chill that was not caused by the wind clasped him. He gazed back at Khotel, remembering the angry exchange of words he had overheard. That was impossible, he thought. Khotel would never push Gelim off the trail to death.

His knowledge of Khotel based on months of close contact told him that the man was intensely loyal, a splendid officer, ambitious for advancement but only through hard work and good conduct, not by treachery and murder. He had little understanding of the intricacies of court politics at Karakoram, yet it seemed that Khotel would have little to gain by Gelim's death. Khotel as second-in-command would be held responsible for anything that went wrong on the journey. He would still have to serve out his time with hundreds of other subordinate officers before he became eligible for the rank of general, and the Il-Khan could easily keep back his appointment because of the loss of Gelim.

But the thought was obliterated from Baignault's mind as he stood staring in sudden awe at the sky. It had just marvelously appeared and sunlight poured down from it. Far aloft, there had been some violent and swift change of wind direction. The storm had veered off and left this valley. Snow still fell, but spangled with sun and in thin, lacy flakes that dissolved in a spattering shower.

Litei laughed, and there was hysteria in the sound. "You must allow that I was right," she said. "You must! We shall be able to reach the summit before darkness."

Khotel shoved her almost roughly aside, as he moved to the edge of the trail and stared down into the lower part of the pass. "Sir Jean," he said softly, not looking around, "take these people into whatever safety above that you can find. Chagan and Litei will be in your personal charge. I must see to the general and the troops."

The vibration was already in the air, ominous, repetitive. Snow is about to slide, Baignault realized. Then rock. There will be avalanches all up and down the valley. Litei and Chagan, attracted by the sound, came to the edge of the trail. They gazed wide-eyed where snow dislodged by the tremendous temperature change began to slide, with a growing roar, straight downward onto the trail below.

"The men . . ." Chagan's voice was hoarse with horror. "They will be swept off the trail. They have no place to go."

Baignault watched, paralyzed by the sheer drama of the tragedy below. The men of the detachment, the troopers and herders and servants, had emerged into the open with the end of the storm and were slowly mounting the trail. Most of them were trapped where they rode, blinking helplessly upward. Tons of snow cascaded over them from the upper slopes, then shale, then rock. Some few were hurled off the trail, one trooper still clinging to his horse's mane in a spasm of terror. Clouds of snow vapor rose from the valley floor. There was a great reverberant echo, punctuated by a single, thin scream.

Baignault grasped Litei and Chagan by the shoulders and swung them back across the trail to the protection of the rock wall. Then he glanced at Mustaf. "Go ahead, sir," Mustaf called. "I will fend for myself."

"Move!" Baignault ordered. He saw the senior guide run up the trail and throw himself beneath the overhang of a dark, broad ledge. He thrust Litei toward it and shouted to Chagan to take cover. Then he stooped and forced Litei's head down while over them, around them, past them, the avalanche dropped in frightful descent.

Baignault lay heavily stunned. When thought began again for him it was as though he rose from the nether regions of confused nightmare. He was aware first that he could move only with great effort. The vast crash of the avalanche had deafened him and when he shouted he was unable to hear a sound. But his body was free. He was not penned in, or trapped. There was open space around him

137

and he groped out into it tentatively, took one step and another, then tripped over loose shale in the absolute darkness and sprawled prone.

"You are a clumsy fellow." That was Litei; the husky, low-pitched voice could not be mistaken. "But you have no need to move so fast. We shall not die quite yet."

"Where are you?" Baignault said.

"Up against the ledge. In the same place that you flung me."

"Stay there," he said. He was moving again, reaching his hands upward and around him. Snow in great, ragged but solidly locked chunks formed a ceiling overhead. It sloped off from the ledge, in a thick mass to both right and left, locking them in a triangular-shaped cavern. Rock had come with the snow, and rubble torn from the mountainside; he touched the limbs of shattered trees that had been ripped loose, and bits of lichen, fragments of moss. Then, groping, his fingers were on a body.

He knew the man from the turban and padded coat. It was the Kirghiz guide and he was dead, his neck snapped at the base of the spine. Baignault searched the body with almost frantic haste. He was beginning to be afraid of the darkness. His nervous control was almost spent.

The Kirghiz had worn a leather pouch on a belt around his waist. It was still in place and it held flint and steel. Baignault took them out, struck them together and there was an orange lick of flame. He struck again and stared swiftly and saw Litei where she crouched. Chagan was near her and she had knelt down by her brother, holding his head on her knee. "He is still alive," she said. "Can you bring your light here?"

"Yes, I can." He went gradually to her, stooped down so that he would not dislodge the snow from above. The slightest shock, he knew, might bring the cavern roof down upon them and they would be instantly crushed. He struck the flint and in the spurt of light examined Chagan. A piece of rock had caught him a sidewise blow across the brow; he was unconscious but breathing with ease and not seriously hurt.

Baignault drew Chagan's fur-lined cap down slowly and arranged the big coat around the body for warmth. "He will live," he told Litei.

"I am aware of that," Litei said. "He has as much chance

138

as ourselves. But how much do you believe remains to us?"

"A good amount," Baignault said. Then he crouched beside her in silence while he recalled a story he had heard often during his boyhood. It was famous in his family, and told usually by his grandfather. It concerned a tremendous, weeks-long snow gale that had once hit the Norman coast.

Houses were submerged; cattle starved in the barns because fodder could not be brought to them. But on a farm near the Baignault estate when the men finally dug themselves out they found a prize herd of sheep intact. It was the barking of a farm dog that led them to the drifts on the lee of a cliff by a seaside meadow. The herd was safe under the snow, warm in their confinement, unharmed except for extreme hunger.

"Listen," Baignault said to Litei, then told her the story. She laughed at the end of it. "So make me warm, Crusader," she said. "I am about to become an ice woman."

"Be patient," he said sharply and got up. With the light of the flint he crossed to where the trees lay tangled. If he worked carefully, he could perhaps cut firewood to keep them alive and still leave the roof intact. He pulled at the trees delicately and then cleared his sword, and hacked at limbs and branches. But in the darkness he almost wounded himself; he stopped and in desperation sought the Kirghiz.

He stripped the already frozen corpse, ripped the turban and shreaded it, setting it alight with the flint and steel. Then he returned to his chopping and heaped bark, chips and pieces of limbs upon the little blaze. Litei came forward as he nursed the blaze. She watched him spellbound, her breath a white, fine cloud about the somber oval of her face.

When the flames leaped high she said, "You are a real man, Crusader. I was resigned to death. And I am much too young for that."

Baignault smiled at her. He felt a great sense of exultation. The darkness, the cold were gone. Here were light and warmth and life. The roof was not disturbed, would hold. There was plenty of air and the chance that help would eventually come from outside. "Why should we surrender?" he asked her. "We must still go on to Rome."

"Now," she said, "we will."

He lifted up Chagan and carried him close to the fire. With the rest of the clothing that had belonged to the

Kirghiz he wrapped Chagan from head to foot. Litei pushed wood into the fire, then said, "Now you must take care of me. I am still cold."

Baignault knelt motionless and stared at her across the flames. He read the thought that was in her mind and sensed the force of both her will and her desire. He remembered what he had told himself in the past about her imperious, selfish nature, and he sat unmoving, wary. She would lose in any comparison with Subeyla, he knew. Subeyla was much the better woman, and certainly, absolutely, he should stay away from this one.

But the horror of what had happened today rested heavy at the center of his thought. He looked around him into the shadows that the fire could not thrust back, and at the snow, the rock which were beyond them. He would quite probably die here, he and this woman and Chagan. Help was far away. Nobody even knew that they were still alive. So why not go to her? Rome, religion, duty, honor, all the other splendid words that had led him on so long should be forgotten while there was a bit of time left. Chagan was lost in coma, would not come forth from it for hours. . . .

As Baignault moved to her side, the hem of his cape brushed through the flames. It began to smolder and he tore it off and pitched it aside. Then he seized her and forced her mouth open with his kisses. "Do not be rough, Crusader," she murmured. But her fierce movements only encouraged him as she drew him down on the cape. . . .

Sleep dragged through his passion even while he clung to her, and she writhed aside and said, "Enough. Enough of you for now."

"You are not satisfied?" he muttered.

"I give nothing more to any man," she said. "And you need sleep and I need sleep. Move over. I would like to be closer to the fire."

He slept lightly, his thought troubled by disturbing images and doubts, and he awoke and heard Chagan stirring. He rose to move to Chagan. "Rest quietly," he said. "You have been hurt. But we are safe here, your sister, you and I. Snow has formed some sort of cave over us. But help will come soon."

"I hope so for your sake as well as mine," Chagan said. But his glance was on Litei by the fire. "Do not give yourself to her. She means only trouble. Let me tell you this again."

140

"You need not," Baignault said dully, aware that Litei listened. "I already understand."

He sat hunched by the fire after that, stoking it with the butts of the logs he had cut. Litei watched him for a while, her eyes hard with anger. But Chagan had gone to sleep, and if she had anything to say to him, Baignault thought, there was nothing to restrain her. She chose to sleep, however, her body at ease, the uneven firelight across the petulant mouth, the high cheekbones and straight, strong nose. A woman without shame or remorse. A woman who used a man . . . Baignault let the thought go. He attacked her, he realized, because of his own sense of shame, and to do so merely showed how weak he had been.

He laughed harshly. His training had forced him to think of morality when all that mattered was survival. It was a fool's business and he should get over it. For some minutes now he had heard small, faint sounds that he believed came from the fire. But they were too regular, too loud. He jumped erect and banged with the flat of his sword blade upon the rocks of the downslope side wall. There was a response, and the very faint rumor of voices.

Chagan sat up wide-awake. He shook Litei and roused her. "Do you hear?" he said. "We are about to be saved."

Litei began to weep, and Baignault said, "Come, help me dig." He and Chagan worked side by side to get through the snow and meet the men who tunneled in toward them.

Khotel was the first to enter. His hands were abraded and bloody in his ripped mittens and his face blotched with frostbite. But he smiled as he embraced them in turn. "It was our great hope," he said, "that you were here and alive."

"You have done very well," Jean Baignault mumbled. He found suddenly that he was exhausted. It took the last bit of his strength to speak. "How about the general? And Mustaf?"

"Your man is in good shape," Khotel said. "He will be along soon. He is down below, helping with the wounded and what animals we have left. But General Gelim is dead. We are not quite certain what happened to him, yet he is gone." Khotel's eyes were squinted in the cone of sunlight through the tunnel. "I am sorry that I must tell you this. The general was a very fine officer."

Baignault bowed his head to show he understood. He had nothing to say now, felt nothing except exhaustion.

CHAPTER TWELVE

Baignault kept to himself for some days after that. His nerves were too tight to allow him much contact with the others and he got Mustaf aside and tried to explain. "See that I am left alone," he said. "Tell whoever asks you that I am saddened by the death of the general. It is as good an excuse as any."

"And better than most," Mustaf said. "I'd still like to know what happened there on the trail."

"Hold on to your curiosity," Baignault said. "That is for the Mongols to put straight. It has little to do with us."

"Yes, sir," Mustaf said. "You won't have to tell me again."

The weather had cleared and, slowly, the party came down from the Suget without trouble, the wounded borne on litters. Then they negotiated the lesser pass of the Sanju and were out in open country. But Baignault was very conscious of Litei. He could not keep his eyes from her while they rode, and at night after the evening meal when he left the fire and went to his tent she stared after him with a brooding intensity. He had been deeply wrong, he realized, to have anything to do with her. Never, never would he repeat that. The old phrase was to be careful of a woman scorned, and she was not merely a woman, but a Mongol princess. . . .

Khotel ordered the column to halt on the edge of the open country. He wanted, he told Baignault, to send couriers back to Karakoram for further orders and he needed replacements for the men who had been killed and wounded. "I agree with you," Baignault said. But for him it would be a difficult time, he sensed. He had been able to stay clear of Litei on the trail. Here in this camp being pitched alongside a little nomad village it would be more difficult.

He walked quickly from Khotel's tent toward his own; Litei and Chagan were calling to Khotel behind him. They were mounted and Chagan had just bought a falcon from the village headman. It was their idea to hunt game in the alder thickets past the camp. "Later," Khotel said. "I have

142

work to do, dispatches to write. Go ask Sir Jean, though. He is free from duty."

"Rather we ride alone," Litei said in a harsh voice. "I have no desire to seek him. Ride now, Chagan. Let me see what that sorry-looking bird can do in the air."

But Litei rode back alone from the hunting. She stopped beside Baignault's tent and rapped on the front pole with the handle of her crop. "Step forth, Crusader," she said, "and talk with me."

He came out reluctantly, angry because he knew that the attraction for her still held him. She sat her horse framed by the background of the lush Turkestan valley. Her face was flushed by the exercise of the chase, her eyes and her lips were bright and she looked at him with a speculative, almost mocking glance.

A surge of passion over which he had no control took his thought. He imagined himself disrobing her, his hands passing over her breasts again, as they pulled tautly together in the act of love. But the deliberate harshness of her voice broke the thought.

"You are a fool to remember what happened between us up in the pass," she said. "Also, you are stupid to attempt to keep away from me in public. I have no feeling about it. You are not the first man to have lain with me, nor will you be the last. That, in Cathay, is the right and privilege of women of royal blood. Quite probably, your simple Druse sweetheart treated you in a different fashion—like a little boy given a magic apple, and you are not to be blamed for your childishness."

Baignault wanted to reach up and pull her from the saddle, throw her over his knees and smack those handsome buttocks until she yelled for mercy. But this was no ordinary woman and it was a very special circumstance. He looked aside and saw that Khotel watched them here. Muscles knotted along Khotel's jaws; open jealousy burned in his eyes. Be careful, Baignault thought. By his own admission, the *ming-bashi* is an ambitious man and might very well hope, when the right moment comes, to make love on his own to the royal princess.

"Let me say only," Baignault told her in a quiet voice, "that when you gave me your body I did not think that you had fallen in love with me, or ever would. But I will obey your wish and no longer try to stay away from you."

143

His ability to control himself hurt her pride, he realized. "If other Christians are as simple as you," she said, "Rome must be a very dull place indeed. Khotel has told me that your Druse is quite pretty. I am surprised that she even looked twice at you."

"Please," Baignault said, rough-voiced, "let be. Now you ask too much of my patience."

A *kourroun* had begun to blow at the end of the valley. The sergeant of the guard was running toward Khotel and with him was a courier who wore the Il-Khan's silver chestplate and whipped a spent horse. Litei swung her horse around and rode at the canter to join Khotel. The courier slid down from the saddle before Khotel, saluted him and then put in his hands a scroll wrapped in sheepskin. While Khotel read it, the man scraped the dust from his face, and he was young and handsome and broad-shouldered. Litei was smiling; she allowed the courier to help her from her horse, then talked gaily with him.

Baignault felt a sensation of relief. She would go on from man to man, he thought. Her dislike of him would not last very long if her vanity was satisfied elsewhere.

Khotel came quickly striding across the camp, bringing the new orders from Karakoram. Mustaf with an old soldier's sense of movement appeared from the back of the tent and stood silently as Khotel said, "I have been given command of the detachment. General Gelim will not be replaced." Then a hard, bitter note came into his voice. "I stay in my own rank, though, and have been given no advancement. You and I will remain on the same terms, Sir Jean. When we are back on the road, let us see more of each other than we have since we left the mountains." Khotel paused. Baignault was abruptly conscious of the tension that gripped Khotel; the *ming-bashi* stared levelly into his eyes. "I think I offer you much the same invitation that Litei offered a bit ago."

"You do," Baignault said. "But let me tell you that I am happy you have been given command. What will our route be out of here?"

"We are to pick up fresh troops in Kashgar," Khotel said. "Then we keep on straight over the Silk Road. I hope it pleases you, Sir Jean."

"Whatever takes us most quickly to Rome," Baignault said.

144

Mustaf stood wordless beside him until Khotel had gone. Then he said, "You have changed toward that man. He used to be your friend. No longer, though. It must be because of what happened up there in the mountains."

"Ponder it all you want," Baignault said. "As for me, the man is still my friend. But I am weary of waiting and I miss my own people. Let us get on to Rome, then home."

The party broke camp that afternoon and started out right after the tent gear was packed. This was still the famous Silk Road they followed, but it no longer seemed endless as they marched westward. Jean Baignault had the impression, odd and perverse after his feeling of depression, that they passed over it almost too fast and that he would find himself unprepared for the problems that would confront him in Rome. His ease increased, as he rode with the rest of the party and was often in casual conversation with Chagan and Khotel, and sometimes Litei. She showed the best side of her nature, and was obviously charmed by this stage of the journey.

They went through Yarkand and then Kashgar and fabulous, incredible Samarkand, past that Bokhara where the bazaars had a jewel-like luster. She recited the names of them aloud. "They remind me of the sounds of temple bells," she said.

"I can imagine them," Baignault said, "being put into song by some troubadour." That was a remark she could pick up and twist to her own advantage, he thought. But her smile in response was without mockery, and she only said, "How romantic of you, Sir Jean."

It was Khotel who turned in his saddle and said, "You should know that in their land the Christians hold what is called a Court of Love."

"I should be charmed to see it," Litei said, and Chagan told Khotel, "Why not? We could make use of such ourselves. You might even be a student there."

Khotel did not answer, his mouth drawn in tight, angry lines. Then he spurred his horse forward, muttering that he wanted to look at the trail ahead. "Our *ming-bashi* has become a man of moods," Chagan said. "His pride must have suffered when father refused to advance his rank."

"So let him be," Litei said. "You and I were given by birth a great deal more than he can ever hope to hold. The same is true for the Crusader."

145

"Very true," Baignault said, relieved that she had not taken the chance to attack him and eager to have the conversation changed.

The whole party was in good humor as they went on from Bokhara to the Caspian. A broad-hulled boat with a flapping, blazoned sail was ready for them there. They sailed at night and it was moonlight and all night long the crew danced on deck and Litei was enchanted. She clapped her hands in time to the music, rose up from her chair and made Khotel dance with her, then Baignault. It was difficult for Baignault to take her in his arms. Her scent aroused erotic images, her body was vibrant, too close, and with the undulant motion of the boat they were thrown rhythmically together. Khotel stood by the mast and watched them, with him the other Mongol officers of the detachment, their eyes curious. Baignault bowed to her at the end of the dance and said hoarsely, "Thank you, Your Highness."

"Not another?" she said.

"No." His voice was low in the wild thrum of the music. "What would you do? Make Khotel jealous?"

"You are smarter," she said, "than I had thought." Then she whirled away from him and pulled Khotel onto the open deck.

Baignault was very careful in her presence afterward when the boat came alongside in Abaku and they went ashore. But the governor of the province had formal ceremonies arranged for her and Chagan and Baignault was able to sit in a tavern with Mustaf and quietly drink mint tea. "We move quite fast," Mustaf said. "It goes smoothly enough too, hey, Sir Jean?"

"As well as I had hoped," Baignault said. "Even somewhat better. Next we have the Caucasus, but those mountains will be nothing after the Suget. We will be through them while the season is still late spring."

"Khotel, though," Mustaf said, "he—"

Baignault gave a small, shrugged gesture of warning and Mustaf broke off. One of Khotel's lieutenants had entered the tavern. He came to their table and saluted Baignault. "The *ming-bashi* sends his compliments, sir, and are you and the sergeant ready to move? The detachment is in formation at the palace. We wait only for the prince and princess before we take the road."

"Tell the *ming-bashi*," Baignault said, "that we shall

146

be with him at once. But, wait, lieutenant. We will leave with you."

The sloping valleys of the Caucasus were lovely in the soft spring weather. Baignault and Khotel rode together at the head of the column, Litei and Chagan just behind them.

Khotel turned suddenly toward Baignault. "What do you believe we shall find in Rome, Sir Jean?"

"I have often attempted to tell you," Baignault said. His voice was quiet and yet his nerves had begun to tighten. He sensed that Khotel asked the question for some particular, hidden reason. It could not be simply that Khotel was jealous of him still because of Litei. For many weeks she had paid a great deal more attention to Khotel than to him.

"But you mistake me," Khotel said. "I have small interest in the city as such. I would like to hear instead about the people we shall meet there."

"His Holiness, the Pope, of course," Baignault said. "Then the Cardinals and the other high officials of the Church. All of them should welcome us."

"But I understand from what I was told in Byzantium last year," Khotel said slowly, "that the Pope is no longer the leader of Christendom. He has been pushed aside. He takes orders from the wealthy merchants and moneylenders. They are the same men who command you."

Baignault rode along the trail for a full minute without speech. He studied the faces of Chagan and Litei and their eyes did not leave him. Rage had ripped into his calm. He measured the distance between himself and Khotel; his right hand flexed and lowered toward his sword hilt. Khotel had offered him deliberate insult. The man would mock him, demean him, and the reason for it was far past any point of petty jealousy.

"You are mistaken," Baignault said, his voice careful and unhurried. "But even if you were right, why do you ask this of me now?"

"We are only a few days' march from the Iron Gate," Khotel said. He sat a bit sidewise in his saddle so that he might freely draw his sword. "Then, in another short space of time we shall be in Rome. I want that the prince and princess should know the truth about what is ahead of them. And it will do you no good to call me a liar. That—" Khotel was smiling at him—"would violate your sense of honor, and it is about all that sustains you."

Baignault took a long, gradual breath. He put his sword

147

hand on the saddle pommel and gripped it hard so that he would not reach for the weapon. There was shocked surprise in Chagan's eyes, while Litei watched with faint, amused contempt. But he must not draw against Khotel. That would win nothing, lose all. And he had been asked much the same kind of questions by Subeyla. It was barely possible, too, that Khotel was right and that His Holiness was no longer the absolute ruler of Christendom. Still, he could not leave himself so exposed and proven, if not a liar, at least a fool.

"My masters," he said, his voice full of passion, "are the chosen leaders of the Knights Hospitalers. I make my allegiance to them and through them to Jesus Christ, the Savior."

"You talk fine words," Khotel said, "and I admire you for them. But in each of the Crusader cities in *Outremer* the best and the largest quarters are given to the Venetian merchants, and the Pisan merchants, and the Genoese. They keep their own laws there. Your people accept orders from them, and live on what they pay you. No matter how honest you may try to be, Sir Jean, trade and not the word of Jesus Christ commands your world."

"You blaspheme," Baignault cried, and he was up from the saddle, sword drawn. "This is the talk of the antiChrist!"

But Chagan had ridden quietly and swiftly between him and Khotel. He took the blow of the big Crusader sword upon his scimitar blade before it had gained momentum. Then he leaned forward and put out a restraining hand that clasped Baignault by the shoulder. "Not here," he said; "not now or ever, Sir Jean. You and I are friends and I must say it to you." He released his hand, then sheathed the scimitar. "Please put away your blade."

"Thank you," Baignault said.

Chagan turned to Khotel. "If you have made sense," he said, "it is in the best interest of all of us. But which of us has been in Rome, and is aware of the truth? What you heard last year in Byzantium could have been only the stories of drunken courtiers."

"They were more than that," Khotel said. A rough note of violence was in his voice. His face was pale with fury and his scimitar half-pulled from the scabbard.

"No matter," Chagan said. "You must take them from your mind until you have more proof."

Litei's voice was soft, surprisingly gentle. "This has done us no good, *ming-bashi*," she said. "I must agree with my brother. Having come so far, I should feel greatly cheated if for any reason I did not reach Rome."

"As you wish," Khotel said. He bowed to her and saluted Chagan.

The next morning Khotel came to Baignault as he rode out on a flank of the column with Chagan. The *ming-bashi* was openly embarrassed; he spoke in a nervous and rapid voice. "I must make my apologies for what happened yesterday, Sir Jean," he said. "My temper tricked me. But let me say that the success of the mission means a great deal to me. A full year of my life will have been given to it by the time we reach Rome. Should it fail, without doubt some of the blame will be attached to me. My advancement would be held back, and, like you, I look forward to a life of military service."

"That I can understand," Baignault said. "Let us have no more talk of apologies, though. You were not the only one to lose your temper; I did the same." Then he extended his hand and Khotel took it and Chagan said, "Messires, you please me. My father would tell you that allies should always first be friends."

But, Baignault thought, he did not put anything like full belief in Khotel's explanation. Khotel could have expressed long ago whatever was in his mind about the rulers of Christendom. He was still convinced that the man had been moved by sheer jealousy, had somehow guessed the degree of intimacy between him and Litei and become gradually infuriated by it.

Yet Khotel was too strong-willed, too determined a man to be swayed by emotion alone. There could be some truth behind what he had said. That was hard to establish, for as Chagan had pointed out, none of them had been to Rome. Let the matter be, Baignault told himself. And, as much as possible, keep away from Litei. The old Syrian saying makes sense in her case; she is the kind of woman who can start trouble in an empty tent.

It was easy for him to discard thoughts about the mission, for this part of Persia through which they marched made his dreams of Subeyla very real. He would see her soon, he realized, in just another few days.

He said her name softly to himself. He saw her, heard her, embraced her. What had happened since he had last

149

been with her disappeared from his mind. It was as if he crawled once more to the Iron Gate, dragging Mustaf from the desert after the long fight with Ibn Aud Aghaf and the Wahabi warriors. Then he and Subeyla were alone playing chess and he could not take his eyes from the shape of her breasts. He watched her ride off from the camel line, so thrilled that her beauty and skill brought him a sort of ecstasy. And, after the polo, in the moonlit night, they rode forth and came to the hilltop where there was the nest of vipers. Subeyla was in his arms, responding with vast, passionate delight to his passion.

His horse sidestepped a rock in the trail and he looked up to see that the column was about to ford a narrow river. Muleteers whacked the pack animals. Khotel called the order of march, and Litei and Chagan were already in the stream, swimming their mounts neck and neck. Mustaf had turned at the rear of the column to look back at him.

Baignault realized that what had held his thought was only dream. Idle, empty stuff. By now Subeyla was very likely back in her home mountains of the Druse range, married to some strapping young sheik of a neighboring tribe. There was small chance that he would ever meet her again. The course of his life had gone far from hers, was profoundly changed. The mission led him far off still; he had to return to Karakoram after Rome. He would be lucky if he ever caught up to Ibn Aud Aghaf and paid back the score the Wahabi owed. "Ride, Crusader," he said wearily. "Get along at least to Rome."

On the other side of the river, Chagan waited for him. "What kept you, Sir Jean?" he said.

"Dreams," Baignault said bluntly. "I became lost in them."

"Then I have good word for you." Chagan was gently smiling. "A clan of the Jebel Druse is at the Iron Gate. They are the same people with whom you stayed on your march to Karakoram."

"No," Baignault said, "it is unbelievable." Then he leaned toward Chagan and his voice was harsh. "How do you know this?"

Chagan kept on smiling. "Remember if you would that at Karakoram you told the Il-Khan of the Druse clan that helped you. As my father's son, I sent a courier some days ago to the Iron Gate. We need fresh mounts to take us to the coast. The Druse are at the pass and ready to sell. They wait for us."

"Thank you," Baignault murmured. "Again, I am grateful to you, Chagan."

Time had never seemed so long, Baignault thought. Each hour passed with excruciating slowness. This, the old Roman road, he had remembered as being only a brief part of the journey, and yet it went on, on, and the next ridge when he reached it was empty and there was no sign of the Ruada camp or the Iron Gate cliffs. He rode as though upon an invisible treadmill, and his eagerness was dulled, and he did not even raise his glance when the lieutenant of the advance guard galloped past him to make a report to Khotel.

Mustaf came forward and said, "The next ridge is it, Sir Jean. Some of the Ruada are there."

"Then ride with me," Baignault said and gave his horse both the spurs and the quirt. Mustaf could not keep the same pace and he was alone as he topped the rise that revealed the ridge ahead. There were the neatly spaced black tents, the camel and horse corrals, the warriors on sentry duty. And on the road below rode two figures, Subeyla and Akhu-et-T'ib, the sheik.

Baignault felt a pulse beat in his forehead. His chest constricted as he breathed, and he wanted to laugh and shout. Then, suddenly, he began to wonder how he would look to Subeyla. She had seen him first blood-crusted and filthy, a spent wreck. He was in fine physical shape now, and greatly changed. But he wore Mongol clothing and that not even clean. There would be a time, he promised himself, when he would appear before Subeyla properly dressed as a Knight Hospitaler, his armor and leather bright, the huge cross of the order emblazoned on his shoulder.

Mustaf rode up. "Why do you hold back, Sir Jean?"

"A good question," Baignault said. He shook the dust from the folds of his cape and burshed his long hair away from his face and tilted the white felt hat in place. "This is the answer; I lack the clothes I should be wearing."

"But you have your sword," Mustaf said, "and she will still know you, sir."

"She should," Baignault said. "I am not that much changed. Stay here and wait for the others. I would ride forward alone."

He rode with his horse on a short rein and at a deliberate

lope. Subeyla and Akhu-et-T'ib were motionless. They sat their camels in the center of the road and did not gesture or call out to him and he was forced to admire their dignity even as he tried to form the words he knew he must say.

He dismounted onto the sunken, cracked stones of the road. Then he salaamed, and his voice was steady enough as he said, "It has been quite a while since I have been with you. But I would think that all has gone well for you, Subeyla. And you, Akhu-et-T'ib, seem in much better health."

"We thank you," Akhu-et-T'ib said. "You are welcome among us again." But Subeyla was silent. She kept the same rigid posture in the deep saddle on the camel, which was not An Najm but another long-hocked mount. Her eyes searched his face and he met them, aware that his glance was filled with longing. She wore a soft white riding cape, and beneath that her favorite costume, a short velvet jacket, a thin blouse and loose, light trousers.

He told himself that she was lovelier than he had made her in dream. The sun set a sheen over her hair, made little shadows that accentuated her high cheekbones and the wide, rounded line of her lips. But this silence had almost taken his wits away. Then she said, "It would seem that you have done well on your journey, and that it has led you far. But, tell me. Do you still work as a clerk?"

A grunt of laugher broke from Akhu. Then he touched his camel with the riding stick and swerved around Baignault. "Better that you two are alone," he said. "And I must greet these other people. Do not be too long, Subeyla."

"With this man?" Subeyla said. "No. . . ."

Baignault advanced wordlessly to Subeyla's camel and reached and pulled her down from it and kissed her until she kissed him back with passion. "Listen to me now," he said after he released her mouth. "You know full well that I am no clerk, never worked for a Pisan merchant. But I could not tell you; I had been given a mission to perform that still engages me."

"So you return," she said, "with a Mongol prince and princess of the royal blood. That is what their courier told us, and some story of your going on to Rome with them. What am I to think?" She was panting from emotion and lack of breath. Baignault tried to clasp her to him again and she fended him off with both hands.

"Give me time and I will explain everything to you, Sub-

eyla. The mission can bring you and your people no harm.
It will—"

"Start new war, that is all," Subeyla said swiftly. "We
have learned enough of it, Akhu and I, to recognize that
your people in *Outremer* would make alliance with the Mongols. Then you hope to drive the Saracens into the sea. Am I
not right? And do not give me any more talk of duty, and,
for the first time, let me hear your true name."

"Sir Jean Baignault," he said with pride, "of Beth-Haggan."

"Very well, Sir Jean," she said. "Then, as a knightly gen-
tleman, consider how you have made me appear to your
Mongol allies." She nodded and he stared around with her.

Akhu was at the crest of the ridge to the east, alongside
the mounts of the Mongol party. Baignault could recognize
Chagan and Litei and Khotel as they talked with the sheik.
But Litei had drawn slightly apart from the others, and
gazed down at Subeyla and him.

"Now tell me," he said, "may I be with you alone
tonight?"

"That," Subeyla said, "depends upon our other guests.
The Mongols have bought a great many camels from us in
the past. They have always been our friends. Akhu has a
feast prepared. Just when I shall be able to leave it I do not
know."

"Promise me, Subeyla, that I may come to your tent." His
hands were extended in a beseeching gesture.

"Yes," she said. "Be cautious, though. We have already
made ourselves look like lovelorn fools here."

He bowed to her and she mounted her camel. Then he
swung into the saddle and followed her along the road toward the Mongol party. Akhu introduced her gravely to
Litei and Chagan and the two women scrutinized each other
with instinctive, inspecting glances and exchanged a few
formal words. Khotel fell back alongside Baignault at the
rear of the party. "The princess and the Druse have very
little to say to each other," he murmured. "But Litei was
quite interested in the greeting you were given along the
road. She seemed to be surprised that you are so much in
love."

"You are kind to tell me," Baignault said. "But I cannot
see how it concerns you or Litei. Mind your duties, please,
and let me be."

153

"As you wish," Khotel said, his voice uninflected. "I simply had the thought that I might warn you."

Anger had begun to pluck at Baignault's nerves but he checked it. He would have no more trouble with Khotel, he told himself. Not now, certainly, and not here. But the reception he received in the Ruada camp both pleased and calmed him.

Old Ibn Rahim, then the other senior warriors welcomed him warmly and with real respect. "We have not forgotten how you fought against the Saracens," Rahim said.

"What of them?" Baignault asked. "There was a sheik among them, a man named Ibn Aud Aghaf, who escaped me, and for several years I have sought to kill him."

"You would mean the Wahabi chieftain," Rahim said. "He got away. You must wait to settle whatever is between you and him."

"As I must in several matters," Baignault said, but did not dare look at Subeyla.

She was intent upon being the hostess for her brother and for the clan. She took Litei to a carefully prepared tent. From it she went to the cooking fires, then to the wide-winged tent where the feast was to be held, and on to her own.

He wandered through the camp, disconsolate because he could not be with Subeyla, afflicted by memories of the past, and, in a strange way, homesick. Beth-Haggan, for the length of the journey he had made, was not far from here. But he would not get there. Rome called him first. Rome claimed his life, would very soon take him again from Subeyla.

Then he forced himself to go to the tent assigned to him and put on fresh clothing, and afterward he sat with the senior warriors. They asked him questions about the mission and he parried with talk of combat and camels and weapons until a slave came to call them to the feast. It was held in Akhu's tent. Dozens of slaves served huge platters of mutton and rice and passed little cups of sweetened mint tea. Baignault sat tense, fascinated by the contrast that Subeyla and Litei made.

Subeyla wore her familiar costume of short velvet jacket and loose trousers. But tonight there were heavy, hammered-silver bracelets on her arms. Her delicately designed pearl earrings picked up the lamplight. A great deal of attention had been given to her hair and it shimmered deli-

154

cately. Litei in comparison seemed quite exotic. She wore miniature artificial flowers in her hair, a Chinese brocaded coat that showed the exact shape of her breasts, black silk trousers that were slashed at the sides, and emerald, diamond and jade rings and a superb pearl necklace. Akhu sat close to her and kept up a steady conversation that Khotel translated. Her glance veered from him as she answered; she stared aside at Subeyla and then, swiftly, from her to Baignault.

It was not vanity on his part, Baignault thought, to tell himself that Litei was jealous. Her subtle mind was keenly at work, assessing the precise degree of Subeyla's hold over him. Ambition prompted her more even than jealousy. She was determined to know everything, this woman, and bend what she knew to her own will and purpose.

At last the feast was finished. Subeyla asked permission of Akhu to leave the tent. She and Litei rose up and moved forth together while the men still sat with their teacups. Akhu signed to the slaves for more tea and when it was poured began a discussion with Khotel about the merits of various breeds of camels. Now, Baignault thought; now it is time. . . .

"You will have the goodness to excuse me, sheik," he said to Akhu. "I have a matter that takes me from you."

Chagan added, "I believe that Sir Jean would send off a message to his own family. He has been far from them, and for some while."

"Of course," Akhu said. "Go with him please, Rahim, and put writing materials in his hands. Then see that he is given a messenger."

"I thank you, sheik," Baignault said, "but the turcopole will serve as my messenger. Let me wish you all a good night, messires."

Ibn Rahim walked in stride with him through the cool night to his tent, then called a slave to bring a scroll, a camel's hair brush and ink pot.

Baignault wrote stiff-handed, clumsy from lack of practice, and the words he set upon the scroll made a simple message. He told the Sieur Amboise that the mission went well and that within a month he expected that the party would be in Rome. Then he added his love, sanded the parchment, rolled it and tied it and handed it to Mustaf, who stood waiting. "You are still a tulwar ambassador," he said, "for the same pay."

"But where do I go?" Mustaf asked. "Straight to Beth-Haggan?"

"Wherever you find my father," Baignault said. "This tells the Sieur Amboise of the mission. Should you lose it, give him the words I now say to you. He will pass on the information to his superiors and they will have a ship made ready for us at Alexandretta. You will rejoin us there, and in no more than a fortnight's time. Are you sure, though, you are able to reach *Outremer* from here alone?"

"Better alone in the open country than with a guard," Mustaf said. "Let me have a fast horse and I will ride around any Saracens. I can start before dawn, Sir Jean."

"Then ask Ibn Rahim for a mount and meanwhile catch some sleep. I will not see you again until Alexandretta. But, if you are too tired, you need not come along to Rome. You may stay in *Outremer* and make up tales to tell the kitchen maids."

"Rome for me," Mustaf said. "I wager you that my legs are so bowed that the dogs there will take them for the front door of St. Peter's and run right on through. And, with your permission, I want to try the Roman wine."

"All you can drink," Baignault said.

Mustaf had knelt and shaken out his sleeping bag and began to crawl into it. Baignault clapped him gently on the shoulder. "The best of luck to you," he murmured, "and for them at Beth-Haggan every bit of my love."

"Yes, Sir Jean," Mustaf said.

Baignault snuffed the lamp before he left the tent. The thought of Subeyla drew him and he knew that she waited in her tent, and yet he stood for some minutes motionless in the darkness. Memories of home held him. He smelled the Beth-Haggan orchards and he saw the fields and heard his mother's voice and she took him in her arms. He sat and talked with them of prosperity and peace. . . .

But Subeyla was waiting, he repeated to himself, and homesickness did him no good. His breathing accelerated as he crossed to her tent and his loins throbbed and he no longer thought of home. When he knocked softly upon the tent pole Subeyla said, "Come in, Sir Jean Baignault."

He let the door rug fall into place behind him before he moved toward her. She sat half-reclining, her back against her camel saddle. Rugs were piled beside her and he sat down among them and stretched out his hands for her body. She kept aside from him, though, and when she spoke her

voice was harsh. "You have kept me waiting quite s۔
time."

"There was a message to be written to my people," he
said. "The turcopole rides with it before dawn. And I could
not get up at once and leave the feast. Akhu and the others
would have been displeased."

"The princess, though." Subeyla was almost whispering.
"You did not stop for her pleasure along the way here to
me?"

Baignault sat very still. His fingers pulled at the fringe
of one of the rugs on which he sat. Anger started in him and
subsided, and dismay took its place. Somehow, he thought,
Subeyla had been told. She had been informed about what
had gone on between him and Litei, and her pride was hurt,
quite possibly also, her love.

"Why do you ask such a question?" he said.

"For a very good reason," Subeyla said. "You have passionately protested your love for me. I have accepted it,
and dismissed from my mind that I know little about you
and most of that lies. Do not try to lie to me again. I have
kept myself from other men because of you, in the hope that
you would make good your word and return."

"I am done with anything except the truth," Baignault
said slowly. "And I am here. What would you have me tell
you?"

Subeyla gazed gravely at him. Her face was white, her
lips pale, and he sensed that she was close to tears. She said,
"I do not want to act the shrew and ask you questions that
give pain to both of us. Rather—" she smiled bleakly—" I
would like to make love. My pride is engaged in this matter,
though, and I feel that I should fully know the truth. So,
Sir Jean Baignault of *Outremer,* tell it to me."

"About me and the Princess Litei?" he said. "You have
been told already of the mission. . . ." His voice was low
and uneven. He spoke staring at the rug-strewn floor, his
eyes mechanically tracing out the patterns. But in his mind
he saw the Suget again. The avalanche ripped and crashed.
Everything was darkness. Death pressed in on him from all
sides.

"It made no sense," he said to Subeyla. "We were like
animals which destroy themselves before the trap destroys
them. That was not love—nothing but a moment's escape
from death. The guide lay dead, frozen there, near us.
Chagan was deeply gone in coma, and the cold, the dark,

the snow stole meaning away. I was like an animal, I suppose. Call me that. I deserve it. But since then I have not put a hand on Litei."

The sounds of Subeyla's soft weeping wrenched Baignault out of memory. The weeping became sobs and he moved to touch her, comfort her and she squirmed aside. "No," she said, "no!"

He sat dully, hands between his knees, filled with bitter rage against himself. There was nothing he could do to change this, he realized. It had all been done in the snow cave on the Suget. Love had been stripped from him along with his pride. He should add them to the cost the mission had made him pay.

Subeyla's grief was spent. She looked at him red-eyed, but her voice was steady. "Leave me," she said. "What was between us cannot be repaired. I can hold no love for a man like you. For you, life means war and you give yourself to it without thought of anything else."

"You are wrong," he said. "I am a Christian, a Crusader." He gestured violently. "My life is devoted to my religion, not war."

"Words," she said, "that are worn so thin that they no longer have meaning. You and your people from the West picked up centuries ago one of many Eastern religions. Then you changed it, made it your own, used it to justify rapine and pillage and the seizure of lands that never can rightfully belong to you. You have chosen your peculiar fashion of making a Christian convert of the Mongol princess—if she may be called that. Burden her with your empty talk. Not me."

"Please, Subeyla," he said, "listen. Let me explain."

But Subeyla pointed to the tent doorway. "Get out," she said, "before I must summon slaves or the warriors of the guard."

"You give me no choice," he said. He was on his feet and moving toward the doorway.

"You deserve none," Subeyla said. "Seek your Mongol. She should be able to console you."

Baignault nodded, then bowed and went out into the night. He walked aimlessly back and forth across the camp. His emotions were unclear; all of his life, he thought, had become a turbulent confusion. The values he had faithfully respected were shaken; they did not now have their same meaning. Still, he was a Christian with solemn vows to be kept and a mission of great importance to perform. He threw his Mongol hat to the ground in a fit of frustration, stamped upon it and cursed aloud.

His voice brought Ibn Rahim through the mist that gathered in this hour before dawn. "It might be, *roumi*," Rahim said, "that I can help you. I have some small knowledge of your trouble."

"How?" Baignault said.

"Last night at the feast," Rahim said, "I was seated close enough to hear the talk that passed between the senior Mongol officer and Subeyla. I mean the *ming-bashi*, Khotel."

"Go on," Baignault said quietly. He had picked up his hat and was slapping the dirt from it. This could be the side of Khotel's jaw, he thought. "The *ming-bashi* has already made me trouble."

"About that of course I have no knowledge," Rahim said. "But Khotel took care to tell Subeyla about some mishap during your journey. An avalanche pitched onto the trail. You, the Mongol prince and princess and a guide were trapped in a cave formed by snow, where you passed some hours together until you were rescued."

"A culvert trick," Baignault said. "A low, mean way of paying me for something I do not deserve."

"Then settle with the *ming-bashi*," Rahim said. He laughed, his hand on Baignault's taut arm. "If you were able to bowl down the Saracens as I saw you, then you have the skill to tend to the Mongol. Take him forth here at dawn and put a lance through him."

"That I will." Baignault said. "I most certainly will. . . ."

But some of his surge of rage against Khotel subsided while he waited for dawn. Mustaf came out of the tent, and stared in surprise at Baignault. "You should be asleep, Sir Jean," he said. "While you won't ride with me, still you also need your rest."

"Granted," Baignault said. "But the morning can be given to sleep, and I wished to say another farewell to you. Now mount and ride. Dawn is close enough."

He knew, watching Mustaf mount and spur around toward the Iron Gate and the trails that led to Beth-Haggan, that he could not simply accuse Khotel of unwarranted meddling in his affairs, then challenge him and take him out and fight him. The mission meant too much to allow him any such satisfaction. Challenge Khotel and he affronted the

159

dignity of the Golden Horde. Wound the man in a fight or kill him, and he wounded or killed an ally. No, Baignault told himself, again he must wait. This was not yet the time to settle his score with Khotel.

But he still walked along the horse line in the dawn when Khotel emerged yawning to inspect the Mongol guard. "You do not look like a man who has spent a very happy night," he said. "This for you was supposed to be a most pleasant halt on the journey."

"You changed it for me, *ming-bashi*," Baignault said. Then in a low, rough voice he cursed Khotel. He told the Mongol that he was a swine and descended from swine. He leaned forward, the weight on the balls of his feet and his body set if Khotel should make any movement.

Khotel stood motionless. He did not smile and let the scorn show only in his slitted eyes. "You would draw me into blows with you," he said. "Your knightly pride has been damaged, Sir Jean, and in your thinking the laws of chivalry should be satisfied. I refuse you, here alone and privately, and I will do the same before witnesses if you press me. I am not of your kind. My life is not bound to the past. I live fully in the present and look forward to the future. What has been done was in the best interests of my people. You needed chastening and you have been given it. Not so much by me, however, as by Subeyla. You do not stand betrayed so much as that you are a fool. Learn the fact now and the mission might well succeed. Fail to regard it and you will meet failure. Should you seek me further, should you choose to make sense, I shall be in my tent. Take care, Sir Jean. You have fallen into a deep pit of your own making. When you are out of it, we will go along to Rome."

"You—" Baignault began. But then through the haze of his rage he saw that Khotel had left him. He stood here alone.

He walked across to his tent where he sprawled against his saddle and after a time, from sheer fatigue, he dropped into sleep that lasted until midafternoon. Chagan awoke him. The slender young Mongol came into the tent and shook him and said, "What would you have us do, Sir Jean? We fret for the road and are eager to leave. All of us have had enough rest."

"Then," Baignault said, "we will be out before dusk." His head was cleared by the sleep. He could think straight again and act with decision. "It might be well that you and Litei

160

make your farewells to the sheik. Meantime, I will find so..
food for myself and see that the mounts are made ready for
the road. Where is Khotel?"

"He is at the picket line," Chagan said. "He has picked
the mounts to be used to take us to the coast. The Druse
ask a good price for them, but they are fast and in excellent
shape and Khotel has paid without argument."

"So if Khotel has taken care of that," Baignault said,
"there is not much else for me to do. We can leave almost at
once."

Chagan gave him a short glance. "I would think," he
said, "that you would be reluctant to go. Had I a sweetheart as handsome as your Druse, I should like to spend at
least another night with her. Even Litei admitted she is most
attractive this morning in my presence."

"Still, Rome comes first," Baignault said flat-voiced. "And
last night here was sufficient for me."

He ate a quick meal at one of the cooking fires while
Chagan and Litei and then Khotel said their farewells to
the sheik. Then he ordered a slave to gather his gear, went
to the picket line and stood there with the Mongol troops.
There was no sign of Subeyla. When the others emerged
from Akhu-et-T'ib's tent he mounted and rode over and saluted from the saddle. "My great thanks to you, sheik," he
said. "May we sometime meet again."

"That is also my hope," Akhu-et-T'ib said. "Good luck
with the venture. Ride in peace. But you do not wish to say
farewell to Subeyla?"

"No," Baignault said quietly, "I do not." He tightened
the reins to swing his horse. "There is, sheik, no reason why
I should."

The march-out was at dusk. Picked Ruada guides had
been assigned by Akhu-et-T'ib to take the column through
the dangerous country beyond the Iron Gate and to the Syrian border. He had assembled all his other warriors as a
guard of honor. They formed a double rank at the edge of
the camp and the *kourrouns* were sounded.

Baignault rode in numb, stiff silence. He kept apart from
Chagan and Litei where they trotted their mounts with Khotel at the head of the column. All he hoped now was to leave
without being given further pain by the sight of Subeyla.
But she sat her caparisoned camel beside Akhu-et-T'ib at
the right wing of the guard. She was expressionless, made
no gesture as he passed. Her face bore the same pallor as

last night, and her eyes were still red-rimmed from weeping, dark with the sorrow she could not conceal.

He loved her, Baignault told himself fiercely. Always, he would love Subeyla. He jerked his horse around and made some of the warriors move back in rank as he rode toward her. The words he said came from deep within him, carried all his longing:

"I will be back for you. Do not forget me."

Her lips trembled. A flush of color was up against her cheekbones. Then she was in command of her voice. "I could never do that," she said.

He rode fast through the Iron Gate to overtake the column. And beneath his breath he hummed a troubadour love song he had learned as an esquire at El Kerak.

CHAPTER THIRTEEN

They came to it steadily over the shining, calm sea in the great galley they had boarded at Alexandretta. A hundred rowers on each side of the vessel hauled the long sweeps. The huge silken sail, blazoned with the cross, trembled under the pulsation of the land breeze, along with the banners at the masthead and the stern pole. The captain and his quartermasters were in rank on the gilt-scrolled poop, cross-bowmen in chain armor below them and the musicians gathered in the waist. This, Jean Baignault knew, was a majestic sight, and the perfect way for the mission to arrive in Italy.

Looking around him, he saw that Chagan and Litei, and even Khotel, were vastly impressed. He felt a soaring satisfaction. The doubts that had lain so heavily in his mind were gone. No matter, he told himself, that the word Mustaf had brought from Beth-Haggan was bad. He could discount most of the message written on a scroll for him by the Sieur Amboise. Mustaf had carried it and the Sieur Amboise asked that it be given personally to the Pope. It told of Saracen forces large enough to be called armies massing on the borders of *Outremer*, and of the threat of invasion from Egypt while the Hospitaler and Templar commanders still bickered aimlessly and King Henry rested indolently on Cyprus. For in Rome everything would be put straight. Christendom . still a powerful force and with the knowledge of Mongo. help the Pope would very quickly take any action that was necessary.

Chagan, Litei and Khotel stood side by side at the landward rail and stared intently ashore. Baignault crossed the deck to them with a slight swagger. He smiled as he spoke. "This is Civitavecchia," he said. "Rome is only a few hours' ride away. Those horses—" he pointed toward the cobbled dock—"are for our use."

"They seem to be fine animals," Chagan said. "Shall we reach your Holy City before dark?"

"Without doubt," Baignault said.

"For me, though," Litei said, "it is yet no more than dream. I will not believe it until I see it."

Baignault shrugged. Mustaf had just leaped from the rail onto the dock. The sergeant wore bright new clothing he had picked up in *Outremer* and he strutted as he walked to the group of horses and pushed past the grooms who held them and saluted the officer in command. "I have told Mustaf to ask the lieutenant for a cart to carry your luggage," Baignault said. "Rome may still be dream to you, but tonight, should you be invited to some great palace for dinner, it would be well to have your best gowns with you."

The red tile roofs of Civitavecchia shimmered with sun when Baignault led the party from the galley. Birds sang in the olive groves and pine trees along the road. There had been few moments in his life when he was as happy as this, he thought. This was more than coming home. It was the realization of a tremendous, stubborn hope which he had often come close to losing.

Then cloud covered the sun. Rain began to fall. Mud spattered Litei's cape; she swung up the hood over her head and rode in silence. Chagan was glum, and Khotel sat slack in his saddle. "Will it last all afternoon?" Baignault asked the lieutenant.

"More likely all night, sir," the lieutenant said. "Would you care to stop at one of the roadside inns?"

"No, we will keep on," Baignault said. "We have come very far. For us a halt would be worse than the wet or mud."

He moved his horse at an unbroken canter, but the others dropped behind until only Mustaf was near him. "Foul luck," Mustaf grunted, rain sliding from the end of his nose.

163

"I have a little Greek wine I brought from the ship, Sir Jean. The stuff stinks of resin but it warms a man up and drives off chills. A small sup could do you no harm."

"Not now," Baignault said and spurred forward from Mustaf. Through the thin, gray sheets of the rain he had seen Rome. He was struck with shocked disbelief. Rome, the Holy City, City of Eternal Light, was half in ruins. The ramparts stretched drab brown, stone tumbled from stone. He had heard in *Outremer* about the wreckage of the Forum and the Colosseum. But St. Peter's seemed to be the one building which was intact, and that rose spectral from the miasmatic mists. Further on, the Lateran Hills were dim shadows, and the city rested like a sluggish hulk between them and the marshes he had just crossed.

His mouth was dry and bitter. The others must have seen by now, he thought. They have made a journey across half the world to become converts to Christianity. And here, this tumble of ruins, is Rome. They can only tell themselves that they have been duped into some monstrous, stupid joke by madmen.

He turned in the saddle and looked back. The Mongols refused to meet his eyes. They rode with their heads averted, as if to duck the rain. But Litei showed her feelings when she cried at Mustaf, "Have those dogs taken from me!"

Mustaf swung his quirt and the troopers of the escort slapped with the flats of their swords. But when the scrawny dogs retreated beggars filled the road, mean and foul and clamorous. Mustaf gave them the quirt, cursing, his voice savage with disgust. And he cannot be blamed, Baignault thought. Even for tough old Mustaf, this is terrible.

Now the party was in the city. They had entered through a gate where people pressed around them and yammered and clawed and plucked. Baignault wheeled his horse and called to the escort lieutenant, "Take us by the shortest way possible to the Vatican. Clear the street. *Dieu me damme!* Does your city always stink?"

"Yes, Sir Jean." The lieutenant saluted. But he was young and a Roman. "No worse, however, than some of the towns in *Outremer*."

Baignault took his sword from the scabbard and let the lieutenant measure the length of the blade. He was aware that the man had resentment of the broad Hospitaler cross he wore on his shoulder. "This street," he said, "will soon

164

be sluiced with blood, Lieutenant. Make a way for us, or I will!"

The burst of rage eased Baignault's tension. He could sit his horse quietly the rest of the distance to the Vatican. But when the party had entered the outer courtyard and he had dismounted he could only bring himself to speak to Mustaf. "Take care of these folk," he said in French. "Remember that here they are our guests. Make them comfortable."

"If you come back," Mustaf said, "and find that my head has been chewed off, don't be surprised, Sir Jean."

"How could I be?" Baignault said. "I am about ready to behead myself." Then he turned and went forward to enter the palace.

Guards halted him inside, and suave-voiced priests, and finally a bishop with sunken eyes, a cold, pale face and an impenetrable austerity. "Not today, my son," the bishop said. "Nor tomorrow. His Holiness has many duties to perform. Among them, he cannot receive heathens in audience."

"You will excuse me," Baignault said quite slowly, the tension out of him, and the last traces of the rage. All he felt as he stood here was a dismal, weary numbness. "Let me repeat. . . . These people come from the Golden Horde. They are the prince and princess of the royal blood and a trusted courtier. Their emperor has offered us alliance and will back it with a million warriors. The prince and princess are eager to take our faith. If you please, Excellency, could not an audience be arranged with His Holiness for tomorrow?"

The bishop stood with his hands clasped in his sleeves. He extended one, yellow and prominently veined, to Baignault. "I bless you for your good service, my son. Now give me the message that you have said you carry from *Outremer*. Then return to the hostages."

"They are not hostages, Excellency."

"Return to them," the bishop said evenly, "and wait in the antechamber. I will see to it that quarters are given them and yourself in a palace next to the Hospital of the Holy Spirit. When His Holiness is ready, you shall be called."

Baignault knelt to receive the blessing. He stayed so as he took the scroll from inside his surcoat. Then, his head bowed, he waited until the swish of the bishop's robe died out along the corridor. He could not let the bishop see the rage that shook him. Waiting—a little more of that was nothing after all that he had done. He could only wonder how long the Mongols would persist before pride took over. *Outremer* was not their country. The Golden Horde was in no danger of attack, and when the Mongols chose, they could simply go home. They were not the petitioners here. By some strange and cruel circumstance far beyond his control, he was. . . .

When he rejoined the group in the antechamber he found that his sense of haste was far greater than their own. Now they were over their initial disappointment, the hurly-burly, the disorder, the weird mixture of magnificence and decay fascinated them. Their pride was restored, he believed, by the quarters to which an equerry led them from the Vatican in the last of the rain.

These were in an old palace in the Borgo alongside the Hospital of the Holy Spirit. Rich hangings draped the walls, the furniture was worn but in splendid style, fires burned in the huge marble fireplaces and a large staff of servants under a major-domo with a silver chain around his neck greeted them. "We shall stay here for all of our time in the city," Baignault said. "And in a day or so, when His Holiness is free from some of his most urgent affairs, he will have us in audience."

"Very fine," Litei said. "Let us not hasten him." She had gone to stand on the curving steps of the main staircase. The rain had molded her clothing closely about her body and her hair lay tousled in small, tight curls. Her eyes flashed with delight. "I think this quite adorable. Beside it, Karakoram is a dusty cattle corral. Tell the servants, Sir Jean, that I should like a goblet of spiced, warm wine, and that I am hungry."

Chagan frowned up at her from the hall below. "We are not here merely for pleasure," he said. But she did not heed him, running on up the stairs. Then Baignault caught Khotel's somber glance, and he said, "A little wine might do us all good. The major-domo can bring some to us near the fire."

"Who pays for such?" Khotel said.

"The Church," Baignault said. "We are the guests of His Holiness. That is not an uncommon practice in Rome."

"Then he is a generous host," Khotel said. But Chagan, his back to the blaze of the fire, laughed at him. "Be less solemn and much more frivolous, *ming-bashi*. Tonight, tomorrow too, we should celebrate. We have come a long way and done well."

166

Rome claimed all of them in the morning. The day was fair and they went out early into the city. Baignault shared the curiosity the others felt, and he was able to forget everything except the majesty of the past when he stood before the Colosseum, walked the banks of the Tiber and climbed the Quirinal Hill. He laughed, too, almost as freely as the Mongols at the hawkers outside of St. Peter's. Those people peddled fragments of "the True Cross," "the True Hair" and "Teeth" of Christ, and fragments of "the True Spear." Their stories were unabashed; no amount of questioning could change them.

"A fantastic and wonderful place," Chagan said. He had his arm linked with Baignault's and behind them Khotel helped Litei along the rubble-littered street. Beggars and palmers and pilgrims and thieves and prostitutes swirled around them. The day was split by countless cries. "I will regret leaving it. None other of its like can exist."

"But you have seen only one part of life here," Baignault said, suddenly grave. "All of the religious activity of Christendom is governed in Rome. And if the mission is to succeed, you and Litei and Khotel should begin your Christian instruction. Friars of the Trinitarian Order are in charge of the hospital next to the palace where we stay. They are men of great quality; for over two hundred years, it has been their duty to work among the captives held both by the Moslems and my people. I am sure that you will respect and listen to them when they talk with you."

"Lessons," Chagan said, "books." But he was not smiling. "I will make myself listen and make Litei and Khotel do the same. I am aware as well as you, Sir Jean, that we are not here simply for enjoyment of the Roman scene. . . ."

The first religious instruction was given that afternoon in the Borgo Palace. A pair of lean, sun-brown Trinitarian friars in white habits sat with the three Mongols and quietly explained the precepts of Christianity. Baignault stayed for a time, then slipped away. The friars had impressed all three, he realized, and he had his own duties to perform.

He asked for Mustaf before he left the palace. It would be good to have Mustaf here as a guard during his absence. But the major-domo said, "The sergeant has been gone since noon, Sir Jean."

"Should he come in while I am not here, tell him that I order him to stay and await my return. Tell him also that I have gone to the Vatican."

167

Baignault spent the rest of the day and then a succession of days in unbroken attendance at the Vatican. He disregarded the fact that Mustaf came stumbling back drunk to their quarters and that, isolated most of the time in the great, musty palace, the Mongols became gradually restive. He was stubbornly determined that he would gain the audience that had been promised by the Pope. But he was one of thousands of petitioners. He was shunted through a maze of minor officials, told blandly that he should not lose patience. Then, after Mustaf had been missing from the palace all one night and had taken Khotel with him, Baignault recognized that he must change his plans. Time of incalculable value was being wasted. He gave up, left the Vatican and went to seek support from the people of his own order.

Sir Hugh Gregor, dour, lame and English, was the ranking Hospitaler officer in Rome. He received Baignault in his monklike quarters and spoke with absolute candor about conditions in *Outremer*. "The matter is much different than in my early life," he said. "We and the Templars both started poor. The Templars now hold unbelievable wealth, more of it in Europe than in *Outremer,* and we cannot any longer claim poverty for ourselves. So we are feared in Europe. We are looked upon almost as enemies."

"But we keep the last bastion outside Europe," Baignault said. "That must be known to His Holiness. If we did not defend it, *Outremer* would be lost to Christendom perhaps forever."

Sir Hugh Gregor ran a hand meditatively over his scarred, bald head. "The answer in Rome is, let us take care of our own. It is said that we are the vassals of the merchants, grow wealthy from their trade. Support for us should be given by the merchant class, not the Church. It is a riddle without end, Sir Jean."

"Except," Baignault said, "that it is not true that the merchants rule us. Nor will they give us men who will fight. For such, we must turn to the Mongols."

"I can only agree." Sir Hugh's voice was weary. "Our need, too, is for leaders like Louis of France, Richard the Lion-Hearted of England. They do not exist any longer. So I can only counsel you to go back to the Vatican and wait your time out to be received in audience by His Holiness. Do not be overly dismayed. There is still true Crusader spirit left and men of the caliber of your father are proof of it. But before you return to the Vatican talk with some of

168

the younger knights who are in the city. They will tell you more than I can, and among their number is, I think, one of your cousins. He is named Sir Genvilliers Baignault. You will find him at his villa on Monte Celio. My groom will show you the way there."

Baignault rode a horse borrowed from the Hospitaler stables to Monte Celio. He was in a happy mood. Who this cousin of his was, he did not know. There were many of his name who had never left Normandy or gone out to serve in the Crusades. It would be pleasant to meet the man, talk of anything other than the fate that hung over *Outremer*.

A pretty, bare-armed maidservant let him into the villa on the crest of the ridge at Monte Celio. "Tell Sir Genvilliers," he told her, "that Sir Jean Baignault of *Outremer* has come to call on him."

The maid was back in a moment. "Go along the hall to your right, sir," she said. "You will find him in the room beyond."

The hall was dark and chill, but the big *sala* at the end of it was filled with sunlight, warmed by a fire. Half a dozen men, all of them young, none of them very sober, sat in deep chairs or stretched on couches. A tall blond youth, bearded, his hair long, stood in the center. He wore only doublet and hose, but the gold spurs of a knight were chained to his boot heels, and he was undoubtedly Sir Genvilliers Baignault.

"So," he said in broad Norman French, "you are my cousin. Enter, Sir Jean. Excuse me for a moment, though. I am busy. Five hundred and fifty florins are bet on this."

He held a half-dozen feathered, steel-tipped darts in his hand, and Jean Baignault noticed a darts board in a corner. But his cousin took aim at tapestry that covered the wall opposite him. He threw a dart and the tapestry quivered and there was a muffled shriek. *"Damme!"* Sir Genvilliers said. "My aim is bad." He threw four times before the dart brought a cry of real pain, the tapestry was flung aside and a naked girl stepped out, a smirch of blood upon her buttock.

"Pay me," Genvilliers Baignault said to the seated men. "No more credit to any of you, and I would have you meet my cousin. Go dress yourself, Gina. If you were not almost on the fat side, that last shot could have cost me a great deal."

The girl went pattering out of the room laughing and the men who were Genvilliers Baignault's guests stood up and acted sober. They were all of them knights, Jean Baignault saw as he was introduced. But none of them wore the habit of any order he recognized although the swords they carried were those of fighting men. Some of his curiosity showed, because his cousin said, "Do not look for holiness among us. We lost that long since."

"I have had my plenty of such," Jean Baignault said. "I am here on no more than a friendly visit. Sir Hugh Gregor told me of you, and I was interested to meet one of the Baignaults of Normandy."

"You find here a strayed sheep," Sir Genvilliers said. Then he clapped his hands and Gina, dressed, came back into the room. "Bring wine and olives and some *pasta*," he told her. He stretched in a chair, his glance speculative upon Jean Baignault. "I have not been home for years. Nor these men. But what of *Outremer?*"

"Nothing that counts in the moment," Jean Baignault said. "Except that here in Rome I find that it is given little thought."

Sir Genvilliers smiled and was silent, but one of his friends, a man with a freshly healed scar on his jaw, said in a soft voice, "Little is considered in Rome these days other than what concerns Rome itself."

"And you men?" Jean Baignault said. He understood now, or he began to understand, why Sir Hugh had sent him here.

"We are what are called 'free swords,' " the man with the scarred jaw said. "We serve various masters—for pay."

"You lie, Phillipe. Pay does not touch our hands." Sir Genvilliers laughed, pouring wine. He passed the goblets, then lifted his to Jean Baignault. "To men like you and the simple life. Our masters are hard to satisfy. They fill our sword scabbards with gold, but it is spent fast, and we must fight to make more. You see Phillipe. Many who were just as good with a blade are dead, killed in the service of some hilltop baron."

"But," Jean Baignault said, "you could have joined an order such as mine and gone forth on churchly service."

The man with the scarred jaw swore in vehement Italian and banged his goblet on the table. Some of the others laughed, and Sir Genvilliers was one of them. "Let me tell you, cousin," he said. "When your people and mine went out to the Crusades they were land-poor. They sold a great lot of it for whatever price the money lenders would pay to take themselves to the Holy Land. Those they left behind

170

went deeper into debt. Now the moneylenders or their companions in wealth, the merchants, own the ancient properties. Only a few huge ducal estates are left in Normandy. People have moved into the towns. The guilds are strong because of it, and they struggle with the merchants and the moneylenders, and for men of our kind there is only the sword with which to make a living."

"I have heard some of this before," Jean Baignault said. "Stories have been told in *Outremer*. But I—"

"You are a fool," Sir Genvilliers said blandly, "and you chase a dream." He poured more wine, and his face was flushed and his eyes hard and brilliant. "I do not mean to insult you, cousin. Yet fact is fact. The old days are gone. Feudalism belongs to the past. The power of kings is small, and the power of His Holiness less."

"That last I cannot accept," Jean Baignault said. He drew himself upright from the couch where he had been sitting. "I hold to vows for which I will give my life, and what you talk is close to sacrilege. You will excuse me, please, and allow me to thank you for the wine."

"Go, then," Sir Genvilliers said. He stood, staggering just a bit. "We do not wish to besmirch you with our rottenness. For, after all, we are a gang of *condottieri*—paid to kill, and taking the pay of whoever offers the most. Good luck against the Saracens. Smite them with might, and when you are about to die, smile."

Baignault offered him a short bow, bowed to the other men and went rapidly along the hall. While he and Sir Hugh's groom rode down toward the city the groom said, "And how did you find your cousin, sir?"

"One of a strange lot," Baignault said out of profound bitterness.

"There are many of the sort in Italy, sir. France, too. If I may say it, they are a plague. But they are like the street dogs here. They fight themselves in the main, kill off each other."

"Not fast enough, though," Baignault said.

Memory had sprung from the bitterness he felt. Subeyla had warned him that he served a useless cause. But he had persisted. Then Khotel had told him that he lived in the past, not the present or the future. And yet he had gone on and risked losing Subeyla forever to reach here. For what? What possibly could he gain in this place of evil, corruption and intrigue? He must talk with Chagan tonight and in the

171

morning take Chagan with him to the Vatican. They would insist upon an audience with the Pope, refuse any delay. Time had ebbed out already past the danger point.

He hit his horse a sudden lick. "I must get on," he told the surprised groom. "I have matters to tend to before the night is gone."

But there was nobody at the Borgo Palace except the servants. He ate a gloomy, solitary dinner, drank what he thought was enough wine to put him to sleep and went to bed. Then, near dawn, his sleep was broken by sounds of revelry outside. He got up and saw by the light that it was nearly dawn and stepped out onto the balcony in front of his room.

Torches still burned in cressets at the courtyard gate. He was able to see Litei clearly and, behind her, Chagan and Khotel and Mustaf. Litei had just left a litter that bore a ducal crest. She wore a new, low-cut gown beneath the cape thrown loosely about her shoulders. Chagan and Khotel and Mustaf came toward her singing an Italian peasant song. They were full of wine and their voices were raucous. Chagan swayed as he bowed to her. "And where have you been?" he said.

"Out to be amused," she said. "Just as you. Now, lacking more questions, may I go to bed?"

"Yet the Il-Khan would not be pleased," Chagan said, "if he were to know of this."

"He would laugh at the entire affair," Litei said. "He would summon us home at once. This is a fool's business and you know it. We were greatly wrong ever to have left Karakoram. You pass your time in wineshops and with common soldiers and prostitutes. While my host of the evening is one of the richest and most powerful men in Rome."

"I must ask that you stop your talk," Khotel said. He took Litei by the arm and turned her through the gateway. "Better indeed if all of us slept."

"My thanks to you, *ming-bashi*," Litei said, her eyes flashing in the cresset light. "I am pleased that you hold onto your wits. Such is rare here." Then she went on into the palace and they followed her, none of them willing to speak.

Baignault forced himself to return to bed, but he stayed sleepless. He lay tense while the cocks crowed, the church bells tolled and the street noises began. This had gone far enough, he realized, if not already too far. He must arrange

172

or an audience with the Pope today, see him alone and plead with all the eloquence at his command. There was, quite simply, no more time. . . .

He sought out at the Vatican after hours of search the same bishop with whom he had talked on his first day in Rome. The bishop listened with patience and at last with understanding. "Remain here, Sir Jean," he said. "I will arrange it for you, then come back. But—" his voice was very soft—"do not give your cause too much hope. You may meet disappointment, although I have made your story known to His Holiness."

"My great thanks to you, then, Excellency," Baignault said.

He walked the shadowy corridor for a cruel time until the bishop returned. Cardinals in red hats passed him, and he was jostled by equerries and pages and dignitaries whose vestments and ranks were unknown to him. Then the bishop was back and he was led through further corridors and a great, bossed door was opened. "Go in, my son," the bishop murmured.

Pope Nicholas sat within a shaft of sunlight. He was unmoving while Baignault made his genuflection and then came forward to kiss the ring. "From *Outremer*," Pope Nicholas said. The voice was immensely tired. It had no tone; it reached Baignault as though from a distance. "You have with you a Mongol prince and princess of the royal blood and one of their officers."

"Yes, Your Holiness."

"They would accept our faith. The Il-Khan would become our ally."

"So he has most solemnly promised, Your Holiness."

"Yet I have only little to tell him, Sir Jean Baignault. I can say to you no more than that you return to him and ask that he receive baptism. Once he has become a Christian, perhaps we may talk again."

Baignault's voice was harsh. "Not before, Your Holiness?" He had begun to tremble, and a sick, hollow sensation was in his stomach. "While *Outremer* is about to be attacked and we have huge need of the help the Mongols would give us? They have the power to put a million men into battle at our side."

"There is no more that I have to say to you, my son."

"Your Holiness—if I might tell you. The message I

173

brought to Rome has been seen by you. Surely you are aware of the danger. Should help be held back, the *Outremer* lands can be swept from end to end by the heathen."

"There is no more I have to say to you, my son."

"Yes, Your Holiness."

Baignault genuflected. He backed toward the door. He stood there for an instant and glanced at Nicholas. The Pope slouched in the huge chair. The gold he wore gleamed. Sunlight made the purple of his chasuble brilliant. His face, though, was without color, and the hands on the arms of the chair were so fragile that they were almost transparent. Beneath the arches of the brows the eyes were dark and dim in the sockets, stared off blankly into space.

Baignault knew he had done all that he could, and that had not been enough. Rome was another dream that had failed. Only one more thing was left to him, to go home and take his place beside his people in the defense of *Outremer.*

But when he was out in the corridor the shock of defeat overcame his sense of fatality. He walked blind and almost weeping along the corridors, down the staircases. Out in the sunlight, he stumbled and then caught himself and walked straight. He had been warned, he told himself. He should not take this so hard. And he had others than himself to consider. The Mongols were still his responsibility. And he had a promise to keep to Subeyla. He could never go seeking her again if he were forced to admit defeat.

The streets through which he moved, the people he passed, were a blur to him. He was thinking of what he must tell Chagan, and Litei also, and Khotel. The truth could not be disguised; he must tell it as it was.

The major-domo let him in at the main door of the palace and then swiftly disappeared. Baignault recognized the reason for the man's haste when he stared across the sun-splashed hall. A sharp family quarrel was in progress here. Litei stretched among silk cushions upon a divan and Chagan was with her, nervously flicking at a wall tapestry, his mouth hard and his face haggard. "Do not mind us, Sir Jean," he said. "Yet it is difficult for me not to strike her. The princess is unhappy with Rome. She would like to go home."

"And why not?" Litei said. She sprang from the divan, her gown riffled about her knees. "What is in this mass of ruins for us? We are lost people here. The Pope will not even receive us. I wish to leave for home at once—at once!" She took a pillow from the divan and hurled it spinning. "I am bored beyond distraction, yearn for Karakoram."

"You would not be greatly welcome there," Jean Baignault said slowly, "should you go from Rome without the permission of the Il-Khan. I assure you of that."

Litei moved rapidly to stand in front of him. "But what went on at the Vatican for you today? Do not tell us that His Holiness received you."

"Yes," Baignault said, "I do."

"He might, then, have accepted the alliance?" Litei asked. Her voice was scornful. "Still, you do not have the look of success about you, Jean Baignault. And you are such a Christian that you cannot lie well. Tell us of your audience."

They are both highly strung, Baignault thought, Chagan as much as she, and their pride has been ripped raw. Tell them and there will be grave, instant trouble. "What has happened to Khotel?" he said. "The *ming-bashi* was supposed to wait for me with Mustaf."

Chagan shook his head. He stood rigid, his glance sharp. "Tell us straight out. Do not delay until the return of Khotel. He has taken Mustaf off to the Campo dei Fiori to find the boar hunter with whom we caroused last night. Khotel is like us; he has also lost patience. So, Sir Jean. Let us know what His Holiness had to say to you."

Baignault spoke in a voice that he tried to keep low and controlled, but it broke. He was forced several times to stop; grief locked his throat muscles. Then, as he went on, he gained a strange eloquence. "I too am homesick," he said. "I dream without end of my birthplace. Visions possess me— the trees, the fields, the flowers, the house set in the gardens which my mother dearly loves. . . . For more than a year I have been away. Now it seems that I am too late; I shall never again see it. Alliance with your people would have saved mine and only that. The Saracens will be able to smash us, grind us and finish us between their armies. *Outremer* cannot stand up against them alone."

"But we will not permit such to be," Chagan said passionately. His hands reached out and clasped Baignault's shoulders, gently shaking the taller, stronger man. "For if the people of *Outremer* fall to the Saracens, then our own suffer great loss. The next Saracen attack will be upon us. Find me a scribe at once, Sir Jean. I will send a message

175

directly to the Il-Khan. The Il-Khan will send troops at my asking. We need not be Christians to protect ourselves by aid to you."

"This, though, is wrong," Litei said. "What you would do takes far too much time, Chagan. The Saracens could take *Outremer* while our troops were being gathered. You are wealthy; so am I. We hold the taxes of entire provinces in our own right. Duke Carlo Maglione, the man whose guest I was last night, is among the wealthiest merchants in Rome. He has great interest in the East and Cathay, and would enter the silk trade. Should we promise him repayment, he could persuade His Holiness. There would be a new Crusade. Within the space of only a few weeks, thousands of troops from here could land in *Outremer*."

Jean Baignault stared at her. Hope flooded the blackness of disaster from his thought. He wanted to kiss her hands from a rapture of gratitude. But some caution remained. He said slowly, "Why, after what has happened to you, do you suggest such a thing, Litei?"

Her smile was gentle. "Chagan and I are not without pride. We have no liking to return home to be called fools and dupes. Chagan has already told you. Your loss would be our own."

"Yet this duke," Chagan said, "this Carlo Maglione. You are certain that he will help us?"

"Him," Litei said, "you may leave to me." She turned and looked into a pier glass between two windows. Her hands ran across her hair, then down over her bodice. "Duke Carlo is most eager to become a very close friend of mine. I shall send off a servant to him with a small word from me. Tonight he will entertain us at his villa. You see nothing wrong in a call upon the duke, Sir Jean?"

"Nothing whatsoever," Baignault said and took her right hand and bowed over it and kissed it. "You have my deep gratitude."

"Khotel should be kept from knowledge of what we do, however," Litei said. "It would seem somewhat odd were I to arrive with three men when, truly, the duke's interest is only in myself. Let Khotel go out and take Mustaf and hunt boar, as he plans. It will be better for us if they are not here until tomorrow. The *ming-bashi* might well have thoughts of his own and try to change our plan."

Chagan was laughing with excitement. "Then we hold talk of it from Khotel. He will pass a happy night in the

Campagna without worry. And with Mustaf handy to pour the wine for him."

Baignault chose to remain alone in his own room during the afternoon. He pondered whether he should go and see Sir Hugh Gregor, tell him of his audience at the Vatican and the decision he had reached with Litei and Chagan. But Sir Hugh could help him little now, he realized, and had warned him of the probable outcome of the audience. Further, nothing was yet resolved; if tonight were successful, then tomorrow would be time enough to inform Sir Hugh. Rain slanted against the windows of the room. Fog from the Tiber filled the piazza outside. Stay here and rest, Baignault thought. He stretched out upon the canopied bed, shut his eyes, and fell into almost instant sleep.

Servants were lighting the courtyard cressets when he woke. Then, after the candles were lit in his room, Litei's personal maid knocked at the door. "Her Royal Highness would see you in her apartment, Sir Jean," she said.

"At once," Baignault said.

Litei was dressed in canary satin, and wore emeralds nearly as fine as the one in the hilt of his sword. She sat at her powder table and looked over her shoulder at him. "All is arranged," she said. "Duke Carlo will send his litter for me within the hour. He has his villa upon Monte Giordano and it is not far. You and Chagan need not take mounts. You can walk beside me. The duke has asked us to dinner, and now do not lose your temper. Have you no better clothes than those? Must you always carry that great, clumsy sword?"

"You should know," he said calmly. "I am a sworn knight. The rules of my order are that I wear such clothing. And I must always carry my sword."

She pouted her lips and then rouged them. "Chagan will vastly outshine you," she said. "He has a splendid new scarlet costume trimmed with fur. We are still heathens, you know, and should be permitted a little barbaric display."

"You are quite beautiful," he said. He meant that sincerely, he realized; he had never seen her more so. But curiosity prodded him. "Tell me. How, exactly, did you happen to meet Duke Carlo?"

"It was last week in the Piazza Navona." She spoke easily, flicking the rouge along her upper lip. "You were at the Vatican on one of your long visits. Chagan was being instructed in holy matters, and Khotel and the sergeant were off together. I entered a shop to buy a frock that took my fancy. The duke saw me and sent in his page so that I might be helped with the language. It would seem that the Duke has such a habit."

"Gathering up women who attract him, you mean."

"You told me that I was beautiful. Can you dispute the duke's taste?"

"No, I cannot," Baignault said, and bowed to her. "I shall be in the main hall with Chagan."

Baignault walked in silence through the dusk to Monte Giordano, letting Chagan talk with Litei in the ornate litter the duke had sent. Litei had explained sufficiently, he thought. It was not uncommon practice in Rome for handsome women to be approached more or less discreetly by some nobleman's page. His interest now was centered upon what sort of man the duke might be. That was of pressing importance, not Litei's willingness to flirt.

Duke Carlo Maglione was small and soft, with protuberant, red-shot eyes. His villa was garish yet magnificent, filled with many fine pieces of Moorish art. He greeted his guests in Arabic. The language was well known to him, he said, and so they should speak it. Then he clapped for his major-domo and the musicians, and, his hand high on Litei's bare arm, led the way in to dinner.

Baignault sat silent at dinner. He felt an extreme tension that he could not release. It was his role to speak, he knew, and put the conversation in the right channels, yet he could not. He had a natural dislike, a deep distrust of men like Duke Carlo. In their presence he was forced to think of himself as a rough soldier and rely upon his strength and his sword instead of his wits.

But Litei and then Chagan were discussing freely the problem of the Mongol alliance with Duke Carlo. They talked quite skillfully, Baignault thought. Their voices were ardent and persuasive; they spoke in open terms of the wealth they possessed and the use they were eager to make of it.

Duke Carlo listened with only an occasional question. His interest seemed keen and he nodded at various points. Then he signaled for more wine to be poured. "I am in agreement with you," he said. "This I will do. Tomorrow, early, I will make out a list of what should be offered in what can be called payment. It will entail so many hundred tusks of ivory, and chests of spice, of incense, and bales of

178

silk. Then I shall call for you in the Borgo and take you to see His Holiness. There should be no delay. Nicholas, above all, is practical in his views."

Duke Carlo looked obliquely over the rim of his wine goblet at Baignault. "Is that not how you have found him, Sir Jean?"

"It is," Baignault said. He got to his feet. "Now let us bid you good night, Highness, and greatly thank you."

"But do stay longer," Duke Carlo said. "You have not yet seen my troupe of dancers. Neither have you tasted my best wines."

"Some other time," Litei said. "My brother and this great brute of a Crusader fall sleepy. That is what your wines have done for them. I shall come back, though."

Duke Carlo kissed her hand, then her cheek. "I am certain of it," he said.

Mist rolled over them when they went out into the courtyard of the villa. It clung close, grayish green and thick, and they could hardly see the torches that the duke's linksmen carried. The litter was ready for Litei, and she entered it, giving the order for it to be lifted. "Stay close to me, Chagan," she said, "and you, Sir Jean. It is a miserable night and I do not wish you beyond my sight."

"Have no fear," Chagan said. His voice was clear, firm. He pulled the folds of his cloak around him and glanced at Baignault. "Which side would you like?"

"Where I am," Baignault said. "Do not slip and fall down in that new costume. You will have need of it tomorrow when you go to the Vatican."

The pair of linksmen went slowly ahead into the mist. It closed behind them swiftly like an immense, mysterious door. Baignault could not see them for minutes at a time, only heard the squelch of their sandals over the muddy cobbles. The four litter bearers grunted, slipped in the steep and narrow street and once Litei cried out in alarm. But she was quiet when, down at the bottom of Monte Giordano, the group of men sprinted from an alley.

Baignault heard rather than saw them. He counted what he believed to be five. They were armed with thin-bladed Italian swords and attacked without warning. He thought first of Chagan who tonight had discarded a sword for an ornamental poniard to wear on the belt of his new costume. He yelled, "Move back, Chagan. Stand against the litter. Let me take them."

But Chagan was already fighting; he had the poniard drawn and was in among the darkly dressed men. Baignault drew the three-foot-long Crusader sword and whipped it left and right waist-high. The Italian blades shattered under it. He could not make out the men he struck, as the sweep of his blade formed a barrier inside which they were unable to reach.

One man went down screeching profanely and crawled away. Then another tripped with a blow; two more ran. The tallest man was left and he had the heaviest sword. But the linksmen were back with their torches. Baignault stared into congested eyes and a scarred, broad-boned face beneath a steel cap. This, he thought, was a trained killer intent upon earning his pay. He stepped back a pace and his foot grazed Chagan prone in the street. The sword up over his shoulder, he swung for the crown of the cap.

The man was too fast. Baignault took a blow in the shoulder that deflected from the bone but almost pitched him headlong. That made his own blow wide and he caught himself and turned in the parry position. Then the man was gone, running along the alley.

"Bitch's son!" Baignault bawled at him. "When I find you, I will split you to the crotch!"

But the pain from his shoulder sapped his anger and Chagan was moaning in the street and Litei calling wild-voiced from the litter. He cursed the linksmen and told them to stand close while he examined Chagan. There were two body wounds through the new doublet, although neither of them was deep. He said, "Do not worry, Litei. Your brother will live."

"Live and take those fellows," Chagan mumbled. "They were not even able to stand up to me when I met them with a poniard. If I had my sword, we would have killed the lot of them."

"Be still," Baignault said and lifted him into the litter beside Litei. She was quick to take her cloak, stanch the wounds. "Who were they?" she asked Baignault. "Who would attack us?"

"I have no way to tell," Baignault said. "But very likely they were *leones*—street toughs. They are everywhere. Nobody is safe at night in this city. Let us get back to the palace."

The surgeon called to the Borgo Palace gave Baignault a potion after he had cleaned and dressed his wound. It

180

was effective. He slept through late into the next afternoon. He roused and looked up and Mustaf stood beside the bed, hard-eyed and solemn. "My place was with you," he said, "not out there in the Campagna. Something has gone wrong with the matter, Sir Jean, and I began to reckon it yesterday. But—" He looked around him and shrugged.

"Go on," Baignault said in a low voice. "Tell me."

"Khotel could ha' chosen another day than yesterday for hunting. His place, too, was here with you."

"But we kept from him what we were about to do," Baignault said. "We did not wish for him to know of it. As an officer responsible to the Il-Khan, he could have refused that Litei and Chagan visit this duke. I cannot see how he might be given any of the blame for what happened."

Mustaf stood silent, obviously unsatisfied, and Baignault grimaced at him.

"Very well," Baignault said, "I also remember the fashion in which General Gelim died. You have never been satisfied with what went on there in the pass of the Suget, have you? Somehow, you bear suspicion of Khotel. Why?"

"Out in the Campagna yesterday, Khotel made to kill me. I came through a thicket while we hunted and he let loose with a spear. That I'm alive is only for the reason that I ducked faster than he handled the weapon. He was then very sorry, and said it was a mistake. But, while I'm not of your stature, I'm too big to be mistaken for a boar."

Baignault lay motionless. The effort to concentrate sent pain from his shoulder to his brain. This cannot be, he thought dully. Khotel is not the man to strike such an evil blow. But neither has Mustaf reason to speak falsely. Great harm has been done to Khotel's pride since he has been here. He might have lost his sense of loyalty because of it. There is only one thing to do, though—make sure.

He looked up at Mustaf. "What is the name of the wineshop in the Campo dei Fiori where you have spent so much time of late?"

"The Two Swans," Mustaf said.

"Go there and learn what you can of a tall man who has a scar on his jaw and the habit of wearing a round steel cap at night. He served me this stroke in the shoulder and I am given to think that he was the leader of the attack last night. Take care of yourself, though. Play the part of the hunter instead of the boar."

"Mustaf will look after Mustaf. But I'll have need of

money, Sir Jean. Those *leones* have a great thirst for wine."

"My purse is yonder," Baignault said. "Take what you wish. Stay sober. I do not have to tell you that you will be in some danger."

Mustaf bent and grasped his hand. "Rest easy, Sir Jean," he said. "I'll be back."

Baignault's rest was broken often during the afternoon. Litei came to call upon him with fresh fruit, scented wine and sympathy. Then soon after she was gone Khotel entered the room. Khotel seemed more enraged than Baignault had ever before seen him. He drew a chair alongside the bed and sat in it and stared squarely into Baignault's eyes. "I was grievously wrong not to have been with you last night," he said. "My place was at your side. You would not be mistaken to make report against me to the Il-Khan."

"I have no desire to do that," Baignault said quietly. He studied the other man for a moment in silence. Khotel and he had ridden thousands upon thousands of miles together. They had shared great danger. If Khotel went home with the mission a failure it would do him no good and again his advancement in rank would be held back. He and Khotel were in no way friends, yet he respected the *ming-bashi*, and looking into the wide and angry eyes, the tanned, bony face, he felt a sense of shame. Khotel was not a traitor.

"We have each of us made our mistakes, *ming-bashi*," he said. "Mine was not to tell you yesterday that I was given audience by His Holiness and refused immediate aid. Yours, if it exists, is small, and forget it. Go talk with Litei and with Chagan when he is able. They will explain to you what went on last evening at the home of Duke Carlo Maglione. Put your thought to that, and forget the street fight. It means very little now."

"I accept your word," Khotel said, "and I am grateful for it. The duke of whom you speak is here in the palace now. He would like to see you."

"Send him in," Baignault said. "He must have news from the Vatican."

Duke Carlo entered with Litei at his side. He was shocked, he said, to hear of last night's attack. His protest had been made at the Vatican and to the civil authorities. Rome had become a vast arena for thieves and murderers.

"What did His Holiness have to tell you?" Baignault said.

"I could not gain audience to him," Duke Carlo said.

182

"That must wait at least until you are well enough to appear with me. Such was the advice given by the Vatican officials."

Baignault noticed in the candlelight the way Duke Carlo's hand reached out slyly and then retreated. The fat little man could not keep himself from caressing Litei; his fingers had just run along her thigh. There was the attraction for Duke Carlo, Baignault thought, not what might be done at the Vatican.

"You will excuse me," Baignault said. He turned his head aside upon the pillow. "I am very tired. Perhaps if you were to return tomorrow we could talk again, Highness."

"But of course," Duke Carlo said, and Litei said, "Poor dear, last night he fought like a lion to save us." Then they were gone. The door was softly shut.

Baignault sat up in the bed. He cursed Duke Carlo harshly by name. The fat man with the groping hands aroused all his sense of caution. He must get out of here and find Mustaf. Whatever the duke schemed, it put Mustaf's life in danger, and the attack last night had already cost enough.

Baignault waited until midnight, but as the church bells tolled the hour he got up and bolted the door. Then he dressed and buckled on his sword. He left the room in traditional style, the bed sheets knotted together, and dropped from the balcony rail into the courtyard. He squatted panting in the shadows and decided that he was wrong to attempt to find Mustaf alone. He was a Hospitaler and it was best tonight that he ask help from Sir Hugh Gregor and the others of his order.

Sir Hugh welcomed him in his cell-like quarters. After he had given Baignault a long glance he insisted upon pouring wine. Then he said, "Speak slowly, Sir Jean, and explain the whole matter to me."

"I do not know the answer to any part of it," he told Baignault at the end. "Yet I have downstairs here a veteran lot of men-at-arms. They spend their pay in the same fashion as your sergeant in the Campo dei Fiori wineshops. It is my suggestion that we enlist a few of them and go out upon a hunt. You are fit for it?"

"Fit enough, sir," Baignault said.

They had no luck at the place called the Two Swans or anywhere else in the Campo dei Fiori. But right past it, under an archway, one of Sir Hugh's pikemen talked shortly with a street thief he knew. He took them to an alley off the Piazza San Pietro and asked them to wait. He came back at a slow, sliding walk, in front of him at the point of a dagger another man.

Baignault's patience was gone, and his shoulder sorely hurt. There was a little light at the door to a cookshop. "Take him to it," he said. "Let me look at him." But the man tried to break and run. Baignault knocked him semiconscious with a hammer-like fist blow at the base of the skull.

"Pick him up," he told the Hospitaler men-at-arms. "Hold him against the wall. Now open his clothing and lend me that dagger."

The scar-faced man cursed, writhed, and talked. He said that his name was Luigi Gambora, and he was from Milan, had worked for some years as a *condottieri* in Siena and Ravenna. But for him Rome was a poor city fit only for pickpockets. He had been starving when he took last night's job.

Baignault applied pressure to the dagger. "Who hired you?"

"Some fellow I could hardly understand."

"Describe him."

"Please, Highness, I wouldn't know him if I saw him again." The man's voice was close to a scream. "Ask them at the Two Swans. He used to go there."

"With a companion," Baignault said. "A little fellow with mustaches like this. He is named Mustaf. What happened to him?"

"I don't know, Highness."

"Listen," Baignault said quietly, "you are going to die. Nothing will save you. But talk and it will not be made too painful. Tell me of Mustaf."

"I stabbed him." The man was breathing hard. Sweat and spittle were on his lips.

"Where?"

"In an alley alongside the Swans."

"Is he dead?"

"That I don't know. He fought hard. Once I got the dagger into him, I ran."

Baignault looked around at Sir Hugh. "I should like to go to the alley," he said. "And have this man taken to it—alive."

Sir Hugh beckoned to the men-at-arms. "Bring the knave," he told them.

The alley alongside the Two Swans was in total darkness. It was littered with offal; rats, cats and dogs roamed it and fought and killed. Baignault entered groping and he came upon Mustaf before a pikeman moved forward and lifted a torch. Mustaf was alive; he lay with his knees drawn up against his stomach and he breathed very slowly.

Baignault knelt and put the fingers of his good hand on Mustaf's face. "Let me know," he said. "We have the man who did it. He is here."

"Three of them," Mustaf whispered. "With swords. They backed me into the alley. Then one got behind. He used both dagger and sword. . . ." Mustaf was squinting in the torchlight. He had seen and recognized the scar-faced man. "You gutless bastard," he said, and his voice was strong. "You struck your blow and ran. I will tend to you."

Mustaf jerked past Baignault. He lunged and scrambled, and out of the filth he had taken his tulwar. But the effort sent blood gushing from his punctured lungs. He slipped to his knees, then lying face downward, he died.

Baignault lifted the body, propped it upright. He cleaned the face and arranged the clothing and slid the tulwar into the scabbard. He felt no emotion in this moment except all-possessing hatred. It was not right, he knew. There was more that he must learn from the man who had killed Mustaf. He went slowly along the alley.

A pair of pikemen held the man. He strained against them in his terror. "Please, Highness," he said to Baignault. "Make it quick."

"Tell me," Baignault said. "What of the men who helped you here?"

"They were supposed to dump the body in the Tiber, and were paid for it. But they ran. They must be running yet."

"Who paid them and you?"

"The same fellow who hired me for last night, Highness. He—I don't know his name. But him and Mustaf used to come together to the Two Swans. They talked Arab together."

"So," Baignault said. "Now I know the fellow you mean." He made a gesture to the men-at-arms. "Take this away," he said. "Do whatever you wish, but be very thorough. I will leave some drinking money for you with Sir Hugh."

Sir Hugh stood at the head of the alley. He stepped away with Baignault as the scar-faced man was led out sagging but silent. Then he said, "I shall see that your sergeant's body is given proper care. Once my lot are finished with their present task, it will be taken from here."

"I thank you," Baignault said, caught suddenly by grief and almost ready to weep. "The sergeant saved many Hospitaler lives, my own among them. He should be accorded all Christian rites."

"You have my promise," Sir Hugh said. "Now what have you learned? May I help further?"

"The matter can only be settled by me," Baignault said. "A good part of it has become personal. I shall be at the palace in the Borgo. The man with whom I wish to talk should be there. Let me report later to you, Sir Hugh."

Sir Hugh answered his salute. "I will look for you at my quarters," he said. "Good luck in what is ahead of you." He turned then and stiff-legged and slow, took the opposite way from Baignault along the Campo dei Fiori.

Rage sustained Baignault as he walked back to the Borgo. Yet it was a much different emotion than any he had ever before experienced. Great hatred was in it, and shock, and loathing, and contempt. Treachery was new to him; he had only encountered a little of it for his dominant principle had always been his sense of knightly honor. He had endowed Khotel with that same sense, he realized, and he had been grossly wrong. Khotel was a traitor; Khotel was beyond all else a foul, scheming murderer. And for what he had done Khotel would be paid by him, the man who had given trust, lived in the belief that honor had meaning no matter what it might cost.

His life had reached a climax, he recognized, and was changed beyond repair. After tonight, he would perhaps enter into the maturity which Subeyla had told him he lacked. Now he was given to a single purpose—find Khotel.

Baignault came to the palace, but avoided the main gate. He went around into the side street and with the point of his sword snapped the lock of the door that led to the servants' quarters. The fire was banked in the huge, hooded kitchen fireplace. A scullion snored on a bench and Baignault moved past soundlessly and up the rear stairs.

He did not hurry as he walked through the upper corridors. He came to Khotel's room, his hand on the sword hilt and beginning to tremble a bit with anticipation. Tapers

186

burned in the room, but it was empty and the bed had not been used.

Baignault moved on quietly, his hand still on the sword. Light from a wall cresset showed him the maid who sat dozing at the end of the corridor. She was Litei's personal maid and Litei held her at call all night long. Baignault touched the woman on the shoulder. She started up at the sight of the blood on his hand, but he said swiftly in a low voice, "Be still." Then he took a handful of ducats from his purse and gave them to her. "Is the princess alone?"

"No, Sir Jean."

"Then go to bed. She will not need you again tonight. And do not be alarmed."

"Yes, Sir Jean." The maid curtseyed, the money clasped in a fold of her skirt, and went off very quietly along the corridor.

Baignault opened the apartment door by degrees and made no sound. He is here, he thought. Khotel is here with Litei. So it is likely that she is in the thing with him. Watch her too, and give her small mercy.

A short hall led from the door. It was covered with thick carpet and Baignault walked slowly in his soft boots. He could hear Khotel's voice and Litei's laughter in response. Then he stopped. He drew his breath and told himself that he must be absolutely sure.

Litei sat at her dressing table in the room ahead. She wore a loose silk robe and faced her mirror and combed her hair. Khotel stood a few feet from her. He had been careless, Baignault saw. Khotel had come here unarmed. For this was a meeting between lovers, and Khotel wore only a shirt over his hose.

Baignault stepped forward a single stride. It brought him beside the bed and Khotel turned from Litei in the big, brightly lit room. Khotel's eyes squinted glaring. His face became ugly, pallor up against the high cheekbones, his lips away from his teeth. He raised his hands as though to grasp an unseen weapon. Then, as Baignault spoke he smiled and lowered them. "Tell me," Baignault said. "I do not yet understand your reason."

"You will never do that." Khotel put scorn into the words. "For you are a fool, a great, blundering swine. Leave us. Get out. Go back to *Outremer*. Attempt to make trouble here and you will be killed."

For a second, Baignault recalled Khotel as he had seen

187

him in the past, smiling as they first met on the road past the Iron Gate, in the snow while the wolves attacked and the insane howled in The Land of Shadows, along the slopes of the Suget, and here. They had gone a long way together, he and this man, and they had come to the end in treachery and tragedy. For Khotel would not live to leave the room. He was going to kill Khotel, and somehow, along his nerve centers, Khotel knew it and was about to become afraid.

"Tell me," Baignault said. "Mustaf gave you no harm. I have trusted you, wished to remain your friend. Why is this?"

"Are you stupid enough to think that we would keep on accepting vague promises, lies and delays? Pride is of vast importance to you. And we have our own. Behind ours, though, is sense."

"I should like to hear," Baignault said slowly, "that you do not hold with him, Litei."

But Litei sat motionless and silent. Her glance reflected from her mirror stayed inflexible, hard and shining. Khotel moved toward her. Baignault did not stop him; he wanted to hear all that Khotel had to say.

"So you plotted my death," Baignault told him. "And Mustaf's. You would even have taken the life of Chagan. The Il-Khan will at least make you answer for that."

"Once more wrong," Khotel said. "What the Il-Khan thinks or would do is a small matter. He will not be on his throne much longer. What has happened to the mission and his trust in it are enough to destroy him. Many men in his council already oppose him and they have had messages from me. When he is gone, Litei will rule. And I with her. Chagan has fallen into your fool's ways. He is of no worth to us or to himself."

Baignault's fingers tingled with the desire to draw the sword, leap at Khotel. But he stood still, wanting this to be full and every detail in place. "What of Duke Carlo?"

Khotel and Litei smiled at each other. Khotel stood very near the table. A small, silver-hilted dagger lay next to her rouge pot and she was sliding it within Khotel's reach.

"Duke Carlo is another fool," Litei said. "He will help us return to Karakoram. That is all."

"The pieces fit," Baignault said, his voice low and weary. "Then you killed the old general on the mountain, Khotel. He too was in your way. So you pitched him from the cliff."

"Of course," Khotel said. "But go home, Crusader. You

"are needed there, and here you do no good to anyone."

"Put down the dagger," Baignault said.

Khotel was stooped, the dagger in his hand. "While you hold your sword? Last night, you used that very well."

"Put down the dagger," Baignault said. "I am wounded, Khotel. You take advantage of me." Then he drew the sword and hurled it.

Khotel sprang for him with a swift, sidewise motion. The sword made a whirring, chirruping sound. Khotel went to his knees beneath the blade. The hilt passed his head and struck the mirror.

Glass shattered and showered across the room. Candles fell in sputtering curves, then went out. Litei screamed as she tumbled to the floor. "Be quiet," Khotel told her in the darkness. "Let me find him."

Baignault followed Khotel's voice. He took off his cloak as he moved and wound it thickly around his wounded arm. Then he prodded with his foot, heard Litei murmur and Khotel rise up to stab. The first and the second blows he managed to receive in the cape. The third grazed his good arm, and he groped and had Khotel by the wrist.

He gave all his strength to the hold, remembering a Levantine wrestler's trick he had learned at El Kerak. He bent down and jerked and spun and pitched Khotel upward and then let go. Khotel, from the sound, landed against a wall, and some of his bones were broken. He could only fumble around on the floor for the dagger. Baignault went to him and seized him by the throat and dug his fingers deep.

Khotel died kicking, his back arched, the dagger snapped beneath his body. Baignault left him while he still flopped and sought Litei. Her slippers crunched glass shards; he got to her at the door. She fought and clawed and jabbed and raked her fingers across his eyes. He beat her mercilessly till she lay quiet and then dragged her into the corridor.

"No," she said, "you cannot."

He looked steadily into her fear-wide eyes and his voice was rough with disgust. "I will not kill you," he said. "Chagan must hear of this, though. You are to tell him."

"But what will happen to me?" She lay panting. A dribble of blood was on her chin. Her body was wet with sweat.

"I am not sure." Baignault said. "Still, as long as he wishes to feed you, I imagine that you might serve Duke Carlo as a whore."

CHAPTER FOURTEEN

Sir Hugh Gregor sat in the main hall of the Borgo Palace after Baignault sent for him in the early morning. He listened to Baignault's story without any show of emotion. "Such things happen," he said. "The life we lead seems often to be filled only with plot and counterplot. I have been more grievously hurt in backstairs intrigues than on the battlefield. But what has become of the princess since you got hold of the truth?"

"I let her maid go off to Duke Carlo," Baignault said. "And he had his litter here for her almost at once. I hope that he is not disappointed in her. She took along all her clothes, her jewels. But last night I beat her the way the Mongols beat their drums. She will not look attractive for weeks to come."

"What of the body of the fellow you killed?" Sir Hugh said.

"It is still in her apartment above. The servants are frightened and will not enter. Most of them have already left. I regret, sir, that I cannot offer you breakfast."

Sir Hugh grunted and got up and limped around the hall. "You are cool enough," he said.

"It might be," Baignault said, "that I suffer from such shock that I will not until later realize the full meaning of this." He sat brushing his bruised, lacerated hand through his hair. His head hurt, and beneath the fatigue that pressed at his brain was an enormous sense of desolation.

"Christendom has been dealt a most severe blow because of it." Sir Hugh was suddenly grim. "There is little chance now for *Outremer* to survive. Still, it does no good to dwell upon the subject in the moment. I will call some of my men, the same lot we used last night. The body upstairs will be dumped into the river by them. I will go also and demand an audience with His Holiness."

"To what purpose?" Jean Baignault said bitterly. "Nothing can be gained. Even if there had not been treachery, we were too late to win."

"Let us have no more talk like that," Sir Hugh said rough-voiced. "Never is it too late to win a battle."

"You mistake me, sir. After last night, I am eager to return to *Outremer* and fight."

"Tell me of the young prince, Chagan. How much consideration have you given him?"

"He knows nothing of this yet, and has not been disturbed. I had the thought that in your presence I would go to him and attempt to make him understand. You see, sir, he has been a good and true friend to me, and he is still weak from his wounds. It will for him be very painful. And if I am to go back to *Outremer*—"

"Enough," Sir Hugh said. His voice had changed. It was low, and soft. "Do not feel ashamed. You are not at fault for what has happened. I will see that the Trinitarians at the hospital take the best of care of Chagan. And I give you my knightly oath that when he is recovered I will arrange safe passage for him home to Karakoram. That he deserves, at least, for the good faith he has proven and for the friendship that is between you and him."

"Then I am ready," Jean Baignault said. He rose from his chair and with Sir Hugh beside him slowly climbed the marble staircase.

Chagan still slept in the shaded room, the drapes pulled closely about the tall bed. Baignault opened them, then stooped and touched Chagan on the shoulder. Chagan awoke by degrees, stiff in his bandages and yawning. But his eyes widened when he saw Baignault's lacerated hand and the somber figure of Sir Hugh at the door. "What has happened?" he said.

"A very great deal," Baignault said. "Sir Hugh Gregor, here, was witness to part of it last night." He paused, drew breath, and when he went on his voice was flat so that he could keep from it the hatred and feeling of desolation. He finished at last and stood staring down at Chagan.

"So, then," Chagan said, "Mustaf is dead. And Khotel . . . Khotel, whose traitor's name will always keep an evil stink in Karakoram. But he sold himself cheap. My greedy little half-sister must have stolen his senses from him. Curse them both, Litei in particular. Should she end up as the fat duke's whore he will pitch her out in time for others. Then she will walk the streets, prowl with the alley cats to stay alive. She is where she belongs."

Chagan lay quiet. His face was gray, exhausted. "I can

191

only guess at the men who have plotted with Khotel and Litei. The Il-Khan, though, is certain to discover them. I will send him a message today and inform him. And in that he will be told that Sir Jean Baignault has acted throughout with honor."

Chagan stopped. He was not weeping, but tears were in his eyes, and he turned his head away on the pillow. Sir Hugh Gregor moved to the bed. He stood massive and silent until Chagan looked up at him. He bowed to Chagan. "I am here, Highness," he said, "to assure you of all the aid that is in my power. You may use in any fashion you see fit the services of the Knights Hospitalers. I shall be exact. Care will be given you till you have recouped from your wounds. Then safe passage to Karakoram arranged. Christendom has fallen on hard days, yet some small ability is left us."

"But my concern is not for myself," Chagan said. "It is for Sir Jean and men like you."

Sir Hugh gave him a grave smile. "Your generosity allows me to tell you," he said. Then, briefly, his glance went from Chagan to Baignault. "News was brought me at my quarters before I was called here. Sir Jean has not heard it. My thought was that he should speak with you before he was told."

"You would mean—" Jean Baignault forced the words— "that *Outremer* has been attacked."

"Yet," Sir Hugh said, "none of us should be surprised." His voice was clipped. He spoke as though he read aloud from some routine military order. "The Saracens under the Sultan Kalawun have started siege against Acre. Very near all the rest of *Outremer* has been abandoned to them. Should we lose Acre, our defeat will be complete. We have troops on the way to aid in defense of it. Sir Otho de Grandison represents the King of England among them. He will sail tomorrow with several hundred English and Picardish knights."

Baignault took a long breath. "From where, sir?" he said.

"From this coast," Sir Hugh said, "out of Civitavecchia. The port at Acre is still open to us. Members of the Teutonic Knights and the Knights of St. Lazarus and St. Thomas will follow in their own ships, and after them Hospitalers and Templars as soon as they are assembled. Sir Otho loads today his horses, his gear and supplies."

192

"You would not object," Baignault said, "if I offered my services to Sir Otho de Grandison?"

"As a Hospitaler whose duites hold him in Rome, I envy you the chance."

"My father and my mother," Baignault said very slowly, "are in *Outremer*. It is my hope that they have taken refuge at Acre. Should they still be at Beth-Haggan . . ." His voice dulled, dropped. He stood staring blindly at the floor. The image was for the first time vivid to him. His mother dead in the wreckage of Beth-Haggan. The Sieur Amboise a captive of the Saracens, taunted, tortured, or dead beside her. No, that could not be. The Sieur Amboise would have taken her to safety at El Kerak, and if the citadel had since fallen, to Acre.

He regained the power of his voice. "I must go to *Outremer*," he said. "It is my homeland. You understand, Chagan?"

"I would be vastly astonished," Chagan said, "if the fact were otherwise." He was struggling to rise from the bed. His hands gripped upon the thick side drapes, he drew himself erect and stood beside Baignault. He reached out and put his arms around Baignault. They embraced as though, truly, they were brothers.

"Then, good-by," Baignault said. "I can only tell you that I have done my best. When you are again in Karakoram, pay my respects to your father."

"Give the Saracens of your best," Chagan said, "and you will chase them into the sea. Good-by, Jean, and use the big sword well."

Baignault wheeled, his glance on Sir Hugh. He started to salute, but the old knight moved forward and kissed him on the cheek. "I will not see you at the ship," Sir Hugh said. "I will be busy here."

At the doorway Baignault looked back and saluted both men. The future was dark chaos. His mind was battered by many thoughts. But he was certain that never again would he see Chagan.

CHAPTER FIFTEEN

There were women among the company Sir Otho de Grandison commanded and led to *Outremer*. Some were the wives of officers whose devotion was too great for them to stay at home, others nuns assigned to routine duty at Acre. The rest were without pretense camp followers, and to them this was a jaunt to be filled with pleasure, drink, song and love-making. They and the men aboard the clumsy, richly decorated galley amazed and enraged Jean Baignault. He was forced against his will to thought of Subeyla.

She had warned him more than a year ago that he was mistaken to continue in the tradition of his family and his people. War was wrong, she said, and secretly he worshiped it instead of his religion. And now he returned, bitter at heart, sorely defeated, and still persistent, claimed by loyalty. What else, though, he asked himself, might he do? Despise these people and he did nothing to save his father and his mother and gain back *Outremer* and Jerusalem and the other fine, proud cities that had cost so much bloodshed, so much faith and courage to win.

But he could not hide from himself that his shipmates sailed as though to some tourney. The chivalric tradition of the time of King Louis still persisted, Baignault realized. Pages had lined the ship's bulwarks with the shields of their masters. Banners, pennants, gonfalons flew from each mast and yard end. Carpets were spread on the upper decks; ladies entertained under silk canopies and musicians played and there was dancing; jesters pranced through the bright, soft spring days and starlit nights. The dice clucked in the leather cups and the pages ran the ladders with jeweled flagons of spiced wine.

Down in the hold were the stalls that held the great battle chargers. The smell of manure and urine rose from them, and on the main deck fletchers worked at making arrows and armorers and blacksmiths were at the forges, swords sharpened, arbalests set up tight and lance points fashioned while the men-at-arms crowded close to watch. Many of the men-at-arms were veterans; they knew the

Saracen strength, and their faces were somber, they drank little wine.

But Baignault kept apart even from them. He felt himself to be almost a stranger in this ship. French was his native tongue, and a number of the English knights were of Norman stock and related to him in one way or another. Sir Otho de Grandison had also sought him out and asked him shrewd questions about the Saracens. Still, he was different, he recognized. He returned to his homeland and his home was gone; up above Beth-Haggan, the Saracens walked the ramparts of El Kerak as conquerors. These people who were his shipmates had their family ties in Europe; they were European-born. Win or lose at Acre, those who survived could go back to their homes. For him, victory would have small meaning unless all of *Outremer* were restored.

He made it his habit to go and stand at the bow of the vessel. Only a few of the crew came near him, and meeting his hard, brooding gaze, let him be. He exercised the arm that had been partially lamed by the shoulder blow. After dark each night when the ship lay at anchor offshore he drew the sword and practiced attack and parry. But it bored him, and from aft he heard the hautboys and viols; feet slurred the steps of a dance; women laughed.

The laughter reached deep inside and hurt him. He longed for Subeyla, not the Subeyla who talked of war and peace and politics, but the woman who made love. He smelled her hair. His hands were on her body. They were in close embrace, locked, held, consumed by passion.

Baignault opened his eyes, the dream gone, and stared forward into the pale blue Mediterranean darkness. Subeyla was lost to him. He had relinquished her, denied her because of the other, greatly compelling dream. So now he was alone. He had wandered into a wasteland where he cherished shadows. In this year of 1291, at twenty-four years of age, he was spent, embittered by both defeat and treachery. Acre, he told himself, was nothing except the last outposts of the wasteland. If he gave his life there against the Saracens he would only be giving proof to Subeyla's warning. Live by the sword, and die with it in his hand was the best that he could do. . . .

But in the light airs of the eastern Mediterranean beyond Cyprus a feverish elation came over him. He would make the Saracens pay dearly for his life. And before that he might find his mother, prepare for battle with the Sieur Amboise. It would be great honor to fight at his father's side.

High at the masthead, leaning down from the rigging, the lookout had just given the cry, "Land ho!" The jesters giggled and scampered to get to the bulwark rail on the landward side. But the knights' wives and the bawds were there before them, and on the quarterdeck Sir Otho de Grandison called for the musicians to be silent. Ahead was Acre, and the priests aboard were preparing to bless the company.

Jean Baignault heard no more than a few words of the prayers. He thrust forward and took his place in the second boat that was launched. Then Sir Otho's boat was away and the second was lowered, cutting in across the calm harbor water around the double mole to the quay.

Baignault stood erect and leaped onto the quay. The knights who had landed with him were shorter men; he could look over their heads and see the city. The Tower of Flies, the broad, strong structure that guarded the harbor to the west was still intact. The stretch of marsh to the north and south of the outer walls had not yet been penetrated by the Saracens. But as he strode ahead the throbbing vibration of the immense Saracen siege engines passed from his feet through his body.

That was serious, he knew. The siege engines could in time smash any set of walls. A sweaty Templar esquire stood in front of him and said that he should halt, give his name, his destination. Baignault pushed the esquire back with a sidewise swipe.

Acre had been familiar to him since he was a small boy. He had come here first riding a pony, the Sieur Amboise a pace ahead on his caparisoned charger. Now he waited for nobody. The siege engine impact told him some of what he wanted to know, but not enough.

It was directed against the Maledictum section to the northeast, and the Tower of the Devil and the Tower of the Patriarch. Over toward the Maledictum was the well's weakest point. He would go there. But not, he told himself, until he had found out about his people.

Wounded lay in the streets. They crawled alone or supporting each other. A great number of them had been struck by naphtha and Greek fire. They were blinded and terribly burned, the remnants of their clothing tight upon the swol-

196

len, blackened bodies. He stepped aside to allow them passage. He had thought himself battle-hardened, but he gagged and nearly vomited. It was more than the wounded; the streets beyond were blocked by dead horses that still wore armor and had been left there for days in the heat.

He turned and chose another way, that led into the Venetian and Pisan quarters. He scrambled through a dark, corpse-stinking alley past the Palace of the Patriarch. He came out into a street he knew well and in front of him was the Convent of the Hospitalers. He wiped his hands against the lining of his mantle, brushed the sweat from his face. An archer propped up by a crutch was on guard at the doorway.

"I am named Sir Jean Baignault," Baignault said. "I search for the Sieur Amboise Baignault, my father, and my mother. Might they be here?"

The archer shifted the crutch to salute him. "It is good to see you, sir. But they are not here. The Sieur Amboise has command of the defense at the Maledictum Tower."

"And my mother, Lady Baignault?"

"She is in the tower, sir. That is where we have had it the worst, and where I picked up this. Lady Baignault helps care for the wounded. Plenty of us have been saved by her."

Jean Baignault felt a sudden weakness in his legs. He leaned against the convent wall. "How do we go in the fighting?" he said.

"Not too well, sir," the archer said. He spat at the cobbles and swatted away flies; from within the carved gateway, some man in agony screamed and it was the sound of death. "We need troops. Kalawun, the Sultan, died of the fever right at the beginning. But his son has taken his place."

"That would be Khalil."

"Yes, sir. But Kalawun made him promise that his body would not be buried till they took the city. They have ninety-two siege engines out there. Ninety-two . . . And all huge. And from up in them they throw the liquid fire at us."

"Some two hundred knights landed with me," Baignault said. "More follow. You fellows shall be able to take a rest. We will carry the fighting for a while."

"Good to hear, sir," the archer said. "But if you would

197

see your father and mother, it would be wise to get over there to the Maledictum. It's not what can be called too secure."

Baignault walked swiftly from the Convent of the Hospitalers. His eagerness to be with his parents kept any sense of danger from his conscious mind. But ahead of him now were the Saracen siege engines. They were massive, loomed high above the city wall. Made of great tree trunks, they came with a gigantic rumbling of solid wooden wheels down sloped wooden rails, and delivered awful force. He was nearly knocked from his feet by their shock. Buildings around him trembled. Tiles fell from the roofs, and the wounded being led back stumbled and winced, their faces white with fear.

Baignault understood when he glanced up at the belfry towers at the tops of the engines. Those were manned by picked Saracen warriors expert with the bow. Arrows sent through the tower slits ripped along the street. He ducked with the wounded and they cursed him. A jackman in a bloody chain shirt pointed at his white mantle with the conspicuous eight-pointed red cross. "You make a fine target," the jackman said. "Take that off. Those bastards up there use a hundred-pound draw on their bows. They will drill you like soft cheese."

"Be on your way," Baignault said. But he took off the mantle and folded it and tucked it in the rear of his sword belt. He moved in the same fashion as the wounded, close to the buildings and then sprawling inside doorways after an engine struck. Quite a few of the corpses that he saw in the street carried as many as twelve Saracen arrows in their backs.

But he had almost reached the wall. Smoke swirled over the street below it. There was the greasy, sickening odor of burned and rotted flesh. Naphtha bombs bounced and split and flamed. Casks of oil were flung down into the flame, and jars of molten lead and heated boulders. He locked his teeth tight to keep from vomiting; around him were men without faces who still screamed.

We have no chance, he thought. This is too much for men to take. It is impossible. Here is a page lifted straight from Hell. Then he saw his father, and the black dismay and the sick horror left him. He felt nothing but pride, pride and love.

The Sieur Amboise stood on the cracked and battered

footwalk of the wall beside the Maledictum Tower. He wore a conical, damascened steel cap that must have been captured from a Saracen warrior and his chain mail was black with soot. Jackmen knelt behind him and handed him arrows wrapped in cotton. He dipped them deliberately into pools of the blazing naphtha and set them to his bow and aimed them upward into the belfry slits.

A pair of the closest belfries were on fire, Jean Baignault noticed, and a third was about to burst into flame. His father single-handed beat back the Saracen assault. The tradition made by men like Richard the Lion-Hearted was still strong in this place; the Sieur Amboise lived it and excelled it. While men of his quality could fight, no battle was lost.

Jean Baignault ran up the ladder murmuring in a kind of ecstasy, "Father, father I am here. Let me help you." But the Sieur Amboise aimed and sent another shaft before he turned around. "If you please, sir. My hand is fresh, and I can charge and shoot that."

"So, Jean." It was as if for an instant they were alone and stood in quietness in a side garden at Beth-Haggan. The Sieur Amboise had dropped the big bow. He clasped his son close and kissed him on the cheek. "You have come home." The eyes within the puffed, reddened lids were joyous, and Jean Baignault smiled back and nodded, ashamed that out of tension his first words had been of war. Then the Sieur Amboise stared quickly away at the belfry where flame had begun to bloom. "Yes, find a bow. We have many. What we need is archers for them."

Jean Baignault kept an arm around his father's shoulder. Now, in the swerve of his intense, confused emotion, he felt a protective sense. The Sieur Amboise should not stay here; he might be killed at any moment. After all the waiting, it was his duty to take his father's place. "You might take a rest, sir," he said. "Should you go below for a time, I will relieve you."

The Sieur Amboise tightened the bow without answer. He fitted the arrow, set it ablaze, aimed and discharged it. "Your mother is at the Maledictum Tower," he said. "She tends the wounded under the archway of the street gate. Go and see her. You will make her very glad."

"Yes, sir," Jean Baignault said. But he was unwilling to leave this man. Saracen arrows racked around them. A splitting oil jar splattered them and they were forced to fall prone, crawl in under the rampart. "Have you heard the word from Rome?"

"I have," his father said, but the glance he gave was unchanged, still full of love. "That was brought to us some days ago in a fast galley bearing dispatches. I would understand from it that you did well and that the fault was not yours. A personal note was sent me by Sir Hugh Gregor. Many things are wrong these days, so do not be of faint heart. Now there is no more time for talk, Jean. Go see your mother."

Jean Baignault stood close and kissed his father's cheek before he went down the ladder. "I will be back, sir," he said.

But he walked slowly when he approached the Maledictum Tower. The scene here was worse than his most terrible childhood nightmares of hell. It was illuminated by torches stuck into sconces along the walls. Straw had been spread across the stone paving, but that was soaked with blood and the wounded who lay on it were piled so thickly that there was no room to move between them. The dead were heaped in a corner and past them, under the breadth of the archway, Lady Baignault worked.

She wore a white frock that was encarmined to the shoulders. A turban was wrapped around her head to keep her hair from her face. Jean Baignault stood and stared at her almost without recognition, too shocked to speak. The cheekbones thrust starkly against the skin, and the eye sockets were discolored, dark, the eyes themselves glaring in a fixed gaze, and the jaw muscles clenched, the mouth a compressed, pale line. She is part dead, he thought, the horror cold around his heart. This has stolen the life out of her. If she stays here much longer, she will die.

Then he forced himself to move, knowing that he must and that even now his presence here would lift for a moment the torment that war had made of her life.

She worked alongside a surgeon whose eyes were insane and she was aided by four esquires who were stooping drunk. Some sense informed her, though, and she looked up from the low operating table, then stood erect, and she smiled. "It is my Jean," she said. "They have told me that you would be home. Yet I could not quite believe them."

Home, he thought. This . . . Her heart must have been broken by the loss of Beth-Haggan. Then he was at her side

200

and although the grief would not let him speak he clasped her tenderly in his arms and she clung to him as they kissed.

Rage was in his brain again, coiled like a cruel, powerful spring that drove out all other thought. His mother was pitifully thin; she trembled as she clung to him. Never should she suffer so, he told himself. In all of her life she had done no harm. Unless he fought soon, he realized, and did not release some of this rage in action, he would go mad.

"You know," he murmured to his mother, "I cannot stay. My place is up on the wall. That is why I came here. The other matter was a great failure. I must fight or I will not be able to call myself a man."

"I know, Jean," she said. She had begun to draw away from him, the tips of her bloodied fingers still on his shoulders. "We defend what is ours and there is no turning from it." She made the sign of the cross. "Go in strength. Pay them well, those who have brought this upon us."

He ran when he was out from under the tower archway. He cleared his sword and it was welcome in his hand and he panted in anticipation of the first blow he would strike. But the Sieur Amboise was no longer on the wall and beckoned him back as he started to mount the ladder to it. "Stay below," his father said. "Sir John would speak with you."

Sir John de Villiers, the Master of the Hospitalers, stood tall and awesome in the smoke. He gave Jean Baignault a nod in response to his salute. "Hold with your father and me. We would go outside the wall for a real fight. That would please you, after Rome?"

Jean Baignault grinned. The Master of the Hospitalers was a man who understood his need and would see that it was satisfied. "I should be greatly pleased, sir," he said. "I have been waiting for such ever since the Roman matter came to an end."

"Then find yourself a horse," Sir John said. "We are about to ride out in strength. The lot with which you arrived is to join us and King Henry has just landed from Cyprus. He musters two hundred more knights and five hundred men. We will make the heathen quite busy."

The Sieur Amboise walked from the wall with Jean Baignault. He leaned against him for support and yet he was quick and alert, his brain keen. "Sir William de Beaujeu is in command," he said. "The Templars have a greater force than ourselves, as always. He has a hundred more than us, and we muster one hundred and forty. But the entire number, even with you who came in today, is only about seven hundred knights and fourteen thousand infantry."

"It would not seem that the infantry have done much," Jean Baignault said.

"They have not," his father said. "Their spirit is poor. They fight for pay, and most of them believe that they will not get it. That is why the knights, each a sworn man, ride out."

Jean Baignault asked the question bluntly, "You think we might win by such action, sir?"

"Who can tell?" The Sieur Amboise stared straight at him. "But keep close to me in the fighting. I am tired, Jean, and it will be very hard . . ."

"Say no more, sir," Jean Baignault said, and shifted around so that he almost carried his father's weight.

But emotion left him when he and the Sieur Amboise were in the courtyard of the Convent of the Hospitalers. He was, he told himself, a highly trained soldier, and he was about to engage in the greatest and what might be the last battle of his life. His glance swept sharply over the faces of the men assembled here. There were considerably more than a hundred and forty knights jangling, jostling, shouting around him. Many of them, though, were not Hospitalers. They were lanky and blond Norsemen in winged helmets, and red-haired Scots who bore huge battle axes and swords as superb as his own. Then he realized that they had chosen to fight under the Hospitaler banner and he was both pleased and proud.

But the command to ride out did not come. The grooms who held the caparisoned reins of the chargers stared at their masters. Knights cursed and asked for wine. Jean Baignault said softly to his father, "Sit down, sir. Rest yourself during this delay." He made a place for the Sieur Amboise against the wall, then went into the convent, took bread, meat and wine from the scullery and brought them forth. He squatted beside his father, and ravenously, the late afternoon in their faces, they ate and drank wine.

The Sieur Amboise rested motionless, his face without expression. But Jean Baignault knew that he listened to the sounds from the Maledictum. "We do not do well there, Jean," he said finally. He started to rise to his feet.

Jean Baignault restrained him. "That I understood before," he said.

The siege engine vibration had become so violent that the entire city seemed to shake. Masonry crashed. Bomb burst followed burst with a muffled, hiccupping roar. The Saracens as well as the Mongols had learned the use of gunpowder, Jean Baignault thought. With it they smashed one battlement after another. "We are too late," the Sieur Amboise said. "The Saracens have taken the wall. They are in the city."

But Jean Baignault only nodded. Sir Matthew de Clermont, blood on his face, his mantle ripped to the hem, was at the convent gateway. He was Marshal of the Hospitalers and the men inside were silent as they gazed at him. "St. Anthony's Gate has fallen," he said. "We could hold it no longer. But, in a moment, we will go and drive them from it. That will again be ours. Gentlemen, I ask you to confess yourselves."

They knelt in close rows and the priests passed and moved on to the esquires, the men-at-arms, the grooms and pages. Then the knights stood up and mounted. The horses shivered beneath the weight of the riders; they whinnied and curveted and the steel hooves clanged. Jean Baignault set himself deeply in the saddle and took the lance and shield an esquire handed him. He had no liking for a horse as big as this, he thought. He was accustomed to the fast, stocky Mongol beasts. But today he rode in battle beside his father and the rest did not matter.

They trotted into the street in column of twos, Sir Matthew de Clermont ahead with the white Hospitaler banner half-unfurled. Other groups and formations of knights fell in behind them and Jean Baignault glanced back, curious. He saw King Henry of Jerusalem, the gold circlet of the crown firmly in place above the hennaed hair and next to him a knight who bore the huge Templar banner, the famous *Beau-seant*. It was half-white, half-black, and the symbolism meant that the fair, the white, was carried toward the Christians, and the black, terrible disaster, toward the heathen. The sun touched the violet silk of Lorraine, too, and the blue, narrow battle gonfalons at the lance points. Trumpets flashed, were swung high, then sounded.

The street was empty here. The column moved from the trot to the canter. Jackmen who were survivors from the action at the wall peered out at them from alleys. They grimaced and put fingers to their heads; the knights were

203

crazy. Jean Baignault drew a long breath to curse. He thought of his mother under the archway of the Maledictum Tower. The men who grimaced might have saved her before they ran. Then, strangely, his thought went to Subeyla. She would call this a parade of fools, join in the jackmen's mockery. Prayer, fine words, panoply led only to destruction and could not save Christendom. That would be what she would tell him. . . .

Then the stark, awful fact of battle jerked his nerves, seized his brain. Saracens—infantry archers and pikemen—were before the column. Sir Matthew de Clermont stood straight in the stirrups and lifted his sword. *"Laissez aller!"* he yelled again and again. The Sieur Amboise cried it with him and Jean Baignault stared aside and saw his father's face was dark, rigid, convulsed with hatred.

Jean Baignault was swept into the cry: *"Laissez aller!"* It eased the pounding ache that constricted his lungs. Let us go. Let us go! Let us pay back. . . .

The Saracens at the head of the column were smart enough to run from them. The slow were crushed in the street, stamped out of recognition beneath the hooves. Jean Baignault tossed an archer spinning, arms and legs wide, yanked the lance loose and measured another man. Now the Saracens in this street were gone. The column wheeled abreast of the Maledictum Tower and he leaned from the saddle and saw his mother. She was at the side of the archway, her hands out to support her, and she was unharmed, although her face was ghastly with strain and grief.

He shouted to her and he heard his father shout. Then they were past and the column was making a left turn into the darkness and flame and smoke of St. Anthony's Gate. He rode through with another Saracen archer hanging to his lance, the shaft shattered by the force he had given the blow. "Drop it," the Sieur Amboise said. "Time to use the sword."

But he already had the great sword up and in his hand and he was laughing as he swung. It had been a long time. It had been a very long time. Let them stand and fight. By God's grace, let him meet here Ibn Aud Aghaf and any others like the Wahabi who sought combat. Come on, all of them who would take Beth-Haggan and *Outremer,* defile Jerusalem, squeeze the life from his mother, make his father, lamed and spent and sick, ride forth against death.

Beyond the sally port was the Saracen right flank. Narrow-eyed and dark men on slender horses. Camels beyond, and the green battle banners. Fire rippled around him. Arrows cut clucking and slapping. His horse stumbled on the rubble of the outer wall. He hauled up on the reins and stared aside for his father and saw him and rode on; this was the open plain of Acre, and there was the Saracen camp.

The Templars had begun to chant. They gave the cry of *"Beau-seant!"* and then "For the Temple! For the Temple!" Saracens were being unhorsed. They sprinted for the tents. The battle hysteria hard on him, Baignault spurred to catch them. They resembled rabbits, and when he swung with the sword, they scuttled in the same way. But Ibn Aud Aghaf stood to fight straight-bodied, his head back, a smile of derision across his bloodied face.

Baignault looked at him as though the Wahabi appeared from dream. This could not be so; chance would never allow such satisfaction. But Aghaf had not waited; he made a darting run and his upward blow with the scimitar was for the horse's lungs beneath the curve of the chain armor. The man strikes a felon blow, Baignault thought, in the fashion of Khotel. Meet it, then, and give no mercy.

He raised from the saddle and with all his strength and the weight of his armored body leaped down upon Aghaf. It was a desperate measure, he realized even before he fell thrashing against Aghaf and they rolled together across the ground. The Wahabi was much more lightly armored, could move faster, and it was the sensible tactic of any knight to keep the vantage of the saddle. But he had dazed Aghaf; he heard the grunt of pain in the same instant that the point of Aghaf's poniard started to scrape along his vizor. He struck back with his mailed fist and bone gave and flesh pulped. The poniard no longer pried; Aghaf was screaming.

"You're no rabbit," Baignault said, the Arabic words thick with his hate. "You are a hyena. Yet, take this." He had hunkered over on his side so that he might raise the sword. The blow he gave was slanted and still he drove it with great power. Aghaf's head bounced from the severed, gushing throat.

Baignault got erect with the help of the sword. He let go a great shout and a pair of Templar esquires heard him and braced and swung him back into the saddle of the frightened but motionless horse. He blinked the sweat from his eyes, caught his breath before he thanked them. "The day goes well for us," he muttered.

"For you certainly, Sir Jean," the senior esquire said and saluted him.

Baignault rode forward then, slack, the battle desire spent, wondering why he stayed on the field. His share was done. Saracens of the determination of Aghaf were dead. Duty kept him here, he thought, and curiosity. He had never before entered a Saracen camp of such size.

His loose hand on the reins guided his horse between the tent rows. The beast crushed a discarded cymbal and shied aside from a leopard skin drum. Wounded crawled or waited to be killed. But, he saw, there were still women in some of the tents. Above the face veils, their eyes were blank. They expected death from his hand; he carried the blood-splashed sword across the saddle pommel. A sick disgust entered him. Brute murder would be the name for any more of this for him. Subeyla, if she were among the women here . . . He could not strike another blow today. Not even in anger or danger. He had been wrong to stay upon the field. Subeyla's image filled his thought; he saw her, heard her, and her words were about the horror of war and they were spoken in truth. . . .

He rode back slowly, head down, uncaring where the horse took him until he reached the Hospitaler standard, set up between the Saracen camp and the city. His father was there with Sir Matthew de Clermont. They sat their horses without motion as they listened to the Saracen trumpets. It was the recall that was sounded and with it came the wailing of the mahdis for the slain.

"They want no further with us today," Sir Matthew said. "Our infantry took courage and came out and fought well. We have won a great victory."

"Still, we should get back," Sieur Amboise said. He stared toward the city in the sunset. "The price has been considerable, Sir Matthew."

"Yes," Sir Matthew said, his voice very low, "that is so. You, Sir Jean, be good enough to pass the word to the various commanders. We are to withdraw at once from the field. My order is for every formation to return inside the city walls."

"It will be done, sir," Jean Baignault said. But as he rode to carry out the order he felt no sense of triumph, but instead a peculiar despair. The recollection of Subeyla was coupled with what his father had just said. And all around him was the price of victory. The Christian dead were heaped and strewn along the way that led from the Saracen camp to St. Anthony's Gate. As many as two thousand dead, he thought, and over three times that number in wounded. We paraded as fools and fought as such. A great victory, and yet little has been gained. Now the victorious returned to the city, a place of pestilence and a trap.

His head went forward on his chest again; he almost shut his eyes. But the horse, blowing, shivering, side-stepped among the dead and jolted him and he could not ignore the cries of the wounded. He halted after he had passed Sir Matthew's order to the last commander. Then, harsh-voiced, he called together a force of several hundred esquires and pikemen. "You will take in the wounded," he told them. He swung down from his horse. "Take this beast and any other that is of use. Make litters of the lances and of planks. Cover them with the Saracen mantles or your own. But fetch them into the city."

He entered the gate with the final group and it was dark and he was numbly fatigued. He reeled as he walked, butting into the litter bearers, but aware that the wounded should be dispersed among the various convents. Then thought came to him of his mother. She would know where to send the men. He called an order and turned the group toward the Maledictum Tower. After this, he told himself, he would sit and rest and make her sit beside him. Then they would talk, and not of war.

Engineers were at work around the tower. They replaced the barriers and built up the ramparts against the next Saracen attack. There was much noise and movement and confusion. He did not understand that the man in front of him was his father until he stood beside the Sieur Amboise under the archway.

The Sieur Amboise stood with the stiffness of a church image. His hands were at his sides. His feet were met and his eyes stared forth into the smoke-thick obscurity with a fixed glare. Jean Baignault felt a surge of love, a sense of protection that gave strength. He clasped his father easily by the shoulder. "Sir, do not be troubled," he said. "We have won, at no matter what cost. And all the wounded who could be reached have been carried in. If now my mother—"

"Your mother," the Sieur Amboise said, "has been

stricken. Some sort of stroke came upon her while we were out there at the fighting. It is her heart, and she lies so still, Jean, that I doubt me if she will live."

But Jean Baignault was already moving. He pushed into the torchlit, blood-reeking space and when he saw his mother's face he knelt down. A pallet of clean straw had been given her and the surgeon with the insane eyes was at her side. "It came most suddenly," the surgeon said. "She would not listen to me, and hours ago, days ago, she should have rested."

"Get away," Jean Baignault said fiercely. His mother's eyes were wide. She recognized him. Through the rapping of the hammers, the babel of the wounded, she had begun to speak.

"Jean, my dear," she said, "the man is right. I have been so tired. And the pain here . . ." Her hand, caked black with blood, raised a bit. "I belong at Beth-Haggan, I believe. Among the flowers. After this is over, I should like . . ."

"Yes, mother," he said swiftly, "I promise you." But he was too late, he knew, even as he stooped to kiss her. His mother was dead.

He stood up unseeing. Grief seemed to squeeze his brain into a knot and each blow the carpenters' hammers hit was upon it. He groped out and almost stepped upon a wounded man, then heard his father. "Leave me with her, Jean. I will tend to what must be done."

"But you must rest, sir. You too are greatly fatigued. Come with me to the Hospitalers. Food for us both, and rest. We will have to fight again tomorrow."

"No," the Sieur Amboise said. "My place is with her now, and alone. Go, Jean. Seek me here tomorrow. Do not start into battle without me. We should give her honor side by side."

"As you wish, sir," Jean Baignault said, and took and kissed his father's tear-salt hand.

He veered sagging along the street to the Convent of the Hospitalers. His sword swung out from his side as he pressed convulsively against the hilt and it tripped men who passed him and he was cursed. Sullen, unreasonable rage started in him and he drew the blade, went on with it in his hand. The next man who cursed him, he promised, he would kill.

But he met a solid group that filled the street from wall

208

to wall, and they were Teutonic esquires and herded women between them. He blocked the way, stood staring, scowling. "Who might these be?" he said.

"Some four or five from the Saracen camp, sir." The esquire in front of the group was drunk, still sober enough to be cautious. "My master, Sir Gustave Gerling, has ordered me to bring them to his quarters. If you would step aside, we will with your permission move on."

"That, though," Jean Baignault said very slowly, "I refuse to give."

He pushed the esquire aside and stepped toward the women; in the torchlight he had recognized Subeyla. She was at the center of the group, and like the others around her, moaning and shivering, she was veiled, wore a silk scarf close about her head. No word had come from her; she made no sign. But he knew her by the embroidered Jebel Druse robe, the manner in which she stood, even, he told himself, by her silence.

"I will take this one for myself," he said to the esquire. He beckoned and Subeyla slightly moved.

"But, sir, I cannot," the esquire said. "My master—"

Jean Baignault hit the esquire twice with the back of his left hand. The first blow thumped the man's skull against the wall. The second caught him as he staggered and he dropped and sat down and was still. "Now," Baignault said. He watched the other esquires. "Let her go with me. Offer to Sir Gustave my compliments and my thanks. If he should feel angered, he is aware of where I may be found."

There was no answer, only the muffled moaning, and the rustle of Subeyla's robe as she stepped forth along the street to his side. "Keep going steadily," Baignault said to her in Arabic. "Let nobody stop you. Should I be stopped, run, but do not call or scream."

"I understand, master," she said, and her voice was like a whip. "I trust your Christian mercy."

"Then be silent," he said furiously, "or I shall be forced to gag and carry you."

She touched her forehead in the gesture of a slave, and yet he saw that her eyes gleamed, and that her fury must be equal to his own. Tonight, he thought, there was another battle to be fought—with Subeyla.

CHAPTER SIXTEEN

They were not stopped in the streets he chose to follow. The patrols were Hospitalers and Templars; he was saluted, told to pass on, although some of the men nudged each other and made coarse, quick jokes when he and Subeyla had gone ahead. Baignault hardly heard them. His brain, his nerves had received too many impressions. He felt a lassitude that was close to coma, but his brain registered a chaotic swirl of images: his mother at Beth-Haggan, his mother dead, the tilting yard at El Kerak, and Louvic—it was months since he had thought of Louvic—dying in the desert before the Iron Gate, and Karakoram, the wind, the snow, the Gobi, then Mustaf, Khotel, Mustaf again, and Litei and Chagan.

He leaned against a street wall for support. He groped his hands over his face and gasped. It had been too much, he thought. He was about to lose his mind. Subeyla touched him on the shoulder. "Where would you go?" she said.

"Follow me," he said. "The distance is not great."

He knew a merchant's house in the Venetian quarter where he had visited in the past and which he believed now was vacant. When he and Subeyla came to it through a dark alley it was unlit, unguarded. The people and their servants had already fled the city. He spent his strength to pry open a side window shutter with his sword, then entered, grasped Subeyla by the arm and pulled her after him.

"Sit down," he said. A couch was near and he sprawled upon it and she sat beside him without speech. He dozed and awoke and realized that she was still there, dozed several times more and felt a renewal of strength. He was almost ready, he thought, to talk with her. But before that he would test the quality of her determination.

"Find us food and wine," he said. "There should be some here in the house. Perhaps I need not tell you that if you run from me and go out into the streets alone, you will be surely captured, raped and killed. This, tonight, is not a pleasant city."

"Yes," was all that she said. Then she rose and he heard

her moving in the room and the rooms beyond. A candle flickered; he smelled food over fire and his hunger was almost as great as his desire to learn whether she still loved him. She came in with fried meat, bowls of rice and fruit, a flagon of wine and a jug of olive oil.

"When you have eaten," she said, "take off your armor and I shall massage you." She indicated the oil jug. "That will loosen the cramps which you must feel."

"Why are you so considerate of me?" he said.

"You are my protector," she said. "In this den of mad Christians, you alone might accord me mercy, for whatever that is worth."

He sat higher on the couch and gazed at her in the candle light. "Tell me," he said. "How do you, who hate war so, happen to be here?"

"The Saracen leaders sought us out," she said, her face pale, and her lips. "They threatened to take our herds and our land unless we joined their cause. We, like them, must take part in the final battle against the Christian invader. So they massed hundreds of warriors against us, right in our mountains. It was a cruel matter, and we were all but driven into their ranks."

"And your brother, the sheik?" Baignault said.

"He died today in the fighting. Along with him, the best men of our clan. They had no other choice."

"So you too have felt the weight of the sword, know that it cannot be avoided."

"Not as you do, though," she said. "War for you must still be a form of worship, your religion. Else why are you here?"

"Believe me," Baignault said, his glance fully on her searching, steady eyes, "that is not true. Today, while your brother died, my mother also gave her life to war. She was a woman of tender spirit, and at last, as she worked to take care of the wounded in the horror of this place, her heart broke. . . ."

"Oh, Jean!" she said, and then, without passion, with a gentleness of understanding, she brought him to her and kissed him on the cheek.

"Subeyla," he whispered against her hair. "Subeyla, my darling."

She drew aside from him and stood. "Let us go upstairs," she said. "I would see how well the walls are held against the Saracens." Her voice was grim. "That is important to both of us."

There was a second-story terrace that gave off from a bedroom above. She stood there for some time looking out at the flame-spilled walls and the small, black figures of the defenders and attackers as they struggled on the ramparts. "It does no good to watch," Baignault said. "Morning will decide. The Saracens will assault in force only after daylight."

She still stood silent. The night was warm. Stars showed above the ruddy, piled smoke from the ramparts. Cypress and lemon and olive trees were in the garden below, and a few nightingales called slow and soft notes. A night for love, Baignault thought, and not for talk. First, though, he sensed, Subeyla must talk. Her pride demanded it.

"What," she said finally, "of your mission to Rome and the alliance with the Mongols?"

"Wrecked by treachery," he said. "And stupidity. Some of that my own." His voice was a low, harsh whisper. He clung to the terrace rail for support. "You were right, Subeyla, and I wrong. I should never have gone to Karakoram, or to Rome."

"I did not ask you," she said, "to be told that I was right, and you wrong. Talk can wait. Downstairs I promised to massage you, relieve your pain. Come in the bedroom. Take off your upper clothing. I will go and fetch the oil."

"Thank you," he murmured.

He lay inert, face down upon the bed as she massaged with long strokes of her powerful hands. The bed was broad and smelled faintly of attar of roses. Passion started in his loins with the warmth and relaxation of the massage and her nearness. He rolled over and reached up for her.

She moved back a pace, the oil flagon lifted. She made of it a barrier between them. It was her way of explaining to herself, he thought, why she showed him such care. "Tell me of tomorrow," she said. "You, who have given so great thought to war."

"I will go out," he said, "and my father, and the rest of the men like us, and try to hold the walls. But we will be not enough. The Saracens . . ." He harshly laughed. "This will be a Saracen city. And you, if you are lucky, a member of a princely harem."

"But you?" she said.

He pointed to the sword where he had propped it in a corner. "I have lived by that. Very likely, I shall die with it in my hand."

"Then there is no hope."

"Hardly any, Subeyla."

"No chance of escape?"

"About the same. But it does not interest me. My father is committed to stay here. My pride and my knightly oath still have some meaning to me too."

Pallor was in Subeyla's face. She stood rigid as she stared at him where he lay on the bed. Then, suddenly, she put down the oil flagon and picked up and tossed to him his mantle. "Cover yourself in that," she said. "Let us sit on the terrace for a bit. I will bring out chairs and pillows."

They sat side by side in the deep chairs, her posture now almost as easy as his own. She seemed to doze, but he was aware that she listened to the sounds of the night and he sensed that she turned over and over in her mind what he had just told her. Patience again would help him, he thought. But, loving her, adoring her, he could wait. . . .

She got up from the chair after a time and stood at the terrace rail and he wondered what her reason was. Then he understood, and rose and stood beside her. She had been attracted, perhaps against her will, by the sounds from the houses around them.

This quarter of the city had been occupied by wealthy Venetian merchants and shipowners and bankers. They had lived in luxury, but weeks ago they had abandoned their homes, taking along with them with their wives, their families, their servants and wealth. Since then, the garrison troops—knights who held sufficient rank—had moved in for the duration of the siege.

Candelabras now threw a checkered brilliance over terraces and gardens. There seemed to be, Baignault thought, an intense need for light to dispel the gloom of the smoke pall with its pervasive odor of scorched flesh. Crowds of knights, a number still in armor, lurched from house to house. They were drunk or meant to be drunk and sought women.

He looked over Subeyla's shoulder into the garden next door and understood quite clearly why she stood there. As many as twenty couples were in the garden. The men were all knights of the major orders and obviously some of the women were their wives. The others were camp-follower bawds and the best of the prostitutes remaining in Acre.

They made love on benches, on rugs flung across the lawn, even under the scintillant patter of the fountain spray. It was a bacchanalia; all rules of conduct and morality had broken down tonight, for this might be their last. Couples exchanged partners. A beautiful, full-breasted woman with black hair that reached to her waist danced and rolled and writhed through the fountain pool. A Norse knight pitched his winged helmet behind him, and his outer clothing, then jumped in and clasped her and took her.

A young knight too drunk to sit erect any longer sat with his back against a lime tree. He reminded Jean Baignault of those who had served with him at El Kerak and must be dead. The knight let his viol fall to the grass, but, head back, eyes shut, he sang. It was the famous *Romance of the Rose*:

> Three cruel vengeances pursue
> These miserable wretches who
> Hoard up their worthless wealth: great toil
> Is theirs to win it; then their great spoil
> They fear to lose; and, lastly, grieve
> Most bitterly that they must leave
> Their hoards behind them. Cursed they die
> Who living, lived but wretchedly;
> For no man, if he lack of love,
> Hath peace below or joy above.

Subeyla turned. She stared at Baignault. "You believe in that?"

"They are drunk," he said deliberately. "And desperate. Do not pay them any mind."

"Still, you believe in what the song says?"

He pulled her to him, his hands hard on her arms. "I will be out with them at dawn. They have fought all day. So now they sing and make love. As for the song, it is one our troubadours brought from France along with many others. But, enough of talk."

"Yes," she said, and the fierceness in her voice was from desire, "enough of talk."

He undressed her on the broad bed, slowly, garment by garment, kissing her hair, her lips and her breasts. A cadence entered their love-making, gradual at first, then accelerated and subsiding into a swoonlike ecstasy. After a long interval they drew a little apart though one arm held her against him while his other hand caressed the warm curve of her thighs and the firm, rounded slopes of her breasts.

They lingered there, lost in a violent, ecstatic world of feeling until their shared need of each other drove them together again. And while their bodies found fulfillment and peace the notes of the viol drifted into the room from next door.

Baignault got up from the bed only when dawn light was on the terrace rail. Trumpeters were sounding the assembly at the convents. Down below in the streets of the quarter patrols passed and they knocked on doors, rousted out any man fit for combat.

He dressed and buckled on the sword. Then he stood over her and looked into her eyes. "Wait for me here, Subeyla," he said. "Should we hold them off through the day, we might still win. Then everything will be different."

"Not everything," she said quite softly, "but a great deal." She took his sword hand and pressed it to her breast. "I can't hold you now, so go. This must be. For us, there is no other way. . . ."

He pondered her words as he went from the house. She was still in part strange to him, he thought. Somehow, their love bound them and yet in their minds, secretly, they were apart.

Then the clamor, the haste of battle pressed in upon him. He moved with the rest of the Hospitaler survivors to the Maledictum. Up on the shaky, smoking foundations of the inner rampart he stood and fought all day long. When the last Saracen attack was repulsed and he was relieved and came down, he sought Sir John de Villiers and asked after his father.

"You will find him at the Convent of the Hospitalers," Sir John said.

"I expected him on the wall this morning," Baignault said, a sudden alarm cold around his heart. "No harm has been done him, sir?"

"None except that he will never fight again," Sir John said. "He suffers from a severe shock. While the night passed, he collapsed. A physician tends him and he will be leaving soon for Cyprus."

Baignault had started to move on along the street, then halted. "With what people would my father leave, sir?"

"Those of King Henry of Jerusalem." Contempt was open in the Master of the Hospitalers' voice. His smoke-reddened eyes blinked with rage. "They will sail on the morrow or the next day. A fight such as this is not for them. They are willing enough to die, they tell me, but only if glory is immediate."

Jean Baignault fingered the blade of his sword. It was nicked, dulled by two days of steady combat. His body ached; his throat was so parched that it was difficult for him to articulate. "I would call them cowards," he said.

"I too," Sir John said. "But that will not keep them here. I will see you in the morning?"

"At dawn, sir," Jean Baignault said. "Or whenever you might need me. Our patrols in the Venetian quarter know where I am to be found."

He came slowly striding into the Convent of the Hospitalers, his mind too dazed to accept much more than the fact that his father was ill. The Sieur Amboise sat almost comatose in a corner. He stared blankly before him, and when he spoke it was about irrelevant matters. His thought was garbled: Beth-Haggan and the olive crop, a Greek poem he wished to translate, a new gown for Lady Baignault that had been promised from Antioch, the condition of the barbican tower at El Kerak.

Jean Baignault could only sit beside him in strained silence and hold his hand. But when he rose to go the Sieur Amboise kissed him on the cheek. "Keep fighting, Jean," he said in a burst of lucidity. Do not let them break you as they have me. Better dead."

"Yes, sir," Jean Baignault said, keeping the grief from his voice. "Sleep now. The physician will be along later to fix you a potion. You will feel more like yourself on the morrow."

Subeyla greeted him quietly at the house in the Venetian quarter. She had food and mulled wine ready, and they ate with only a few words between them. She sensed his grief, he understood, and patience prompted her to be still. But at the end of the meal when he reached for the wine and filled their goblets again, she said, "You have news, Jean?"

"Yes," he said, thick-voiced, "and it is bad."

"Still, tell me." She had moved with him to the couch, sat with her thigh against his.

"King Henry and his knights are leaving. They have had all but their full share of battle. Without them, defeat is quite certain. And they might take ship for Cyprus tomorrow."

"You have said to me that there would be no retreat. That it was all but impossible."

"So I thought. . . . The harbor is still free, however, and Henry has his own ships and crews for them." He looked up

216

at her and wearily smiled, and the bitterness was gone from his voice. "I can find place for you aboard one of Henry's ships. You need not stay here for the final, ghastly business."

"If you remain," Subeyla said, "then so do I. That I tried to make clear to you last night."

"But my father is taking his leave." Baignault spoke in a whisper; his head was down; he stared at the floor. The wine he had drunk was sour in his throat and the fumes mixed with the odor of death that was now constantly through the room. "You could care for him, and he is in sore need of help."

"What has happened to your father, Jean?"

"He is a walking dead man," Jean Baignault said. "At last, after all these years, the Saracens have beaten him. His mind has broken. He is no longer himself, he sits and babbles, talks of my mother as though she were still alive. . . ."

"Oh, Jean, Jean! Go with him. Do not stay any longer yourself, then. You would serve no purpose of any worth, should you stay here."

"But, afterward?" Baignault was weeping. "Sit on Cyprus and babble back at my father? Drink myself stupid with King Henry's wastrel knights? No, and forever no." He stood and stalked the room and the sword was in his hands. "I will stay and fight. So long as I am able to hold this, I will give vengeance to what has been done to my mother, my father, your brother, all the rest."

"Very well, Jean." Subeyla spoke only after the fierce clash of his voice had echoed away in the room. "Come to bed. If you would fight, you need sleep."

She half-led, half-dragged him to bed, and he was asleep before she had finished taking off his clothing. He awoke once in the night and screamed, racked by the horror of the men he had seen burned and killed on the ramparts. But she quieted him, her arms around him, her body close, and he slept again while she slowly stroked his hair.

He heard the trumpets at dawn. They brought him upright and fumbling for his clothing, his armor and the sword. She watched him from the bed, but he knew no language for her except to say, "I love you, Subeyla." Then he saluted her and was gone.

He walked numb-legged in the streets, his mind still clogged by sleep, until he reached the Convent of the Hos-

217

pitalers. He heard there at once that King Henry was leaving that morning for Cyprus.

King Henry stood now in the great main hall of the convent. The senior officers of the various orders were around him when Baignault stepped in from the courtyard. "For three days and nights we have had no sleep," Henry said in a low, conversational voice. "It has been too much for us. Farewell, messires." He inclined his head to them and moved forth to join the knights who waited tightly ranked together for him.

"He might well be called a culvert knight," Sir John Villiers said. "But, for myself, I cannot greatly blame him. While here, he fought with bravery."

Jean Baignault had gone to the corner of the hall where his father stood vague-eyed and stooped. He held the Sieur Amboise upright before he said, "Others will be going with that lot to Cyprus. I should be grateful were my father to leave with them."

"Many are about to go, Sir Jean." It was Sir Matthew de Clermont who spoke, his face gray, his body hunched and his hands clenched on his sword belt. "Make your father ready to get aboard the first ship. We send the children and the women, all but the nuns who are kept here by their vows. Should you wish, join us after you have spoken farewell. We are to be confessed and then we will return to the fighting."

"I so greatly wish," Jean Baignault said. "Give me time only to take the Sieur Amboise to the ship."

He walked side by side with his father to the quay. He supported him, guided him through the mute, grief-stricken people who were on their way to board the ships. But there was nothing that he could tell his father, no communication of love that he might make. It was as he had told Subeyla last night. His father was a walking dead man. Beside him was not the Sieur Amboise he had known since childhood. This was no more than the battered shell of what had been a fine body and superb mind. It would be best, he told himself, if very soon on Cyprus the Sieur Amboise died.

They parted from each other on the quay where nuns took charge of the wounded. Jean Baignault squeezed his father's hand; he kissed his brow. "Good morning, Jean," the Sieur Amboise mumbled. "I would visit with your mother. She must be in the garden."

218

"Yes, sir," Jean Baignault said, and nodded to the nun who had his father by the arm. "It is a beautiful morning, and you will surely find her there."

He did not wait even to thank the nun. A compulsion claimed him; his need to fight, strike and kill had become absolutely paramount. Now was the last of it, and in the time left to him he had much to do.

He returned at a loping run to the Convent of the Hospitalers and knelt and received confession. But he was barely aware of the knights around him, the men with whom he would enter battle. He listened with wild impatience as Sir John Villiers gave the orders for combat formation.

King Hugh's Gate was now the weak point, Sir John explained. A force of five hundred reserve cavalry was assembled. They were to be a part of it and were to mount at once and ride forth. "Spare neither your mounts nor yourselves, messires."

Jean Baignault took his place in column on a horse that was half-crazed with battle shock. But it galloped with the rest as the column went toward King Hugh's Gate. Counterattack, Baignault thought dimly, and then set himself in the saddle and took out the sword.

The Saracens had driven camels and donkeys loaded with faggots into the ditch before the gate. They had then slaughtered the animals and used their carcasses as bridges. The knights as they went forward from the gate were met in immediate assault. These men were the Mamelukes, the famous White Slaves of the River, the finest of the Saracen cavalry. With them rode their holy men, the black-robed *mahdis*, and the *mahdis* scorned weapons and carried only the tremendous black battle banners.

Baignault, screaming, cut and slashed and parried, felt blows upon his blade that were too rapid to be seen. Then by sheer weight alone he rode through the Mameluke ranks. But no more than a few Hospitalers close beside him were left. They were surrounded by the conical caps, the dark, sharp faces and curved scimitars. "Back!" Sir John Villiers yelled. "Back through them! Give full rein and ride."

Baignault's horse was killed on the way to the gate. It stumbled at the carcass-clogged ditch, a scimitar blade impaled to the hilt through the throat. He sprawled and crawled, ducked hooves, got to his knees and ran, saw the

219

gate and was inside. Maybe a dozen of the Hospitalers were there. He backed away with them and heard a man with a lopped hand screech that Sir John was dead.

Saracens held the street they tried to take. Other gates had been penetrated, he realized. The city was about to fall. He fought without sense, by instinct, blood on his face, in his mouth, a blur before his eyes and dripping from his sword arm. But he saw Sir William de Beaujeu come along the yellow-walled street to make a passage for them. The Master of the Templars rode his staggering horse as though it were a projectile. Saracen footmen were pinned and smashed supine before a Mameluke lance tore out his throat.

The way he had left was wide enough for retreat. But some of the Hospitalers stood to fight again and Baignault stayed and with awful effort swung the sword. More Hospitalers came from behind. Together they made about a hundred. Sir Matthew de Clermont rode forth from an alley, his horse still miraculously unwounded. He was insane with rage, and would not listen to the knights who called to him. He galloped past their rank and the lances got him and he hurtled down beneath the scimitars.

There was no order given. Baignault sensed what must be done along with the men around him. Together, holding rank and in unison, they started toward the convent. That was their last refuge. While they could, they would defend themselves in the Tower of the Master.

Baignault moved bent almost double. He was wounded, he knew, and he needed the support of the sword. But as he came into the convent courtyard Subeyla stepped to his side. She said, "Sit down. I will take care of you."

"No," he told her. "Get me back on my feet. Push me up along the wall. We can hold them off from here. They will make some sort of truce with us."

She did not answer and he slipped down into a crouch on the cobbles. He felt her wash his face and rip off what was left of his mantle, put a fresh robe around his shoulders. Then she gave him wine to drink. "How did you get this?" he said. "And how did you get here?"

"I knew," she said, "that if you lived you would come to the convent. These I brought from the house where we stayed. Now, Jean, you had better stand up."

"That I can do myself," he said. But he needed her shoulder, and he was still so weak that he staggered. The great

220

iron gate into the street was still open. He beckoned and shouted, "Shut it!"

"Rest easy, Sir Jean," some man behind him said. "The Saracens are coming in to treat with us. Khalil has sent his bodyguard of three hundred men to make a truce and see that it is kept. They can be trusted."

"No," Baignault said. "I refuse to trust them."

"Then come with me into the street," Subeyla said. She walked with him at a slow, shuffling stride. "Let the others make truce. You are very tired."

"So I am," he muttered and went with her.

There was a house across the street which had been barricaded but was empty. Subeyla asked for his sword, then yanked away planks with the blade and they entered and he collapsed upon the dusty floor. He did not know how long he was unconscious. When he emerged he was in a shadowed room upstairs, propped next to a barred, shuttered window. Subeyla was close; he heard her irregular breathing. "This is wrong," he said. "You hurt yourself to carry me. And I should be back with them at the convent."

"No, Jean," she said brokenly. Then he also heard.

It was the nuns gathered in the courtyard of the convent. They screamed and called upon God for help. Baignault got to his knees and stared through the shutter gap. He could look down into the courtyard. Crusader weapons were piled inside the gate. The survivors of the Knights Hospitalers stood bare-handed in rank, kept from the inner courtyard by Mamelukes who carried scimitars. But a nun broke forth and she was part-naked. She was followed by Saracens who held altar cloths and chalices and holy relics in their hands. They threw them to the cobbles and stamped on them, then the nun was caught and thrust down.

Jean Baignault groaned in agony. He seized the window bars to pull himself to his feet. Subeyla stopped him. She clung to him until his strength was gone and he dropped back beside her. "Nothing can help now," she said. "It is too late."

The Knights Hospitalers had left their rank. They moved as though they formed a fantastic, incalculably powerful wave, and they killed with their hands. They battered against the Mamelukes and tore and smashed until they had weapons. Then, in awful silence, they killed the rest of the Saracens within the convent walls.

Jean Baignault prayed. He spoke aloud the names of

the knights he knew who were still alive. There was no hope for them. They would die in that place. Courage could not save them. Saracens by the hundreds were coming in at them from the street. The strongest, the luckiest got back into the Tower of the Master. But bombs were being set. Barrels of oil were spilled. Then naphtha was ignited.

"I have betrayed them," Baignault said. "We pledged together to defend the faith. And I am here and they die with their honor. I must go out. Help me to the street, Subeyla."

She was silent, motionless.

"Help me, please."

"Should you really want to go," she said, "you will find the strength."

He did not answer, but let go his grip upon the sword. He had served it too long, he realized; what he needed now was a shield which could be wrought only from intelligence. And he would need Subeyla in the making of that shield.

Across the street, the floors of the Tower of the Master had begun to buckle as flame caught. They dropped. The walls caved and crashed, and from inside there was no more human sound. The Saracens moved demon-like below, prancing, jeering, shouting with pride.

There in the tower, Baignault told himself, brave men had vainly given their lives. For them, pride, honor, a mystical belief had been enough, and so for those things they were willing to die. They were the last, though, and in Europe no Crusader lot with any strength or true conviction would come forth to avenge them.

Life had changed in Europe. He had seen the signs of it in Rome and learned the reasons along the road to Karakoram. Men were no longer content with the phrase, "Seek and ye shall find." Seek what? Death such as had been dealt them in the Tower of the Master? In the past, that question had always been answered: *"Deus veult."* Yes, God willed. But not blind obedience to leaders like King Henry, who, rich from the inherited spoils of *Outremer*, left those of greater faith and sailed off to safety.

Myth had become twisted into fact in *Outremer*. It had been all but forgotten by those who had died in the Tower of the Master that the first of the Crusaders had been hungry, impoverished men. They had bartered away and mortgaged their land at home to seek fortune from the infidel. Yes, they had done it in the name of the Saviour. Yes, there had been leaders among them who were of pure heart. Yes, also, there had been countless thousands who had robbed, ravaged and gone into combat for mere personal gain.

So now in Europe the proud knight upon his great, stiff-stamping charger was a figure of the past. His power had slipped from him, and the merchant who had lent money upon the knight's lands to pay for a venture to *Outremer* had taken his place. The merchant ruled, and it was no longer in the castle on the hill where power was held, but in the town, the merchant's house, the guildhall.

Jean Baignault brushed his hands over his forehead. His brain ached from too much battle and too much thought. But he had survived here, and Subeyla with him. He was young yet; his life could have meaning in the new Europe he had vaguely sensed in Rome.

There came to him memory of a conversation with Sir Hugh Gregor. The old Hospitaler had talked of conditions in his home country, England. Education was being spread there, Sir Hugh said, and was not confined to the monks. A college had been set up at a town called Oxford in 1249, and then another, called Balliol, in 1263, and a third, Merton, in 1264. Over in France, rather than giving his energies to the Crusades, William of Champeaux had chosen to educate youths who sought schooling.

Pope Innocent III had recognized the University of Paris in 1211, and it was already a great center of knowledge. Young men from all parts of France and Western Europe came there to study. Jean Baignault sighed, then in the smoke-filled darkness, smiled. He would go to Paris. He would take Subeyla with him, and out of his bitterly gathered store of learning prove that he could teach. Not the sword, not the ways of war and death—but what was called geography and the ways and manners and religions of the peoples of the East with whom the Western folk must deal if ever there was to be peace.

"You are troubled, Jean? Why are you so still?" Subeyla had moved. She clasped his hands and stared into his eyes.

"I have been," he said, "but am no longer. Let us go now. If you are willing to go with me."

"Tell me the place," she said softly.

"Paris," he said.

"It has no meaning to me," she said. "Still, I will go. . . ."

He smiled at her, and kissed her. Then he said, "Help me up. A ship, a war galley, is still in the harbor. I have seen it from the window here. We can reach the quay across the rooftops. The Saracens might—"

"Say no more," she said. "I am your woman, and strong enough to use your sword. If there are Saracens on the quay, leave them to me."

But, because of his weakness, it was an hour before they were across the rooftops. The alley beside the quay was dark. They crawled along it and at the far end, legs spread, hands on his hips, a Saracen sentry stood and stared out at the galley. "Give me the sword," Subeyla whispered. "Please, Jean."

He took a long, gradual breath. "Very much better," he grunted, "that I try."

The Saracen turned at the sound of his voice, and using both hands, Baignault hurled the sword. But his weakness was too great, and the blow was only glancing. The Saracen staggered, but kept erect and began to yell.

Subeyla flung forward. She tackled the man around the knees, sent him down onto the cobbles. Her fingers went to the throat and clung and closed. When Baignault got to her, the man was dead. "Come on," Baignault said. "Truly, you are my woman. . . ."

At the boat steps, he was forced to show her how to row. He pointed down into the skiff that bumped the bottom step and said, "Take those. Do this."

"I am mountain-born," she panted. "It is all new to me. Get in, though, and I will do as you say."

She rowed standing erect, facing the bow, and the Saracens who ran along the quay could not find her with their arrows. Baignault sat straight on the after thwart. "Slow now," he said. "We are safe." Then he looked back.

The city was a crater of flame. Acre, he thought, the beloved, the beautiful. But a great sense of peace had entered him. Subeyla rowed with regular strokes. The galley lay low and dark beyond the final cast of light from the shore. Men aboard it called out and he answered, not looking around again at the city. Ahead, in Paris, lay the future. He was young, and he had his woman. Jean Baignault, he told himself, had come a very long way.